THE RED QUEEN

S. Nano

Adventures in Fetishland
The Red Queen
Published in 2024 by
House of Erotica
houseoferotica.uk

an imprint of
Andrews UK Limited
West Wing Studios
Unit 166, The Mall
Luton, LU1 2TL
andrewsuk.com

THE RED QUEEN

S. Nano

HOUSE OF EROTICA

Contents

HOUSE OF EROTICA

1: Prologue

The metal tips of her stiletto shoes clicked against the black and white chequer board floor tiles; each step instinctively, without thought or effort, alternating between black and white. As she made her stately progress across the tiled floor she mused on the aptness of the symbolism that reflected the extremities of the world she inhabited and held sway over: darkness and light, cruelty and kindness, pain and pleasure, humiliation and reward. She commanded over her domain like a chess master playing a twisted and beautifully imagined chess game in which she, the Red Queen with a black heart, orchestrated proceedings and her slaves were pawns. She stood before her gothic mirror and admired her image reflected within its black cast iron frame. The Queen of Hearts was ready.

"How do I look Duchess?" she asked, turning to her transvestite companion and lady in waiting.

"I'm speechless, madam, really I am. You look absolutely stunning, a true fetish red queen," she answered.

She examined her image in the mirror carefully appraising every detail of her dress and make-up to ensure it met her exacting standards. She held her body upright and smoothed the shiny metallic red pvc panel of the ankle-length skirt, straightened her ruby encrusted tiara and made a final adjustment to the black heart-shaped choker around her neck. Yes, she thought, she looked perfect.

She turned and stepped off the black and white floor tiles taking a few steps to face one of the male slaves who served in her realm. His wrists were secured with leather cuffs, which had a rope attached to them and threaded through a metal ring fixed into the ceiling pulled tight so that his arms were stretched out. His ankles were similarly bound in leather cuffs and secured to rings set in the floor, his legs stretched just wide enough to cause discomfort but for the soles of his feet to lie flat on the black carpeted floor.

Hanging from him his balls was a large cast iron ball weight forged into the letter 'N'. 'N' for Nemesis, the Queen of Hearts smiled to herself, the name taken from the Greek goddess of fate and retribution and one of the personas she adopted in the fetish fantasy realm she had created and ruled over. She lifted the weight up and traced her finger along the letter and then let it drop heavily. The blindfolded man gasped as the velocity of the falling weight stretched his balls. The Red Queen merely laughed sadistically at his predicament. She gestured to the Duchess who, silently and secretly, stood behind her helpless victim and lifted the blindfold from his eyes to reveal the vision of his mistress transformed into the Queen of Hearts.

The cruel piercing blue eyes, framed in ruby streaked ebony hair, met her victim's as the blindfold was removed permitting him to feast his eyes on her. He gasped and then moaned in homage at the formidable and ravishing presence before him. She stood there, her heaving cleavage held tight in a shiny electric red pvc bodice festooned with black hearts and framed with a ruff in gold. This is the part I love, she mused. The look in their eyes when she reveals herself; that look of mesmerised devotion mixed with fear, fear of the unknown, fear of the seductive torment they knows she is capable of inflicting on them.

"So, are you ready to submit to the Queen of Hearts?" her voice whispered with more than a hint of playfulness mingled with the malice.

"Yes mistress," was the breathless reply.

"Mistress?" the inflection of her voice was raised and indignant, "Do you think that's the correct form of address for the Red Queen?"

"No your majesty. I mean your majesty. Of course, I mean your majesty."

"Yes, that's better slave. But you know you must be a punished for addressing me so inappropriately."

Her fingers strayed down to his cock grasping it in her metallic red gloved hands to inspect it. At the sight of his mistress revealed in all her shiny fetish glory his cock had instantly sprung to attention and stood firm and erect in her hand. They were so weak sometimes, she reflected. They knew the standards that were expected of them but still they succumbed to their own lusts. She enjoyed not making life easy for them, revelled in the control she had over them, but really, if they could not exercise more self discipline then they simply had to be punished.

"So, slave, does my presence arouse you? Do you think I'm dressed like this just to get you excited?"

"No your majesty. You're dressed as the Queen of Hearts for your own pleasure, your majesty."

"Yes that's right, but then how do you explain this? How many times have I told you about controlling yourself in my presence," she admonished, "I'm not a sexual object for you to ogle and get aroused over, you know that. You are here to serve me."

"Yes, your majesty, I know. I'm sorry."

"Sorry. Hah. Sometimes, slave, I just think these are meaningless words especially when your actions betray you. And look at this, what have you got to say about this disgusting mess?"

She held up her finger in front of his eyes, the traces of pre-cum from the tip of his cock glistening on the tips of her gloved finger. She held it up to his eyes.

"You know what you must do," she said, slipping the finger into his mouth for him to suck off the sticky substance. He licked it off greedily and obediently.

She nestled a flogger made of twisted strips of black and red leather firmly in her other hand and ran it across the flesh of her slave's back-side. His body tensed, tingling in anticipation of the pain that would follow, knowing that she would soon strike. Sure enough five hard strokes whipped across his arse. He gasped and moaned as the flogger struck and the stinging sensation crept across his body. He felt the gentle touch of leather; a series of gentle taps and some gentle rubs against his throbbing flesh before another ten hard strokes rained down on him, fast and relentless.

"Thank you, your majesty,"

She held the flogger up in front of his eyes and then ran it down his chest and stomach. His whole body trembled with that strange mixture of yearning and fear that slaves have when they submit themselves. The flogger was raised and struck hard against his erect penis. His arms wriggled and twisted in their bondage as his body instinctively flinched against the strokes but he was captive and powerless. His erection instantly wilted. She glanced up at him her eyes full of pleasure and satisfaction at the punishment she had inflicted.

"Perhaps that will teach you to address me properly in future and not to get an erection without my permission," she scolded.

The Red Queen retired to her carved wooden throne. The Duchess took up a standing position next to her so they were both facing the man stretched out in bondage his, penis still throbbing in pain. The Duchess was dressed as a transvestite fetish maid, her shiny black and red pvc costume and heart shaped apron mirrored her mistress's own dress. Her white masked face afforded her a sinister and mysterious visage. She was the Red Queen's loyal companion and lady in waiting.

At the Queen of Heart's feet, on all fours at the base of her throne, was another of her slaves, entirely naked except for a black leather hood laced tightly at the back in a criss-cross pattern and a metal studded collar around his neck. She rested her feet on his back side and nestled the tips of the stiletto heels firmly into his soft flesh.

The Queen of Hearts nestled comfortably back in her chair and gently stroked the jet black feathers of her raven, which was perched on the ornate carving on the hand rest of her throne, with her finger.

"And how are you today my sweet?" she said leaning down to whisper at the bird, "Vicky Duchess has a nice little treat for you, don't you Vicky?"

"Yes madam."

The Duchess held out a saucer and tentatively picked out a trail of raw bloodied meat and fed it into the mouth of the raven, which gobbled it up hungrily.

"Yes, that's nice isn't it, some tasty mouse entrails. I have to be keep you fit and healthy for whenever you're needed, don't I?"

She adjusted her feet to get herself comfortable and in the process pressed her stiletto heels deeper into the soft yielding flesh of the man's back-side. The slave expelled a grunt of pain as the sharp metal tips of the heels dug into his skin. The Red Queen lifted her shoes off and quizzically examined the marks left on the man's fleshy rear; deep little red indentations where her heels had left their impression. She turned to the Duchess.

"Sorry, did I hear something? Since when have foot-stalls been able to utter anything?"

A voice came from below her, "Very sorry your maj—oh!"

Her elegant dark eyebrows raised a fraction and her scarlet lips spread into a malevolent smile.

"You may well say, oh, for that little slip up, slave."

"No, madam, foot-stools don't speak," the Duchess interjected.

"That's right, of course they don't. They kneel in silence serving their mistress. They express no opinions, not even when they're asked and certainly not when they aren't asked, do they?"

The Red Queen rammed her heels back down onto her slave's back-side again, pushed hard and then twisted the steel tips driving them into the man's flesh. He gasped with pain and shock dropping his arse slightly as an instinctive reaction.

"Keep your position slave. I'm not very happy with you and, if your behaviour doesn't improve, I shall have you on foot-stool duty for the rest of the day. Do you understand? Now keep still and take your punishment."

The Duchess looked on nervously. Madam was not in a very good mood today. She was always a demanding mistress but Duchess could often be relied upon to share in her amusement of the treatment of her slaves but today she was in a dark mood and the Duchess was anxious to keep on the right side of her in case she ended up in trouble.

"Duchess, I'm in bad spirits today," the Red Queen confessed, "I feel restless and unsettled."

"Madam, I can't understand why. You have a stable of willing slaves who will submit to you in all things and absolute control over your wonderful domain."

The Duchess was right of course. She looked over her private chamber from the comfort of her throne and admired it. Nemesisland was her own creation; a place where she could give expression to her wildest imaginings and where slaves could lose themselves in submission and explore their innermost darkest desires. She knew it was a magical place where anything could happen. And this room was her special private domain. It was a gothic palace decorated with curtains and wall hangings of black and purple and filled with special objects, all of which had some special symbolism or held great meaning for her. There was her unicorn statuette, the porcelain figure of the Chinese goddess, Kwan Gin, the glass chess board and its figures, the Egyptian incense burner and many other precious articles all of which decorated and enhanced her special place.

"Yes all that's true," she acknowledged to the Duchess, "but my world isn't quite complete. I've been reflecting on this for a while and there is something missing from my fetish domain. I want a new play thing for my dungeons and I know what it is I need; a slave girl."

"A slave girl?"

"Yes Duchess. I can see it. I have a vision for how I could use her. But, the girl must have all the right qualities, she must be very special. Let me see, she must be compliant and submissive to me of course, willing to do and enjoy anything that I demand of her, like any other of my slaves. But, it would also amuse me if she wasn't totally submissive, if she had a little dominant streak so that I could use her to punish some of my male slaves. They can be led to believe she might be a plaything for them only to find she is just another instrument that I can wield to torment them. Yes, it would amuse me to see her carrying out all my instructions."

"Yes Madam, I can see how a slave girl would enhance your world."

"There is more Duchess. I have a particular girl in mind. Her story is a complicated and sad one, suffice it to say that she had been chosen by me for a special role and through a series of mishaps, and also the failings of one of my slaves who had been sent to help her, she was taken from me and put to work in a brothel in Manchester by some of my enemies. She was a dedicated and willing girl blessed with both physical beauty and a worthy soul. Now, I have never forgotten about this girl. She was once, and indeed still is, very dear to my heart and I believe our fates are still bound to one another in some way. It is most likely that some of her adventures will exist only in the dark recesses of her memory. She will be a confused soul, Duchess, in need of a guiding hand from a firm but caring mistress.

"This girl has never been far from my thoughts and I have been waiting to find a purpose for her and now I believe I have found it. She is damaged though and I cannot say how much of the spirit that she was imbued with in the short time she was under my tutelage still remains. She may resist my ministrations and be beyond my reach now but I feel it's my duty to do something for her. The time is now propitious for such an undertaking.

"Yes, I have servants in the other world. Duchess, get some of them onto this task to rescue her. Her name is Kim. There cannot be so many parlours and brothels in Manchester that this girl cannot be found. Bring her back to me. I can see it now Duchess. It will be so entertaining. I will instruct her in the ways of Nemesisland. Yes, that's exactly what I need to ease my restless spirit; a nice willing slave girl."

2: Tweedledum and Tweedledee

Kim's client sat silently opposite her on the flowered pink duvet cover. Kim knew she was good at her work. She had been working in this massage parlour for a couple of years now and that was long enough to have developed sound instincts about her customers. She had a bad feeling about this one from the moment he came into the living room to choose his girl; eyeing them all with cool detachment before selecting Kim. Most men she could get a response from, but this one was hard work. He had responded to every attempt at conversation with a monosyllabic grunt. It wasn't unusual to have clients that were nervous but usually, with a little bit of coaxing, Kim was able to encourage them to interact with her. It was true there were some clients who didn't particularly want to chat but there was something different about this one, something obdurate and unsettling about his manner and his detachment.

And why had the madam given her the pink room? She presumed the other rooms were in use by some of the other girls or had been booked, but it felt totally inappropriate. There were some men who wanted a surrogate girl friend experience, who wanted to pretend, or could believe, that thirty minutes or an hour with an escort in a parlour was a romantic interlude. There was nothing wrong with that, it was harmless and Kim was as good as any of the girls at playing along with that fantasy. But, this man wasn't one of these. He was thick-set, with muscles clearly toned from working out in a gym and then there was the knife tattoo with blood dripping from it on his muscular arm. It felt so incongruous against the pretty and feminine pink bed linen and matching furnishings and curtains.

Why hadn't they given her the black room? This was her favourite; it was the one with the black leatherette couch and hooks for tying clients onto. It didn't occur that often but it always gave Kim a tingle when a client asked for some tie and tease or some domination. It was one of her favourite activities and she loved doing it. She liked observing the feeling of helplessness in a man's eyes as she tied him to the two gleaming metal hooks and aroused him, gently stroking him so that he got an erection, but utterly in her control. She loved it when she could see all that masculinity and male bravado just evaporate as men would succumb to the slightest touch and give up control to her.

Often she couldn't go as far as she would like. After all, Kim thought, many of her clients had wives or girl friends and some marks would be rather embarrassing to explain away, so the domination and corporal punishment she delivered was fairly light touch. It usually consisted of a few gentle flicks with the whip across a client's back or arse or, if she was really lucky, on a taut cock; that really made the men flinch. Most of this was done in a fairly playful spirit; it was real enough for the client to have the experience of feeling dominated but never with any actual threat or menace. Kim would have loved to take it further but rarely got the opportunity. Most of her clients wanted oral or full on sex and she was happy to give them what they asked; after all, she was under no illusions, that was what she was here for. But, domination made her feel really wet and by the end of such a session, which usually did end up with sex, her cunt was sopping wet and a hard cock just slid inside her. She didn't often come when she was working but it was on those rare occasions when she did some domination that it was most likely to happen.

And Kim was hardly dressed for the pink room. She usually preferred to wear something a bit edgier, something a bit fetishy. She liked wearing leather, pvc and even latex, loved the feeling of it against her skin and how it made her feel sexy and assertive. But today she was wearing a leopard skin print satin bra and matching knickers and black hold-ups with stiletto heels, which had already been kicked onto the floor. She could only assume that it was her dress that had partly drawn this client to her.

She sighed inwardly. She prided herself on giving a good service and would never openly look bored or indifferent, even when she felt it. Most clients were alright and there were some regulars whose visits and company she genuinely enjoyed and looked forward to. But, she could see she was going to have to work hard to get a response from this one, not a sexual response –that was rarely a problem and she could see he got a hard cock as soon as he undressed, but some connection that might make it at least a bit pleasurable for her. She set to work and right now it felt like work.

Kim turned her naked client onto his back and knelt over him. She had to admit his erection was impressive, he certainly had no problems in that department, she thought. She leant over him so that her cleavage, squeezing out of her tight leopard skin print bra, was hanging over his face and his gaze was drawn to her heaving breasts. This certainly seemed to have got his attention. That's more like it, Kim thought. With a deft and practised motion she expertly unhinged the back of her bra and released her two glorious orbs of pale white flesh. Kim loved this bit. There was always a look of almost child-like wonder in men's eyes when she did this. Her clients were mainly pretty experienced; most of them must have seen women's tits scores of times but whenever she did this they always dropped into this mesmerised state and were completely in her control from then on. And Kim knew she had great tits, beautiful rounded mounds with pert nipples that stood to attention like little guards on sentry duty. She even detected a flicker of reaction from her immobile and taciturn client. Yeah, let's press home my advantage now and get this thing over with she thought.

"Come on, touch them, you know you want to," she whispered.

She took hold of his hands and gently guided them onto her tits never drawing the gaze of her lovely green eyes from her client. His surprisingly soft hands massaged the soft flesh and Kim feigned a gasp and moan to encourage him. Now we're getting somewhere, she thought. OK, that's fine, if you want to play strong and silent that's alright with me, I'll take control of the situation. He's paid for an hour though so I'll have to spin this out as much as I can because I can see that cock's ready to burst.

Kim got onto her knees and gave him an eyeful of her mound underneath her silky satin briefs. She eased a couple of fingers into her knickers and gently, almost imperceptibly, rotated her hips voluptuously. She pulled the gold and black material down a fraction to reveal the top of her bush of yellow pubic hair and then gradually pulled her knickers down so that the fleshy mound of her sex was right in his face. God, I'm good at this she thought, taking pleasure in her own sensuality. Then with a deft movement she stood over him so that he could see right up her cunt, which was now glistening with her leaking juices and then quickly pulled the knickers over one leg at a time so that she was completely naked.

Kim got down again and pushed her tits against his chest letting strands of her tussled fair hair brush against him and then lifted herself up so that she was crouched on all fours above him and started to kiss his hairless muscular torso. It was such a shame, he had a great body, beautifully toned muscles, smooth hairless skin. If only he could find a personality to match it, well any personality at all really, thought Kim. As her lips moved down his body she felt as though she was getting into this now. It was getting beyond the point where idle chat would mean a thing anyway.

Her tongue flicked the end of his cock and then her lips closed around his rock hard member. He was perfectly clean and presentable and, though Kim used her discretion, she had no qualms about doing oral without; many of her regulars chose her for that reason alone. She moved her mouth up and down the long hard shaft of his cock. She'd carry on like this for a few minutes and bring him right to the brink before whipping out a condom and mounting him and then riding him to a climax. Kim was convinced there wasn't a man on earth who could resist her oral; she was an expert after years of practice with various boyfriends and working at the parlour.

She loved that slurping sound of saliva from her mouth rubbing against hard cock as she increased the speed and intensity of the sucking motion. She could feel the veins of the cock throbbing inside her mouth and knew instinctively when to ease off or stop to prolong the ecstasy.

She pulled her mouth away when she tasted his salty pre-cum, not wanting to bring him to climax yet. She glanced up at him but he still looked pretty inscrutable. Most clients would be squirming and moaning in ecstasy at treatment like that, begging her to go all the way or to get the condom on quick so that they could fuck her and release themselves inside her. She reached out for the condom artfully left at the bottom of the bed. You never want to break the momentum by having to fumble around in drawers for a condom, she thought.

"You want to do cowgirl with me on top, darling," Kim gasped still getting her breath back from the lengthy session of oral.

"No."

So, muscle man did have a voice. But Kim was taken aback at the suddenness and abruptness of his reply.

"You want to come on top, mish position. I don't mind, anyway you want."

He grasped her firmly by the arms and turned her around in one powerful motion so she was lying face down on the bed. Kim was disconcerted by the suddenness and force of the movement but decided to run with it.

"OK, doggy style, that's cool with me," she gasped into the sheet as she started to get up onto all fours for him.

"No, I want to take you up the arse."

Kim was furious. She was also worried. She had a bad feeling about this guy from the start but had reached a point where that had passed and she had got on with her job. This behaviour was well out of order.

"I don't do anal," she spat out angrily, "you know that. I told you that earlier. Now get off me."

But he didn't. In fact, quite the reverse, he leant over her and laid his heavy muscular body on top of hers.

"I said I want anal and if you don't offer it, I'll take it."

"Fuck off you bastard. I said I don't do it."

Kim was scared. In the years she had been working in the parlour nothing like this had ever happened. Kim could feel her heart racing and beads of sweat forming on her forehead from the weight of the body pressing down and also from fear. Anal was one thing Kim didn't enjoy and just didn't do. She had a bad experience with a former boyfriend who had insisted on doing it. Reluctantly she had given in to him but it was excruciatingly painful and it made her feel abused and humiliated. She had never tried it again since and had never done it in the parlour. It was something that was definitely off-limits for her. She tried to compose herself and take a different tack.

"Look, OK, if there's been a misunderstanding that's cool, there's no problem. I can go back to the madam and explain and she'll give you your money back. It's no problem, no-one's trying to rip you off. So, just let me up and we'll go back to the lounge and I'll sort it out, OK."

I don't care about the money, I just want out of this situation anyway I can, thought Kim.

"No, you don't get it. I want anal. I'm going to fuck you up the arse, whether you want it or not. You're a whore aren't you, that's what you do."

Kim started to struggle underneath the dead weight of his body but, before she could shout out, a hand closed around her mouth and he pushed her hard and violently against the post of the bed head. She was groggy from the pain and shock and could feel beads of warm blood and a bruise starting to swell on her forehead. She squirmed some more but it was hopeless, he was just too strong and powerful for her as his hand closed around her nose and mouth and he pushed her down into the bed. Kim fought for breath. Her face pressed hard against the pillow, the weight of a body crushing down on her, a hand over her mouth. The hand relaxed long enough for her to take in a long gasp of air, like a free diver surfacing and taking in a long blast of life sustaining breath before going under again.

She took in just enough to sob, "No, please don't, please," before the hand tightened over her again.

"So, you don't do anal. You fucking whore. You'll do what I want. I'll take what I've paid for."

This was what Kim had always feared about her work in the massage parlour, the risk that one day she would encounter someone who was deranged and malicious. She put up with most things, she knew she was good at her job and could give her clients a good time. Most of them were harmless but lurking under the surface was always the threat that one day she would encounter a truly nasty piece of work. That day was here. The hand was removed from her mouth, but her face was still pressed into the pillow until Kim forced her head up for a fleeting moment. There was one desperate card she could play.

"The other girls will hear. You won't get away with this."

But he took no notice. Her face was pushed down even harder so that Kim had to fight desperately for her breath. Kim was terrified. The sweat of fear oozed out of every pore in her body as she struggled for breath and braced herself for the agonising pain in her back-side that now seemed inevitable. She didn't deserve this, no working girl deserved to be treated like this.

She felt the weight of him, took in the smell of sweet sickly after shave. She felt the hardness pressing against the flesh of her naked bottom searching for the right spot. She felt a hand against her, exploring her flesh, trying to find her tight little arse-hole and strong hands parting the cheeks of her bottom. She could feel the hard cock brushing against flesh and then being pushed into the crack in her bottom. He had found the right spot now. Kim braced herself for the searing pain and the humiliation...but it didn't come.

Instead, there was a dull thud. That one of the other girls must have heard something and come to the rescue was Kim's immediate thought. Kim's face was still pushed into the pillow but she could sense movement and other people in the room. She felt her attacker, now an inert dead weight, being dragged off her aching body and heard it fall with a dull thud onto the floor. She forced herself over to see her rescuers, expecting it to be Ruby or Tiffany, who were working today. What she saw surprised her more than the shock of the blow to her head against the bed-head.

She blinked in amazement. What she saw were two funny little men. They would have been rotund figures in normal clothes but they were both enormous, wrapped in bolsters and blankets as they were. They had metal tea trays tied to their fronts and backs in a haphazard way with belts and old pieces of string. One held a massive cast iron saucepan in one hand and a wooden sword in the other whilst the second had a large brass coal shuttle in one hand and an umbrella in the other. They looked like fat bundles of clothes and could barely move.

Kim was amazed they had overcome her fit and muscular attacker though she supposed that they did have the element of surprise in their favour and the saucepan and coal scuttles were quite formidable weapons in a peculiar kind of way. It appeared to Kim both the heavy items of household ware had been used on her attacker, who now lay unconscious on the floor. This reminded Kim of something. She racked her brains, trying to recall stories from her childhood. Then she remembered – Tweedledum and Tweedledee; they were characters from 'Alice Through the Looking Glass'. How odd, thought Kim. What could they possibly be doing in a massage parlour in Manchester?

The two fat little men stood over Kim's assailant with huge grins across their faces looking very pleased with themselves. Kim's client laid in a misshapen heap on floor knocked out cold, a pool of blood oozing onto the carpet from two deep gashes in his head, which Kim supposed had been

12

made by the saucepan and the coal scuttle, but could not be sure and, in her disorientated state, could not really care less. She was just relieved to have escaped, but bemused by her bizarre new predicament.

"Mistress will be pleased with me for saying we should turn up dressed for battle," said Tweedledum.

"Contrariwise," Tweedledee said, "I recall it was my idea to dress for battle."

"No-how, it was me who found all the saucepans and tea-trays."

"And, anyhow, it was my blow that knocked him out. I'll tell mistress that and she'll reward me, no-how."

"Contrariwise, it was my blow with the saucepan that did it and she'll reward me."

The two funny men seemed oblivious of Kim's presence and seemed only intent on arguing about their respective roles in the bizarre fight with Kim's client. Then, all of a sudden, they both looked up and pointed up at the ceiling.

"Mistress's raven!" they shouted out in unison.

"She's sent it to spy on us," Tweedledum called out.

Kim glanced up to where they were looking but could see nothing. It was almost as if they could see beyond the walls of the room into a distant sky. Then the room went dark as if a thunderstorm cloud was passing through it and a jet black bird appeared from nowhere, swooped down and darted across Kim's astonished eyes in a flash. Tweedledum and Tweedledee grabbed one another's hands and ran into the corner of the room where they sat cowering. The black raven perched on the pine-wood bedstead at the foot of the bed, cocked its head and fixed its white beady eyes on the two quarrelling figures. Its beak opened and a voice cawed across the pink boudoir.

"Arguing again boys? The Red Queen won't be very pleased with you. She needs the girl and all you two can do is squabble," the raven said.

Now Kim had seen enough; characters from a children's book and now talking ravens. I must be in a nightmare, she thought. Obviously the blow to the head has made me delirious or I have been knocked out and am imagining all of this. In a minute I'll wake up and everything will be back to normal.

"It wasn't me, no-how. It was him who started it."

Tweedledee, a rotund figure wrapped in blankets, bolsters and tea trays and wielding a coal shuttle, his face screwed up in a look of sheer terror, pointed an accusing finger at his companion.

"Contrariwise, it was him who started it. The Red Queen should punish him, not me," Tweedledum screamed, pointing his finger in return.

Kim's head was in a whirl of pain and confusion. Her violent client, her unexpected rescue at the hands of two story-book characters, the talking raven and the whole bizarre predicament she found herself in conspired finally to overwhelm her. One final thought went through her head; what did the raven mean about the Red Queen needing the girl. Did it mean her?

Then she passed out.

3: The White Rabbit

Kim found herself, still naked, her back propped up against a cold stone wall. It was pitched black, only the barest flicker of light seeped past the perimeter of a thick metal door. Her eyes gradually adjusted to the darkness and in the penetrating gloom Kim saw she was confined in a cell of some kind. There were iron shackles on her wrists and ankles locked with padlocks and iron chains attached to them that were in turn secured to metal rings mounted in the stone walls. Around her neck was a leather collar with a ring in it. She rattled at the chains and found that they still let her stretch and move around a bit. Kim gave an ironic snort of laughter. On the floor was a bottle of mineral water and a big bar of Cadbury's fruit and nut chocolate. Whoever was imprisoning her did not intend that she die of thirst or hunger at least. Her mind drifted back to the advert she remembered from her childhood; 'everyone's a fruit and nut case', the jingle ran through her head. Is somebody taking the piss, she wondered? She didn't care. Kim was ravenous and she set about unwrapping the familiar dark blue foil and biting off a huge chunk of chocolate. It felt like bliss. She let the milky chocolate melt in her mouth to savour it before swallowing.

Kim rested her head back against the wall of the cell as she ate and took a moment to reflect on her predicament. She must have looked a state. Her long fair hair was tussled and knotted, she had a bruise on her forehead and her head still throbbed. What was happening to her? Why was she being kept as a prisoner? And, most importantly, was this real or was it a twisted nightmare? The strange events of the last few hours spun around her head as she tried to piece them together and make sense of them. She couldn't. On the verge of being raped in the arse by a psycho in the massage parlour where she worked, her attacker had been disabled by two characters that looked like Tweedledum and Tweedledee from 'Alice Through the Looking Glass." She remembered the strange words spoken by the talking raven, "she needs the girl". Did that mean her? And if so, who needs me, and why? Then she recalled a fog pass over her as she passed out.

The next thing she remembered was falling down a long tunnel, just like Alice in the book, she thought. It was the strangest experience, like she imagined weightlessness might feel. It was an odd floating sensation as if she were a feather dropped from a great height, but always falling deeper.

Down, down, down she went. Was it a dream? Had the blow to her head traumatised her so much she was now delusional. Kim wondered if her descent would ever come to an end. First, she tried to look down and make out where she was heading and how far she had to fall, but it was too dark to see anything.

Then, she looked at the sides of the tunnel and to her surprise she found that it was lined with cases full of books. She tried to take in some of the titles as she floated past; '120 Days of Sodom' was one. Very strange, thought Kim. One of her clients in the brothel who enjoyed some domination recommended she read it but she had never got round to it. She understood very well that it was a manual for sadists though. She noticed some of the other titles: 'The Golden Bough', 'A Study of Ritual Hero and Goddess in the Iliad'. 'Chariots of the Gods' and a copy of the Egyptian 'Book of the Dead' drifted past her. What an intriguing collection of books, she thought; their owner must have some very odd tastes.

Down, down, down Kim tumbled. Interspersed amongst the cupboards and book-shelves there were pictures on the wall; quirky sketches showing bizarre scenes of bondage and strange rituals. How disturbing, thought Kim. There was also another set of pictures, comic book covers with fairy tale characters, but fairy tale characters like Kim had never seen depicted before. A black haired vamp-like Snow White in a yellow latex mini skirt with massive breasts squeezing out of tight blue top and a tart-like Red Riding Hood in thigh high red leather boots and wearing only a bra and knickers and a scarlet rubber cloak.

There was one picture that particularly caught her eye, a statuesque dark haired woman dressed in red and black in a costume decorated with black hearts, but it was not this that attracted her attention, striking and unusual though the image was; it was the eyes. They sucked her in and captivated her. She felt that they were watching her long descent into... well, Kim didn't know what. But there was more, Kim felt that she had seen them before, had been the subject of that penetrating gaze in some other life. She could not explain it but she was inexorably drawn to that look as she tumbled until the image receded into the distance and out of her sight.

After descending for what seemed like an age Kim had found herself in this cell. She had no idea how she got there and no recollection of how she had become manacled to the wall. She could only presume she had passed out again. It was hardly surprising. Kim's head was still aching from being rammed against the bed post in the massage parlour. Kim's eyes had fully adjusted to the impenetrable darkness by now and she could see that the solid stone walls and ceiling offered no openings or means of escape.

Her terrifying predicament had finally struck home. Here she was chained up and locked in a small stone cell with only a bottle of water and some chocolate, most of which she'd already eaten. Her experience in the brothel and now this even stranger, more frightening, ordeal began to overwhelm her. Was she going mad? And it was more than just the events of the last few hours, traumatic thought they had been. The enforced confinement was forcing her to look further back over her life. In some ways it was nothing new. She always seemed to find herself being pulled along by circumstance, never quite having control of her life and never really finding a place she belonged. It was like the work at the brothel. She never at any point remembered making a conscious decision to do that, she just seemed to drift into it and the reasons for doing it had got lost in a haze of distorted memories. There was a whole chunk of her life leading up to her starting work there she had no clear recollection of.

She pulled her arms around herself, her breasts were heaving with emotion. She felt the tears welling up in her eyes and then the trails of salty water run down her pale cheeks. She began to sob as the emotion of everything overwhelmed her. She needed that. It was most unlike her to give in like that, but her bizarre situation had given her ample excuse for a good cry. Come on Kim, she thought, pull yourself together.

Well, she reflected, I can't make sense of any of this. There is nothing much I can do. Perhaps this is my fate, that I shall be left here to rot and centuries later my skeleton will be found and I will become the source of a great murder mystery. She imagined the cell a hive of activity; full of white boiler suited and masked forensic scientists. "Yes, we know that she was a girl in her twenties. This is interesting; we can tell from a close examination of her pelvic bones that she was a sexually active young woman." Kim supposed that she would rather her life would not be exposed to that kind of scrutiny but she had to find some way of diverting her mind away from her predicament.

The moment of distress had passed and Kim was settling down to accept her fate, whatever that might be, when she heard movement outside the cell door. Her heart jumped a beat. Was she about to be released and would she now find out who her captor was? A window in the cell door was slid back and a shaft of light filled the room. Kim looked up straining and squinting into the dazzling light.

What she saw startled her. A pink nose, whiskers and black beady eyes appeared at the opening. A white pawed hand ran across the whiskered face. I don't believe this, thought Kim, a white rabbit; I really am in a story book.

"Oh dear! Oh dear! I shall be too late," she heard a voice mutter.

She heard the jangling of keys and the metal door creak open. There was a man sized white rabbit wearing a yellow jacket and tartan waistcoat in the frame of the door. Kim pinched herself. It was no crude costume, the man's features had morphed into the white fur as if he had really been turned into a rabbit. Kim was reminded of a theatrical production of the 'Tales of Beatrix Potter' she went to when, through a child's eyes, it seemed so magical that people could be turned into animals and for it to look so real.

"You're late," the white rabbit said to her.

A thousand questions Kim would like to have asked spun around her head but she could only blurt out, "What do you mean I'm late?"

The white rabbit hopped nervously from one foot to another anxiously looking at his fob watch, which he had pulled out of his waistcoat, tapping its face hard with his knuckle as if this act might miraculously make time move backwards for him.

"Oh, Oh, I'm going to be in so much trouble. I'm late, so, so late. Mistress is not going to like this. She likes everybody to be punctual. Oh, I'm going to be in trouble," the rabbit muttered to himself.

"Shut up babbling and tell me where I am and what I'm doing here," Kim demanded.

"No, no, there's no time for explanations, I'm already five minutes late. We must be going."

"I'm not going anywhere until I get some answers," Kim persisted.

"My mistress will explain. Look, please, let's go. I'm already going to get punished; the later I am the more severely I'll get punished. You wouldn't like to see me punished, would you?" the white rabbit pleaded.

Kim sniffed, "Well, I don't see why I should care. If it was left to me, and you were a real rabbit, then I should put you in a casserole and eat you. Besides, it's me who has been kidnapped and imprisoned."

"She's most likely done that to keep you safe." The white rabbit looked one way and then the other. "There are strange and wonderful things happen here. I don't expect she wanted you going off on your own. She probably wanted to protect you."

"Yeah, strange things, tell me about it!" huffed Kim. "Whoever she is, she has a funny way of looking after me. I've been chained to the wall and kept in darkness for hours."

"Oh please," the rabbit pleaded. "I don't know anything. I can't answer your questions. She might do. We're already late. Believe me, we don't want to keep her waiting and anger her any more, that's not good for me or you either for that matter. If you want answers please do as I say and come with me."

Kim decided she was not going to get any sensible answers from this bundle of babbling idiocy. If she wanted answers then she might get them from this white rabbit's mistress. The wicked thought crossed her mind that he rather deserved to be punished and she really wouldn't mind seeing it happen.

"I have to put these on you," said the white rabbit apologetically as he dangled a blindfold and leather lead in front of her.

"No way, I'm not putting those on," said Kim indignantly.

"Oh, but you must. I have express instructions. I want the girl blindfolded she said."

"Oh, well, if you must," Kim sighed with resignation.

Kim's situation was so bizarre that she had got beyond caring. I suppose that being blindfolded by a white rabbit has to be preferred to being fucked up the arse by a psychopath she thought. She would much rather be safe at home, freshly showered in her dressing gown with her cat, Dinah, nestled in her lap and a nice glass of chilled white wine in her hand.

The white rabbit pulled a blindfold over her eyes and adjusted it so that she was in complete darkness and then nervously attached a lead to the ring on the leather collar she was already wearing. Kim heard the jangling of keys as the white rabbit unlocked the padlocks to release her from the manacles.

"Follow me," he said, "I'll take you to my mistress. She's expecting you."

4: The Queen of Hearts

"Here she is mistress," announced the white rabbit.

"What's the meaning of this? You're ten minutes late."

"I'm sorry mistress."

"Do you think I've got time to wait around for my slaves?"

"No, of course not, I'm really sorry mistress."

"Sorry is not good enough. You know what happens to slaves who are late, don't you?"

"Yes mistress."

"Well, what?"

"They're punished mistress."

"Yes, they're made to be kept waiting, aren't they? Usually in some uncomfortable position, usually in pain. Get out of my sight now. You're dismissed. I'll deal with you later."

Kim, still blindfolded, listened to this conversation intently. The first voice was the white rabbit, still in a state of fidgety agitation, speaking with respect and deference. The second voice, the one presumably belonging to the white rabbit's mistress, sent a tingle down Kim's spine. It wasn't loud or hysterical just calmly imperious with a thinly hidden menace. Hearing that voice Kim could well understand why the white rabbit was so jittery.

Kim drew in a gulp of air. Oh well, this is it she thought, it looks as though I'm going to meet the white rabbit's mistress. She felt hands from behind her head lifting up the blindfold. There was so much to take in around her but Kim's eyes could not help but be fixated on the commanding figure that stood before her, a vision in black and red pvc, her red bodice festooned in black hearts. A fetish Queen of Hearts, thought Kim.

"Come here girl," she said gently beckoning Kim towards her.

Those eyes, blue pools of latent and unspoken dominance, gazed into Kim's. They were the same eyes she had seen in the picture on her descent down the tunnel, the same eyes that she had felt inexplicably drawn to. Kim had so many questions, so much that she wanted explaining, but she shuffled forward obediently, not daring to say anything.

"Look at her Duchess, she's lovely isn't she," said the Red Queen turning to her companion, "just as lovely as I remember her."

"She's certainly very beautiful," the Duchess replied.

"I bet you'd like to dress her up and play with her, wouldn't you Duchess?" she asked, with a sly grin on her lips.

"Oh, yes madam, I certainly would."

"I think she'll do perfectly," the Red Queen pronounced.

"She's a bit damaged though."

"Yes, those fools, they got there too late, as usual. They'll pay for that."

"Yes, Madame, they were probably arguing with one another again I expect."

The Queen of Hearts came forward. She ran her pvc gloved hand through Kim's dishevelled hair, across her cheek and down her neckline and then across her shoulders and down to her breasts. All of the time her eyes were fixed on her as if she were live bait and Kim had taken the bite and was being reeled in. Reeled in to what, she did not know. The haunting gaze of the Red Queen and the touch of the smooth pvc against her bare flesh sent a tingle through her body, right down to her crotch. Kim gasped with longing and desire. What is happening to me she wondered; these strange events and now these erotic feelings swelling up inside her at the slightest touch of this dominant woman? Finally, as the pvc clad fingers were pulled away from Kim's flesh, the spell was momentarily broken.

"Please, where am I? Please let me go. What do you want with me? Please let me go," she blurted out.

The Red Queen's gaze hardened and her whole body stiffened; her eyes flashed with anger and the malevolent threatening tone she had used with the white rabbit returned to her voice.

"You will ask no questions of me. You have been rescued from a terrible fate and brought here to serve me. If you submit then you will have nothing to fear. You are a special person and the fates have chosen you for a purpose, my girl. Submit willingly and give your heart up to me and the rewards will be, how can I say, unimaginable."

This was all too much for Kim. She felt tears welling up inside her and she started sobbing.

"But, please, I just want to go home. Please let me go."

The flash of anger appeared in the Red Queen's eyes again. She reached out and grasped Kim's nipples, gripping them tightly between her thumb and fore finger, squeezing and then twisting. Kim let out a squeak of pain. How perfectly horrid, she thought at first. But, the nipple torture had the desired effect, as Kim immediately stopped crying as she focused on the waves of pain that washed over her. Kim couldn't believe she allowed that to happen. She uttered no murmurs of protest, offered no resistance at all. It was almost as if, in some inexplicable way, she wanted to have this

21

awesome figure of a woman play with her and inflict pain on her. Her nipples felt sore and were throbbing and her head was in a whirl of confused torment.

"Contrary to what you might think, I will not keep you here against your will," the Red Queen pronounced. "All who serve in my kingdom here do so entirely of their own free will; they submit to me because they want to. You are free to go at any time you want. But, what I offer you here is the chance to find out who you really are. I don't claim that it's easy for any who serve me and I won't deny that there won't be challenges, some of them severe, but I give you the chance to test yourself, to fulfil your deepest desires and to discover your true self, if you dare. Do you dare Kim?"

Kim was transfixed by the Red Queen's speech. Her commanding presence and her calm imperious voice had left her spellbound. Everything called out to her to go. She had been presented with the opportunity to be let free and to leave this bizarre place, which just minutes ago she had pleaded to do. But yet, there was another part of her that desired to follow this mysterious dark woman and enter the path she held out for her. This powerful figure had some kind of hold over her. And there was the strange comment she had made earlier that gnawed away at Kim, "she's just as lovely as I remember her." Kim was curious as to what she meant by that. How could that possibly be; Kim had no recollection of this person. Kim was tormented over how to answer the Red Queen.

"And can I leave at any time?" Kim asked, seeking confirmation of the Red Queens' pledge.

"Yes, of course, you have my word," she replied, "but if you leave of your own free will you will never be able to return and, then, you may never know what you might have learnt."

Did she dare stay and accept her fate in this strange world? Kim agonised over her answer. She felt some enigmatic affinity with this woman and the world she inhabited like there was some strange umbilical cord connecting them. After all, she thought, what did she have to lose if the offer of being allowed to leave at any time was on the table? Above all, the Red Queen appeared to be holding onto some hope for Kim of understanding those parts of her life that she had forgotten.

Kim took a deep sigh, "Yes, I dare. I'll stay."

The Queen of Hearts face lit up with a broad welcoming smile. She was thrilled her powers of persuasion were skilled enough to capture the girl. I know fate has tied this girl to me in some indiscernible way, she thought, and I want her in my world.

"I am pleased Kim. I don't believe you'll regret your decision." She turned to her companion, "Duchess, will you tidy her up for me? I want to make use of her straight away and she must look her best for what I have in mind."

Kim's heart jumped a beat. What had she done? What strange journey had she just committed herself to?

The Duchess came forward with a bowl of water and some cotton wool. The Queen of Hearts' companion was another bizarre figure, but that no longer came as any surprise to Kim now. Underneath the shiny pvc costume of the Red Queen's fetish lady-in-waiting there was clearly a man. She wore a black skirt trimmed with a metallic red ruff and black apron with a splendid red heart emblazoned on it. Her black wig had streaks of ruby in it, just like her mistress's, and her hair was tied in bunches and perched on it was a little red cap with a black heart on it. She reflected the colours and style of her mistress though, understandably, did not look as striking or regal as her. The eyes behind the white mask she wore to disguise her identity and true sex looked kind and gentle and Kim immediately warmed to her.

The Duchess cleaned the bump on her head tenderly with some diluted TCP and washed her face for her. Her mouth was probably smothered in chocolate after gorging on the bar of 'fruit and nut' earlier she thought, her sense of humour returning to her now she had made this strange decision to remain in this unusual place. The Duchess studiously brushed the knotted tangles out of her wavy fair hair taking great care not to pull on it and taking clear pleasure in touching her and looking after her.

Kim had some time now to take in her surroundings. She had been overwhelmed by them when the blindfold was first removed but then all of her attention became focused on the Red Queen. She returned to look over the room in greater detail whilst the Duchess tended to her. It had the aspect of large medieval barn. She looked high up into the wooden rafters in the ceiling and noted, as she had seen when her eyes were first uncovered, that it was dominated by an iron body cage that hung from the ceiling suspended by chains. This was a fearsome article of captivity and maybe torture she pondered. She was minded of pictures she had seen of medieval torture chambers and the fearsome iron implements of pain that filled them, yet strangely did not feel fearful any more.

The Duchess continued to clean Kim up, washing her gently with balls of cotton wall dipped in a bowl of water that had been scented with essential oils. Kim stood quietly; content to wallow in the sensuousness of the calming scent and the Duchess's touch on her bare skin. She felt a tingle of arousal as her breasts were washed. The Duchess brushed her pubic hairs and ran a gloved finger across her sex. Kim didn't mind particularly, the touch was gentle and erotic. She gasped as she felt a finger exploring her sex, softly parting her cunt lips, and being inserted into her.

"Vicky Duchess! Are you playing with her?" the voice reprimanded.

"Yes, I'm sorry madam, I just couldn't resist."

"Well you can stop that. I know you want to play with her Duchess but you'll have to show some restraint. I don't want her interfered with…yet."

The Red Queen had been adjusting the chains that suspended the cage before Kim's little moan of pleasure distracted her. The body cage had been lowered to the floor alongside Kim.

"Now, girl, I want you to climb into the cage."

Kim glanced across at her quizzically but the Red Queen's authoritative mien and the tone of her voice was such that she knew she would not resist the command. She obediently stepped over a metal bar and into the cage. It was fashioned with wide metal strips moulded into the contours of a body shape. Kim nestled her face into the head of the cage and stood quietly awaiting her fate. The cold metal loomed around her. A smell, like rusting iron, filled her nostrils. The Red Queen stood facing her, the door of the cage open, with that icy penetrating look in her eyes. She was silent. She did not need to speak. She worked herself into Kim 's mind like creeping fingers of ivy reaching into decaying brickwork. Kim had made her choice to submit to this. The Red Queen took the blindfold and pulled it over Kim's eyes and adjusted it so that once again she was plunged into blackness. Kim immediately felt her other senses heightened, the aroma of the iron taking on an intoxicating feeling.

Kim stood quietly for what seemed like many minutes, her breathing heavy and tense with anticipation. The removal of the sense of sight had made every nerve ending tingle and the silent waiting for the unknown was overwhelming for Kim. Fingers reached out for her nipples again and squeezed them firmly. The pain was intense but Kim did not scream or flinch. She embraced it, like it was the only sensation in the whole world. Her nipples were twisted and then messaged and then tweaked again and with every exquisite piece of torture Kim felt her body well up with a combination of pain…and pleasure. The probing fingers were withdrawn and Kim let out a gasp of relief.

But, her respite was short lived. She heard a gentle buzzing sound. What new implement of torment was this? Suddenly she felt a tingling sensation on her breasts like a hundred tiny pin pricks. She could not see the implement that was being used on her but the buzzing and the sensation of an electric current passing over her all pointed to it being a violet wand or similar kind of instrument. She had heard of them and seen pictures but never had one used on her before. Its touch was a mixture of searing pain and sensual pleasure. She squeaked and moaned as the implement was brushed down her body, across her thighs and over her crotch. She expelled groans of pain but, despite that, she didn't want the sharp tingling sensation to stop.

"Do you trust me Kim?" the voice whispered, persuasive and seductive.

"Mmmm. Yes, I do," replied Kim, "at least, I think I do."

"Now the door will close in on you and you will be enclosed in the cold iron of my body cage. You will need to trust me. Stay their silently and listen for my commands."

Kim heard the hinges creaking and the metal door click shut. What will happen now, thought Kim? She heard the grinding and clanking of chains as they were fed through a pulley in the ceiling. She felt the cage move and sway slightly. She felt herself being lifted up high into the rafters of the barn. The sensation was intoxicating. She was hanging there, helpless, powerless, entrapped in a metal cage completely in the control of the Queen of Hearts. She felt the sensation of movement, heard the sound of clanking chains. She could no longer tell if she was moving backwards or forwards, up or down; there was only the intoxicating swinging motion. The cage stopped its gentle rocking movement. Kim felt that it was now on the ground again.

A voice whispered from above her as if it was far in the distance.

"Kim, listen to your mistress. Listen to the Red Queen. The gate of the cage is not locked, you can push it open."

Kim gently raised her hand and pushed against some metal bars, felt them give and the door of the cage swing open.

"Now Kim," the voice came from far away, "take off your blindfold and step out of the cage."

Kim did as she was told. She felt so disorientated. Her head was spinning from the motions of the cage and it took a while before she felt steady on her feet and she could take in her surroundings. She was in a pit. Above her was a metal grill and peering through it she could see two faces staring intently down at her; one the white skin and dark hair of the Red Queen, the other the white masked face of the Duchess.

"Look around you Kim, what do you see?"

Kim looked in front of her now and saw two other figures with her in the pit. She recognised them immediately from their round faces and pot bellies; it was Tweedledum and Tweedledee but they were very different from when she had encountered them before. Tweedledum, or at least Kim thought it was he (it was rather difficult to tell as they looked like twins) was laid out naked on the stone floor of the pit, his arms and legs stretched out and tied with rope to rings at the side of it. There was a ball gag in his mouth. His twin, also naked, was sat on a chair and tied to it with an elaborate criss-cross pattern of ropes. He also had a matching hard rubber ball gag in his mouth. Kim smiled; their mistress was clearly not going to have her peace shattered by their bickering. There was a luggage label attached to the big toes on their right hand feet and Kim knelt down to read the writing on the one tied to Tweedledum. 'Punish me' it read.

The voice from the on-looking Red Queen called down, "Yes Kim, can you read what it says. They must both be punished. It was because of their tardiness and incompetence that you got damaged Kim. You must administer my retribution on them. Can you see the implements I have selected for their punishment?"

Kim cast her eyes around the pit and they alighted on a small round table. Kim stepped over to it and looked at the objects on it. There were two sets of nipple clamps with fierce metal prongs and also two sets of electric massagers with controllers and sticky pads connected to them. Kim knew what the Red Queen meant her to do with these and, bizarrely, she felt a surge of empowerment. She had been jettisoned into this strange world and had so many things done to her that the idea of doing something to somebody else quite appealed to her.

Kim smiled. The eyes of the two round figures widened as they saw her look of anticipation. There were muffled pleas from behind their gags but Kim had already made up her mind; this was one of the Red Queen's instructions she might enjoy carrying out. And she was right, if they had got to the massage parlour earlier, Kim might never have been threatened by her psychotic client or got the nasty bump on her head, so really, they deserved to be punished.

Kim picked up a set of nipple clamps and one of the massager units and knelt over Tweedledum, who was laid out flat, his back against the stone floor. I loved doing this kind of thing in the parlour, she thought, now is my chance to take it a bit further. Strands of her wavy fair hair fell onto Tweedledum's chest. She teased him by holding the nipple clamps and squeezing them open and shut right in front of his terrified eyes. She felt wicked; she know she had a sadistic glint in her eyes. She started by taking his nipples between her fingers, nipping and pulling them just as the Red Queen had done to her. Then she opened the claws of the nipple clamp. They were fearsome, highly sprung little objects with metal claws like crocodile teeth. This will hurt, Kim thought.

She let the teeth close on his nipple and watched for the reaction. Tweedledum twisted and squirmed in his bondage. He was probably screaming in agony behind the ball gag but all Kim could hear were muffled squeaks. She repeated the process on the other nipple, the two clamps being connected by a thin chain, which Kim could tug if she wanted to torment him more. A soon as Tweedledum got comfortable with the level of pain

Kim would give the chain a sharp little pull. I should be ashamed of my behaviour, she reflected, but I'm not!

Kim turned her attention to the little electrical massaging thing. She knelt down between Tweedledum's legs, took the covers off the little sticky pads and stuck them onto his balls. Then, she switched on the control that went with it. She had never used one of these before, but it was perfectly straightforward; one little button to reduce the current and another to increase it. Kim pushed the 'up' button a few times but was disappointed that there was no response. She pushed it a few more times and was pleased to hear Tweedledum moan and watch him twitch. She pushed the button a few more times. Ha! That's better, she thought, now I've got a reaction. There were muffled shouts of pain through the gag and Tweedledum's rotund little figure jerked up and down in time to the electric current. Kim toyed with him, turning the little device down a little bit to give him some respite, and then up again.

She carried on like this for a while until she left the massager in a throbbing position so that she could turn her attention to Tweedledee. Oh no, she must be fair and give some attention to him. Kim wondered which would be worst, to be punished first or second. She rather thought it would be better to go first. After all, poor Tweedledee had all that time to watch his poor companion being tormented and anticipate the agony that was going to come.

"It's your turn now," said Kim, her lips curling into a sadistic little smile, "you didn't think you were going to escape, did you?"

A voice came from high above beyond the grill set in the dungeon floor. Kim had quite forgotten that the Red Queen and the Duchess had been watching her all the time.

"Yes, excellent! Carry on. She's good isn't she?" said the Red Queen turning to the Duchess with a delighted grin.

"Oh yes, madam, she's really good."

"She's a natural. I think I'm going to have great fun having her around my dungeon once I've got her trained properly."

Kim turned away and concentrated her attention on Tweedledee, who was tied to a chair with soft black ropes. There was an elaborate network of ropes that created a criss-cross pattern across his body and legs and secured him tightly to the back and legs of the chair. Kim had only done a little bit of tie and tease in the massage parlour, usually tying a simple rope around wrists or ankles and then onto the bed frame. Whoever had done this was clearly very skilled at rope bondage. The patterns of ropes across his body were carefully thought out and skilfully executed.

Kim started with nipple clamps again, the initial shock of putting them on made Tweedledee strain so hard that the chair nearly toppled over. Then she applied the pads from the electric massager onto his balls and turned the current up. Tweedledee was tied so tight that it was harder to gauge his reactions to the electric current. After pressing the little button higher she could see him strain against the ropes so hard they dug into his flesh and started to leave red impression marks across his torso and thighs.

Kim carried on playing like this, alternating between the two, turning the current up higher, tugging the chains on the nipple clamps every so often to keep them on their toes. She was having a great time and had quite forgotten where she was until she heard noise in the corner of the underground cell. The Duchess had pulled up a hatch door in the roof of the pit, which revealed a set of little steps. Kim presumed that this was a signal for her to stop tormenting Tweedledum and Tweedledee. She ripped off the sticky pads from their balls making them jerk with surprise and pain and, finally, squeezed the nipple clamps to release the tight claws. Kim had always been told that this was the worst part of nipple torture and judging from their reaction she could believe that.

Kim climbed up the wooden steps and came back out into the open medieval barn but it was deserted; there was no sign of the Queen of Hearts or the Duchess. Perhaps the Red Queen had deliberately left her to her own devices to explore this strange place. Kim wondered what she would encounter next.

5: The Black Cat

Kim traced her steps back through the darkness of the medieval chamber with its fearsome cage and pit and emerged into a corridor. Here she faced a difficult choice; to her left was one door, facing her was a short passage leading to another door and across from her was an imposing black metal gate with the word 'Nemesis' welded onto it that led to stairs and an upper floor. Where should she go next? She had already had some strange adventures and she wished she could end up somewhere normal with normal people and hold a regular conversation.

Then Kim noticed something; built into the space under the stairs was a small cage with a wire mesh door that was padlocked. Kim's attention had been drawn by a flicker of movement in this cage. As she approached and her eyes penetrated the gloom she could see a shadowy figure inside.

She peered into the cage through the wire mesh. A whiskered face, pointed black ears and a pair of eyes stared back at her. She jumped back in fright. It was a strange creature, the shape of a man but with the features of a cat. The ankles and wrists of the black cat, if that was indeed what it was, had been shackled and padlocked to hooks on the walls and floor of the cage. His head hung forlornly and his bushy black and white tail spread out from underneath his back-side where he sat.

The black cat looked back at her. It was most odd; it was as if the creature recognised her. It shuffled to the back of the cell and cowered into the corner staring back at her in alarm. It must think I'm going to harm it, she thought.

"I promise I won't hurt you," said Kim, "I like cats. I have a cat at home in my flat in Manchester, she's called Dinah."

Kim held her hand out to the mesh reassuringly and the cat shuffled towards her on all fours. Kim saw that there was a tag on the leather collar around the cat's neck. She stretched her fingers through the wire mesh and tentatively reached for it, hoping that the animal would not scratch or bite her. 'Nano', it read. That must be the cat's name, thought Kim. What a strange name for a cat. She flipped the metal disc around and on the other side was another inscription, 'Property of Mistress Nemesis', it read. This was even stranger, thought Kim. What could that mean?

The cat eyed her warily. She wondered if the cat could speak at all. The strange encounters she had already experienced suggested it was worth striking up a conversation with the animal. It was hardly going to be the normal conversation she craved but she was so anxious to find out more about this world and to use any opportunity to understand this strange place she had committed herself to.

"Hello, my name is Kim. Can you help me? I've lost my way," she asked.

"Well, that's very careless of you," the cat replied.

Kim glared at the black cat. Really, this was so infuriating. Would nobody here give her a sensible answer? She was about to speak crossly to the cat and tell him off for being so rude and unhelpful when he spoke again.

"Besides you don't have any ways, all of the ways here belong to Mistress Nemesis. You'll have to use one of her ways."

At least Kim had got an answer of sorts, even if it was a strange one. But, the black cat named Nano appeared to know something about this place so Kim thought it was worth pursuing him with some more questions.

"So, who is Mistress Nemesis?" she asked.

"This is all her domain, her kingdom, there is nothing that happens in here that she doesn't know about or doesn't control," the cat replied.

"You mean I've no free will in this place at all? I must have some choices."

"No, of course not, Mistress Nemesis controls everything here. You'll meet many characters in this world but they are all doing her bidding. Sometimes they may think they have free will but it will be an illusion. Even when you think you have made a choice it will only be because that's what she desires. Mistress Nemesis is powerful; she will get inside your head and make you do what she wants. Everybody in this world is in her control, they all serve her."

Kim contemplated the answer she had been given. The cat was proving to be most helpful and knowledgeable. Perhaps if Kim could find out more about how this world worked she could find her way around it. This Mistress Nemesis seemed to be the key, especially if the cat was right about the power she wielded over her domain. The cat seemed to have got over his initial nervousness at being approached by her and was speaking to her openly. She decided to get as much information out of the cat as she could.

"So, this Mistress Nemesis, am I likely to meet her at all?"

"Oh yes, almost certainly, but she takes on many characters, sometimes you might not know. Who have you met in Nemesisland?"

"Well, I've met the Queen of Hearts in a chamber with a cage and the Duchess, the white rabbit and Tweedledum and Tweedledee," Kim replied.

"Oh well, you've almost certainly met her then, the Red Queen is one of the personas she takes on as she travels through her kingdom. She has many guises. Most of the time she will treat you cruelly, she is capable of inflicting severe punishments on the people who occupy her world, especially if they displease her or fail to carry out her instructions. She'll laugh at you as well. Even when you are in the most awful of predicaments it will amuse her. Occasionally, if you serve her well and if you're lucky, very lucky, she'll show you some kindness."

"Well, I think she sounds quite horrid," said Kim, "I rather hope that I don't meet her again."

The cat nodded his head and smiled at Kim. "No, you haven't understood this world at all. She's not horrible. When you've been here a bit longer you'll understand, you'll embrace her, you'll do whatever she wants and, however painful or humiliating, it won't matter because you'll want to serve her."

Kim was struggling with this concept. She had been told she had no free will and now she was being told she would have to be servile to the cruel mistress of this bizarre world.

"I'm sure I should not wish to serve such a person."

The black cat laughed at her.

"I bet you've already given yourself up to her. There are none here that don't. Did the Queen of Hearts punish you?"

"Yes, she treated me cruelly. She chained me up in a cage, twisted my nipples and used an electric wand on me."

"And you could do nothing to resist could you? Am I right?"

"Yes, I suppose so."

"Even when you weren't restrained you did nothing to escape, did you?

"Well, you're right, I didn't."

"And tell me, be honest, when the pain was being inflicted, you wanted it didn't you? You didn't want it to stop, did you? I bet you wanted more, didn't you?"

Kim was shocked. It was as if an express train had stopped her in her tracks. All of this was true.

"And did she have you carrying out tasks for her?"

"Well yes, I guess she did. She told me to punish Tweedledum and Tweedledee."

"And you did it without questioning, didn't you? You had to, because she wanted you to and you were powerless to resist!"

Kim gaped as the dawn of realisation hit her.

"You're a character in Nemesisland now," the black cat laughed, "You've been captivated and there's nothing you can do about it."

"But how can I get out?" cried Kim.

"You don't. At least not until she lets you go. Anyway, after a little while you won't want to, you'll want to stay here. Don't worry. All the characters in Nemesisland have been through what you have. Some have accepted their place whilst others still resist. But it's hopeless; she will control you in the end. She's very powerful. Look at me. She turned me into a cat."

"How did that happen?" asked Kim.

"It's a long story."

"Oh, but do tell me, I'd like to hear."

"Well I'll try and tell it as briefly as I can without missing out any of the important parts. Sometimes Mistress Nemesis lets her characters out of Nemesisland. Some privileged slaves are given missions to carry out for her. I have been lucky enough to be sent on such a mission. You have heard of the Celtic Goddess, Rhiannon?"

"Yes, I have. Well at least from stories and myths."

"I had to go to an underground labyrinth in the Welsh borders where the Celtic Goddess Rhiannon and her magical white horse and birds were being held in captivity."

"Ooh, a magical horse, that sounds exciting," Kim interjected.

"Yes and also very dangerous. She was being held captive by the Roman invaders who were seeking to destroy the powers of the Celtic goddesses. My task was to rescue Goddess Rhiannon and her horse. Mistress Nemesis provided me with an elixir which gave me the shape shifting powers of the goddesses. I used this to turn myself into a horse to infiltrate the stables where Rhiannon's horse was held. But I was caught myself and turned myself into a black cat so I could sneak away from my captors. I did eventually escape with Goddess Rhiannon and her horse but, although my mission was successful, at one point I had succumbed to temptation and seduction so Mistress Nemesis kept me in this cat's body as a punishment."

What a strange tale, thought Kim. Perhaps the worlds outside of this place were even odder still.

"But, don't you mind being a cat?" asked Kim.

"Oh no, not really," the cat replied. "I've learnt to accept Mistress Nemesis's judgement in these things. One day, when she's ready and she thinks I've suffered enough, I expect she will release me back into my human form again."

"I should find it very strange to be a cat, "said Kim. "Would she turn me into a cat do you think?"

The black cat smiled, a long broad grin, wider than a Cheshire cat.

"Beware, she is capable of turning you into whatever she pleases and having you do whatever she desires."

Kim sighed, "I don't know if I'm going to like it here, it's so very weird."

"As I've said, the only ways are Mistress Nemesis's ways. You'll have to follow the path that is laid out for you and when you have finished your journey submit to her judgement as to whether she will let you return to your world. Who knows, by then, you might be happy to stay."

The cat had already been helpful and explained something of the strange world that Kim found herself in. She decided on another line of questioning now, one that might give her some practical help.

"Can you tell me where these doors lead?" asked Kim.

"The door behind you leads to another part of Goddess Nemesis's realm that leads to a dark isolation chamber. Upstairs beyond the metal door is the heart of her world. It's a forbidding place with dungeons and instruments of torture. Through the door there," the cat nodded his head in the direction, "there's a tea party going on."

"Oh, just like 'Alice in Wonderland', that sounds fun," said Kim. "I think I should prefer that to dungeons and torture chambers. Thank you for your help. I hope your Mistress sets you free soon. Goodbye," Kim called out as she set off towards the next door.

"Goodbye Kim. I'm sure our paths will cross again. Beware, not all tea parties are such fun," the cat called down the corridor.

But the warning came as Kim skipped out of ear shot, too late for her to heed the cat's words.

6: The Fetish Hatter's Tea Party

As Kim turned the corner, she was thrilled at what she saw. It really was a tea party, albeit a strange one, and there actually was a Hatter, a March hare and a dormouse just like in 'Alice in Wonderland'. In the centre of the room was one of Mistress Nemesis's or the Red Queen's slaves wearing a leather hood down on all fours with a piece of clear Perspex strapped to his back for a human table.

Along one long side of the table were the three figures. At the centre, and dominating the proceedings, was the figure of the Red Queen, who was now dressed in a metallic blue pvc tail coat suit, a green silk cravat and a blue and red checked waistcoat. On her head was perched a top hat with a label reading 'In This Style 10/- 6d' on it. To Kim's eyes it was clearly the same figure as the Queen of Hearts, the shiny black hair lay against the lapels of her jacket and the piercing blue eyes carefully emphasized with eyeliner and blue eye shadow. On either side of her were another two human animals as Kim had come to see them, a March hare with floppy ears in a tatty long tail coat, a spotted bow tie and a monocle in one beady eye. At the other side of the Hatter was a man transformed into a dormouse. The hare and the dormouse had the same features as the Duchess and the black cat. Kim was confused; she could see how the Red Queen and the Duchess could have left the medieval barn and got changed but there was no way that the black cat could have got past Kim without her seeing.

"Come here my dear," called the Hatter beckoning Kim forward.

Kim stepped forward to stand in front of the table.

"Have you no manners girl? Do you always come to tea parties with no clothes on?"

"Well, no madam, least ways not usually," she answered quietly taking up a deferential position with her hands behind her back. Kim had quite forgotten she was stark naked and felt quite embarrassed stood before them with no clothes on. "But, I have had some rather strange adventures and, well, I seem to have lost my clothes along the way."

"That's really most unfortunate and very careless of you. Well, that won't do. You can't have tea without any clothes. Hare! Go and find the girl some clothes."

The hare produced some clothes for Kim. There was a light blue dress made in latex and a white pinafore to go over it, also in latex. Kim was delighted; she would be like a little fetish Alice. She loved rubber, the feel of it on her skin, the tightness and the smell. She used to wear latex underwear when she worked in the brothel and it always made her feel incredibly horny. She squeezed into the tight rubber dress. It was very short and left the fleshy white skin of her thighs exposed. The tight rubber squeezed her tits and pushed them up enhancing her already ample cleavage even more. She pulled over the latex pinafore and finally put on some short white ankle socks and some patent leather shoes. The latex felt tight around her buttocks and breasts but that was a lovely feeling. Kim thought she looked great and was quite looking forward to joining the party.

"That's better, now come and sit over here girl," said the Hatter pointing to a little armchair at the end of the Perspex table where the slave's head was. "Oh, don't worry about him, if he tries to sneak a look at your crotch he knows he'll be severely punished. Besides, he has been told to look at the floor at all times and keep perfectly still and if he tries to ogle your sweet little fanny, my dear, I shall know."

Kim was shocked, she was sure the Hatter in the children's book didn't use language like that.

"And who are you?" the Hatter asked.

"My name is Kim. But, surely you must be The Queen of Hearts?"

"How rude my dear, what bad manners you have."

"Now that's very bad, she should be taught better manners," the hare added.

Do I look like the Queen of Hearts?"

"Well I suppose not but it's just that you do have the look of her," replied Kim.

"Things are not always what they seem girl," the Hatter added with a mischievous glint in her eye, "but of course the Red Queen is a good friend of mine, I make all of her bonnets I'd have you know."

"Have you come far, Kim?"

"Well, I don't know for sure. I have just been talking to a black cat just outside there."

At the mention of the word cat the dormouse became very distressed.

"Cat, where's there a cat?"

"Oh dear, you have to be so careful you know. He's very sensitive and the c—a—t word does upset him so," said the hare, who had gone over to console the dormouse.

"Oh, I'm terribly sorry. I didn't mean to upset him, I wasn't thinking. I suppose if I were a mouse I would get disturbed at the mention of a cat."

"Ahh no, where's the cat?" the dormouse started off again.

The Hatter leaned over, held dormouse's nose between her thumb and forefinger and twisted it.

"Ouch!"

That was terribly cruel, thought Kim, but it did have the desired effect of calming the dormouse down.

Oh dear, thought Kim, this tea party could be very weird. She cast her eye across the table; it was certainly a wonderful spread. There were two huge round tea pots and places set with china cups and saucers and plates. The centrepiece was a large multi-tiered black cast iron cake stand that was filled with a delicious assortment of cup cakes. They were iced in shades of pastel green, yellow and pink and decorated with cherries or walnuts. There was bread, butter and jam, home-baked scones and jellies and trifles. I've not seen party food like this since I was a child, she thought. Kim was ravenous and thirsty, just ready for afternoon tea.

"Pour yourself a cup of tea," offered the Hatter.

Kim picked up the big round yellow tea pot and was about to pour a cup when the hare and dormouse intervened.

"No, No, my dear, you don't want to drink from that tea pot," shouted the hare.

"No, no," muttered the dormouse, "definitely not that tea pot."

"Why, what's wrong with this tea pot?"

"The orange tea pot is for the tea," said the hare.

"And the yellow tea pot is for the hatter's special blend of tea," said the dormouse.

Kim looked surprised, "I'm sorry I don't understand, do you mean I shouldn't drink from that tea pot?" she asked cautiously.

"We don't recommend it," replied the hare.

"Believe us," echoed the dormouse, "it's not very nice tasting."

"Why of course, that tea pot's for them," pronounced the hatter.

She pointed to two of what Kim presumed were Mistress Nemesis's male slaves. Kim hadn't noticed them yet. One had a leather hood on his head, the other an iron cage. They were both sat behind her forlornly. Waiting to be fed perhaps, thought Kim?

"They are probably thirsty," said the Hatter, "would you mind doing the honours, girl?"

"Why, yes, I suppose not."

Kim picked up the huge round yellow tea pot with both hands and walked over to the two men.

"Should I pour them out a cup?" she asked.

"No, no, they can drink straight from the spout," the Hatter said.

"Yes, direct from the spout," echoed the hare.

"Oh, definitely from the spout," confirmed the dormouse.

The hooded slave lifted his head up and positioned it so that Kim, holding the tea pot high over him, could tip the spout up and pour its contents straight into his mouth. She did just that and a stream of fluid came flooding out of the spout. It was a clear golden colour and had a strange mineral-like aroma. Kim wondered if the hatter grew his own tea leaves in his garden. Most of the steaming hot liquid poured straight into the slave's mouth and he guzzled it down eagerly, but some splashed onto his body and quite a bit spilt onto the floor.

"He can't waste any," called the Hatter, "make him drink what he's spilt off the floor."

"Go on, drink it," said Kim tentatively at first and then more firmly, "come on drink it up."

"That's no good," said the Hatter, "he's got to obey you. Kick him in the balls."

Kim did exactly that with the shiny leather shoes. The hooded man howled in pain but soon got his head down onto the floor and started lapping the golden waters up.

"Save some for later," ordered the Hatter. "Now bring the tea pot back here and put it on the table."

Kim did what she was told and took her seat at the table again.

"Would you like a cup cake, my dear?" the Hatter asked, her mouth spreading into a broad grin as she held the cake stand in front of Kim.

"Don't mind if I do," replied Kim reaching out to take a pale yellow iced bun with a cherry on top.

"Don't you mean, 'do mind if I don't'."

"Well, I suppose so," said Kim.

"Or rather, don't you mean, you suppose not."

Kim's head was in a whirl. "Whatever you say," she said, taking a huge bite out of the bun. Mmmm, lemon cake, her favourite!

"Have some bread and butter."

"And some jam."

"And a scone."

The hare and the dormouse piled her plate high with food.

"And there's always some trifle for afters."

"Or some jelly."

Kim tucked in to the delicious home-baked food and poured herself a cup of tea, from the orange tea pot of course.

"Do you think we ought to feed them Hatter?" said the hare pointing to the slaves.

"Well I suppose so," she replied, "but they can only have dried bread. Is there any stale bread left hare? They can have that."

The hare found some stale bread and handed it to Kim, "Would you be so kind?"

Kim wasn't quite sure what to do.

"Just break it up and throw it on the floor for them," said the dormouse.

Kim did exactly that, taking off chunks of bread and tossing it onto the floor. The two slaves crawled on all fours to take it up from the ground with their mouths. The man with the iron head cage had great difficulty and had to position himself carefully so that he could get his lips out of the cage to suck the dried bread up from the floor. The Hatter, hare and dormouse were greatly amused at this spectacle.

Meanwhile, they had started on the trifle and jelly. The hare scooped out a huge spoonful from the cut-glass trifle bowl. Mmm, trifle, thought Kim, delicious layers of whipped cream, smooth yellow custard, sponge cake and raspberries. This was wonderful; maybe Nemesisland wasn't going to be so bad after all.

"Some jelly with that?" said the dormouse as he emptied the wobbly green substance onto Kim's plate.

Mmm, lime flavour. My favourite. How did they know?

"Should we give them a treat?"

"That's up to you Hatter," said the hare.

The Hatter took up the trifle bowl, "hare you bring the tea pot; dormouse you fetch the jelly bowl; girl, you get some cup cakes – strawberry and chocolate, I think."

What a sight we must look, thought Kim, as the procession of them got up from the table and marched across to the two slaves on the floor carrying the food in their hands.

The Hatter started by emptying two scoops of trifle onto the floor. Then, Kim heard the lovely slurping sound of jelly being scooped out of the bowl and dropped onto the floor where it sat wobbling in front of the slaves' eyes.

"Drop the cup cakes onto the floor. Now, hitch your dress up and sit on them," ordered the Hatter. "Make sure you sit on them with your bare arse, my dear."

Kim laughed her head off. She was quite entering into the spirit of this. It was extremely bizarre but she was really up for it. They never did anything as fun as this in the brothel. She ceremoniously held the two cup cakes in her hand and let them drop to the floor. She hitched up her latex skirt so that her lovely round arse was exposed. As an additional little flourish she put her back-side right in front of the faces of the two slaves and wriggled her bum at them. Then she lowered herself down and sat right on top of the two cup cakes, one cheek of her bum on the strawberry one, the other on the chocolate one. Kim wriggled her bottom around in the mixture of butter icing and cake positively relishing in the squishy texture and the sweet smell before working the sticky mess into the crack in her arse.

She bent over and stuck her bum out into the faces of the crouching slaves. The hare had kindly removed the head cage from one of them.

"Now, lick every crumb off of my arse," she ordered, "and make sure you get your tongues right up the crack."

The Hatter, hare and dormouse were in hysterics.

"You were right Hatter. You told me the girl would be perfect for Nemesisland," said the hare.

"Don't get carried away just yet hare, she's still a lot to learn. But, yes, this is wonderful, I'm really enjoying this," laughed the Hatter.

The two men set about their task enthusiastically, a bit too enthusiastically thought Kim. They eagerly ran their tongue across her back-side licking up the mess of squashed cake and butter cream icing. Kim felt through texture of their tongues as they went all over her arse and worked their way up into her crack. God, thought Kim, this was so erotic. She felt herself getting wetter and wetter at the attention she was receiving. She was almost disappointed when every morsel had been licked off her and her lovely fleshy bottom had been cleaned.

"Excellent, but I think the slaves got too much pleasure out of that," said the Hatter.

"I think the girl got too much pleasure out of that," added the hare.

"Get them to clean the floor up, they can't leave it like that."

"Now," Kim pointed at the pink and brown patches on the floor. "That mess has been squashed by my arse. You're going to eat it all up. You've seen where it's been. I don't want to see a crumb left. Do you understand?"

The two slaves got down onto their knees and started licking the floor. The Hatter, hare and dormouse were most amused at the spectacle. They had to clean up every piece of cake, trifle and jelly. At the end of their task they were a complete mess, their faces covered in yellow custard, bright red raspberries and lime jelly.

"Isn't it time for some more tea now?" said the dormouse after the two slaves had licked all the food up from the floor.

The Hatter took the yellow tea pot, ordered the two slaves to lie on their backs and open their mouths and then started to pour all the golden fluid out of the spout; over their bodies, over their cock and balls and then streams of it into their eager mouths until the tea pot had been entirely emptied.

"More tea girl?" said the Hatter after his own blend of tea had been dispensed over the two men.

"Mmm, yes," replied Kim, "I'm thirsty again now."

"How much tea do you think was in the tea pot?" asked the Hatter.

"Too much," said the hare.

"Too much of a muchness," said the dormouse.

"Tell me, girl, how much do you think there is in a muchness?" asked the hatter turning to her.

Kim looked bemused. Was this a trick question? How was she meant to answer that? She thought about how much the huge yellow tea pot might hold and blurted out the first figure that came into her head.

"Two pints?"

"Two pints! Oh dear, that's not right."

"To be honest, sir, I don't even know what a muchness is."

"She doesn't know what a muchness is? She's rather stupid then isn't she?" said the Hatter.

"Well, I don't think that's particularly fair," Kim protested.

"Ask her some more questions?" said the Hatter.

The dormouse asked one, "Now, there were three sisters who lived in a treacle well. If Elsie collected 3lbs of treacle, Lacie, 2lbs and Tillie, 5lbs, how much treacle had they got out of the well?"

"Well," answered Kim, "that would be 10lbs."

"Wrong!" called the Hatter. "It would all depend on the consistency of the treacle. Ask another question."

"What's two plus three?" asked the hare.

"Well that's easy," said Kim, "five."

"Are you sure?" asked the hare, "be careful what you reply."

"But, of course it's five," said Kim.

"Wrong!" said the Hatter, "it's seven."

"No, it's five," complained Kim.

The Hatter's penetrating gaze bore down on her. Kim had a feeling of foreboding. Her voice was slow, deliberate and menacing, "It's whatever I say it is, girl."

"But that's not fair," protested Kim.

"She definitely needs some education," said the hare.

"You should send her back to school," the dormouse said.

"Yes, she definitely needs to learn a lesson."

"You're both right," said the Hatter, "she needs to get some manners and learn some sums. She insulted me by calling me the Red Queen when

I'm not, she upset the dormouse and now she's shown how stupid she is by not being able to answer a few simple questions. You need to go back to school girl."

This was mad, thought Kim. Everything was going so well. She had enjoyed the party, loved dominating the two slaves, and woofed down loads of cup cakes and trifle but now they had turned against her and everything was all spiralling out of her control.

7: The Headmistress

The hare led Kim away from the tea party. Kim was told to take off her fetish 'Alice' dress and change into some new clothes. The hare, or the Duchess, as she saw her, helped Kim tie her hair into plaits and get dressed. This time Kim had to put on baggy navy knickers, a grey skirt, a white cotton blouse and a purple and black striped tie with grey socks and clunky black shoes. The hare handed her a navy blue blazer with a badge on its pocket emblazoned with an 'N' in black and purple and interwoven with a design of creeping ivy. Finally she perched a boater with a purple and black strip band onto the top of her head.

Strangely enough, Kim felt very smart. The cotton blouse was clean and freshly ironed and felt nice against her bare bra-less breasts. She had never had a uniform when she was at school though she had dressed up as a school girl in the parlour when clients made the occasional request for her to do so; wearing such a uniform made her feel oddly sexy. She wondered what new adventure Nemesisland would throw up for her.

The hare pointed to a door, "The headmistress is waiting for you. You really don't want to be late."

Kim stepped up to the door. There was a brass plaque on it that read 'Headmistress's Study' and Kim suddenly felt very naughty. She knocked timidly on the door.

"Enter," came a firm voice from inside.

Kim obediently opened the door, stepped in and closed it behind her. She felt like a naughty school girl and instinctively took up a submissive position, just like she used to when she was told off in school, putting her hands behind her back and lowering her head.

She could see enough to take in her surroundings. Before her was the imposing figure of the headmistress. It was the Red Queen again, or the Hatter, or the mysterious Mistress Nemesis or whatever she cared to call herself. The same piercing blue eyes and daunting presence confronted her. She wore black rimmed glasses which, if anything, made her even more forbidding as she peered over them at Kim. She was dressed smartly in a pressed black skirt, crisp white blouse with an academic gown over it and a mortar board perched on her head. Her dark hair was tied up into a bun making her look severe and very much like a school ma'am.

"Come forward girl," she commanded brusquely, "I have received complaints about your behaviour from the Hatter. From what's been related to me I find your character and attitude most reprehensible Miss Kim. I very disappointed with you. You know how poor behaviour has to be punished."

She stood in front of her desk tapping the floor with the toe of her smart leather shoes, her hands in front of her with her fingers pressed together in an admonishing stance.

"I'm very sorry ma'am," said Kim, wondering how best to respond and deciding to defend herself, "I'm sure I didn't mean to upset her, but I don't see how it's my fault."

"Really Miss Kim, you are incorrigible. I don't know how you have the nerve to say that to my face. You must know that the 'Nemesis Academy for Submissive Girls' expects the highest standards, the very highest standards. Yet I've heard reports that you turned up to the Hatter's tea party without your school uniform, indeed without any clothes on at all, that you insulted the Hatter, upset the dormouse with talk of cats and totally disgraced yourself with your antics involving cup cakes. You know that when the Academy let's one of its pupils out for a special treat their behaviour reflects on the whole school and the highest standards of discipline and decorum are expected from our girls. What have you got to say for yourself now girl?"

Kim recognised from the headmistress's demeanour and the lecture she had just delivered that she was in big trouble, but really it was most unfair. The whole tea party had been quite silly and she'd only done what she'd been told to do.

"I assure you ma'am I didn't mean to spoil the Hatter's tea party and I'm sure I didn't intend to upset her or the dormouse. But it's really not fair. It wasn't my fault I'd lost my clothes and, besides, the Hatter told me to sit on the cup cakes!"

"Don't be so insolent girl. You'll pay for answering me back. Even if the Hatter did tell you to do that you weren't meant to get so much pleasure out of it, which you did, didn't you? Don't deny it girl."

"Yes, that's true, sorry ma'am," Kim hung her head in shame; she couldn't deny she enjoyed doing that.

"And haven't you been taught to behave with discretion at all times. And then I'm told that you got a simple question wrong. What have you to say to that?"

"But ma'am, that really isn't fair. I got that question right. Three plus two is five, not seven."

Kim was prepared to concede her behaviour might not have been perfect, that turning up to a tea party naked was not very polite, but she did know she got the simple sum right. The headmistress's eyes flashed with anger.

"Are you answering me back girl? Remember this is an academy for submissive girls. You idiotic girl, has none of your tuition sunk in? Have you been paying any attention in your lessons or have you been dreaming all day. Probably thinking about getting sexual pleasure I expect. You can't fool me girl. I know what goes through young girls minds in the classroom. You must learn to direct those thoughts into submissive behaviour Miss Kim. Have you learnt nothing about Nemesisland yet that you don't know that when a mistress says three plus two is seven, it is seven."

"But..." Kim stuttered.

"No 'buts' Miss Kim, that's fact. I'm most disappointed in your behaviour Miss Kim. You have the potential to be an outstanding pupil but you have let yourself down. You had a special invitation to the Hatter's tea party and you have disgraced the Academy and yourself with your disgusting, insolent and ignorant behaviour. Have you anything to say for yourself?

"No, I'm sorry ma'am," Kim said, but she was still glowering with resentment, especially about the sum, which she knew she'd got right.

"Don't look at me with that glum expression girl. You don't look as though you're sorry and that really won't do, you're only building up a more severe punishment for yourself girl. You know the 'Nemesisland Academy for Submissive Girls' will never accept defiant and insolent behaviour. It has to be punished out of girls."

"Yes, ma'am," admitted Kim, but reluctantly.

"Well there's nothing for it, I'll have to administer some severe corporal punishment on you girl for such unacceptable behaviour."

"But...," muttered Kim.

The headmistress fixed her steely gaze on Kim, "still protesting girl? Haven't you been listening to anything I've said? Your behaviour is a disgrace and I'll take great delight in administering it personally. Now, take off your school blazer and boater and hang them up," ordered the headmistress pointing to the coat hooks on the wall.

Kim trailed obediently to the back of the study. She cast a glance at the blackboard and noticed the lines of neat writing saying, 'I'm a very naughty girl and I deserve to be punished'. Oh dear, thought Kim, how very weird, what have I landed myself into now. She removed her blazer and boater as she had been told but this only made her conscious of her pert nipples pressing against the tight cotton shirt.

Whilst Kim had been doing that the headmistress had retrieved a chair from behind her desk and sat on it waiting for her. Kim stood in front of her assuming a submissive position again with her hands behind her back.

"Pull your knickers down girl," she ordered.

Kim lifted her skirt up and shuffled the navy blue knickers down her thighs until they hung forlornly around her shoes. Kim felt really humiliated now, stood in front of the headmistress, her knickers around her ankles and her cunt and arse bare against the scratchy grey material of the skirt.

"Now bend over my lap girl."

Kim knew she had no choice but comply with the headmistress's command. When she was at school she had always been a bit of a madam answering back the teachers but suddenly she felt powerless to do anything but submit to the headmistress's order even though she knew what was going to happen. She could invoke her right to leave at any time but strangely, she did not want to do that either and even more strangely, she also had a feeling in the pit of her stomach that she wanted to be punished and deserved to be punished.

She bent over the headmistress's lap. She was on tip-toe and then let her arms drop the other side of the chair so they touched the floor letting her plaits dangle freely in the air. It felt oddly warm and comforting. The smell of lavender mingled with chalk dust, the rough material of the academic gown and the proximity of the headmistress's warm crotch pressing against her body as she nestled into a comfortable position made Kim feel quite turned on. Shit, what's happening to me, she thought. Her cunt was really getting quite wet.

"This is the first part of your punishment Miss Kim. I'll warn you that this is only a little warm up."

The headmistress pulled back Kim's skirt to expose her voluptuous back-side. She ran her hand gently across the soft flesh before planting a firm stroke on each cheek of her arse with the bare palm of her hand. Kim expelled a short gasp. It was a stingy tingly kind of feeling, painful but not excruciatingly so. There was also another aspect to the sensation that was really quite sensual.

The headmistress administered more strokes with her bare hand, ten on each buttock cheek before pulling her hand away and rubbing Kim's arse, now shiny and glowing with the attention it had received. That's not so bad, thought Kim. In fact it almost felt quite warm and comforting. She closed her eyes and nestled down into the headmistress's lap.

The next strokes were hard. Kim could hear the loud slap as the hard bony surface of the headmistress's hand struck soft flesh. She could feel the spongy skin of her arse wobbling between each stroke and a warm, painful glow spread over her. Once again the hand rubbed gently across her back-side, which was now red and hot.

"The final ones now Miss Kim. Another ten on each bum cheek."

The next ones were harder still as the headmistress put even more effort into the strength of each stroke. It was painful and stung like hell but by now Kim had drifted into a state where she had accepted each slap, even welcomed it. The last two or three were really powerful ones and Kim let out little whimpers of pain.

"Get up girl," ordered the headmistress.

Kim slowly and a little dreamily lifted herself up from the headmistress's lap and stood in front of her. Her face was red and flustered and her plaits dishevelled. Her back-side had a stingy hot red glow. Kim felt very humiliated stood there with her knickers still around her ankles and her hands behind her back and her breasts sticking out.

"Look at you girl. You look a disgrace. You look quite the slut. Do you think you're going to turn on the boys of the joint sixth looking like that? You're nearly bursting out of that shirt Miss Kim, it's far too tight."

"Sorry ma'am."

It was true. Kim could feel her swollen breasts stretching the buttons of the shirt and her engorged nipples pulling at the white cotton material.

"Sorry is no good Miss Kim. You'll simply have to be punished some more for being such a wanton slut, girl. I want you to stand facing my desk and bend over so you're touching your toes, then spread your legs and stick your back-side up in the air for me."

Kim's head hung down between her legs with her yellow plaits nearly touching the floor. The headmistress went to her desk, opened a drawer and pulled out a black plimsoll. Oh dear, thought Kim, this might be more challenging.

The smell of rubber and sweaty girl's feet filled the study. Kim felt the rubber being brushed against her arse and then a loud slap as it struck her round bottom. Kim grunted and moaned as the pain spread over her back-side. There were ten strokes on each buttock cheek and the headmistress was a good way through the next ten whacks with the plimsoll when there was a knock on the door. Perhaps Kim would get some respite from her punishment.

"Hold your position Miss Kim. Enter," the headmistress called out.

The door opened slowly. Kim, with her head bent over was able to peer up at the upside-down figure which had just entered the office framed between her legs. It was a young man. Boy would be a wildly inaccurate description and wouldn't begin to do justice to the young hunk stood in the doorway. He was dressed in a school uniform, a black blazer and trousers, but it was smart and worn with pride and his tie was knotted neatly. God, he's a bit fit, thought Kim to herself.

"You asked to see me Madam," he spoke clearly and confidently but with enough reverence for the headmistress not to get him into trouble.

"Yes, that's right. I want your assistance in administering some punishment to this miscreant here," she said pointing to Kim's skirt, "And what's your name lad?"

"Everard, Madam, Digby Everard."

"Do you hear that Miss Kim? Master Everard is the head of boys for the joint sixth form of the Nemesis Academy for Submissive Girls and the White Knight School for Masters. All our pupils enjoy the joint sixth. It's where all our hard training and tuition is put into practise. With your behaviour Miss Kim, I doubt if you'll ever qualify for the sixth form. Do you know how we select the head boy Miss Kim?"

"No, Madam," Kim spluttered.

She was still ogling the athletic physique of the young man. Even upside-down he looked a hot specimen.

"We test all the boys and select them on the basis of a number of things: the length and girth of their cocks, of course, the speed of their attaining an erection, their ability to maintain their hard-on and their skills at dominating a submissive girl. These are all the attributes we look for in training young masters. Come here boy."

The young man stepped forward so he stood immediately behind Kim. She got an eyeful of his long legs and tight trousers, not to mention the bulge in his crotch.

"Drop your trousers and pants now Master Everard," the headmistress ordered.

"Yes Madam," he replied firmly.

He did it slowly and seductively knowing that Kim's head was still between her legs looking up at him. Kim was starting to get uncomfortable and the muscles in her legs were starting to ache, but there was no way she was going to miss this show. He unbuckled his belt first, slowly lowered the zip on his trousers and gently pulled them over his beautiful rounded hips until they dropped onto the floor. Kim looked on expectantly. She could look up at the huge bulge underneath his boxer shorts. He moved the tails of his white cotton shirt to one side and inserted his thumb and fingers in the band of his boxer shorts and tantalisingly pulled the elastic forward far enough to tempt Kim to crane her neck to get a peek but not far enough for her to see anything. He smiled at her, confident in the knowledge that he was toying with her and that what she was aching to see was his erect cock. Kim was getting wet in anticipation.

Finally, after teasing Kim in this way for a couple of minutes, the band of the boxer shorts was lowered over the curve of his powerful hips and muscular thighs and, released from the tight containment of his shorts, the young man's cock sprang up. Kim gasped. It was every bit as huge and magnificent as the headmistress's build-up had suggested. It was long and thick and hard. It stuck out proudly as the young man stood with his hands on his hips with an arrogant swagger knowing how impressed Kim was with his erect member.

"How long is it, Master Everard?" asked the headmistress.

"Nine inches, Madam," he replied with pride.

"Hmm, let me see," she said, picking up a ruler from her desk.

She held it against the enormous object of throbbing flesh.

"Nine and half inches, actually," she said as she read the markings on the ruler.

She pulled the ruler away, raised it up and then brought it crashing down onto the erect member. Kim gasped. That must have hurt, that must have hurt really badly, she thought. But, the young man did not flinch at all. He stood straight and erect with his hands still on his hips with a smug satisfied look on his face.

"Do you see that Miss Kim? He has been trained to maintain his erection even in the face of severe punishment."

She raised the ruler again, this time right over her shoulders and with one mighty swing brought it crashing down on the young man's erect penis. This time there was a slight movement and the boy expelled a small gasp at the force of the stroke. The headmistress fixed him in the eye with an admonishing stare. He turned away from the gaze and looked down at the floor. She took his cock in her hand to inspect it. The object had lost just some of it steely rigidness.

"What's this lad? I don't want to see you flagging boy. I've a task for you to carry out and I don't expect you to disappoint me. I need this to be rock hard," she said gently stroking his member to bring it up to a full tight erection again. "That's better," she added satisfied the cock had been restored to its full potency.

Kim was watching this scene being played out with her head still between her legs. Her back really was aching now and she was relieved when the headmistress told her she could assume a normal standing position. She stood in position with her hands behind her back conscious that the hot young man with the enormous cock was right behind her.

Her attention was drawn by the headmistress clearing a space on her desk in front of Kim. She took two piles of papers, filed them neatly so that the edges of the paper were all lined up and then arranged them carefully on the desk in front of Kim.

"Now, I have a little test of compliance and discipline for you Miss Kim. If you fail it you'll face even more punishment. Do you see those piles of papers?"

Kim gulped, "Yes ma'am," she replied.

"Those are my end of term reports, one pile for the girls that have passed; the other for those girls who need further correction. I think you know which pile you're on, don't you girl?"

"Yes, ma'am."

"Well, which is it?"

"The pile with the girls who need further correction ma'am."

"That's right Miss Kim, you are with the girls who need more punishment. Now lean over the desk. I've arranged my reports so that you should have a tit resting on each pile of papers."

Kim bent over obediently and rested her breasts on the neat piles of reports. The desk was polished and slippery but she was able to rest her tits on the reports without moving them. The paper felt cool and smooth against her breasts.

"Now stretch your arms out so your hands are gripping onto the far corners of my desk."

It was a long stretch but Kim reached out and gripped the desk. She turned her face to one side so that her cheek pressed against the polished wood. The pace of her breathing increased as the torment and anticipation built up in her.

"Good. Now stretch your legs girl."

Kim stretched her legs as far as she thought they could go. The ruler whacked the inside of her thigh with a sharp sting.

"Come on girl, you can do better than that. Wider. I want to be able to see right up your little pussy Miss Kim."

The position was starting to get a bit uncomfortable but Kim tried to shuffle her legs wider apart without disturbing the papers on the desk.

"That's better. Now stick your arse up into the air."

Kim adjusted her position and lifted her arse up into the air. She could not see, of course, but she could imagine the rosy pink flesh sticking up invitingly in the air and the headmistress and the head boy looking down at her.

"Stick it up girl!" the headmistress ordered. "I want to see it sticking right up in the air."

Kim pressed her tits firmly on the piles of reports and shuffled her body so she could raise her arse up.

"Come on girl, you can manage a bit more than that."

Kim was close to tears now with the effort but managed to stick her back-side up just a bit more. She felt so exposed. She was splayed out on the desk like a creature in a lab pinned down for dissection. The soft mound of her flesh was so tantalisingly exposed and her cunt lips hung open and inviting. But Kim was also sopping wet with a mixture of fear and anticipation. Would it be another beating or would she receive the attention of the head boy's rampant cock? She hoped the latter. She really prayed that the cock would be rammed up inside her.

Her dreams were going to be realised. She felt fingers prising her cunt lips apart and the tip of something nudging the entrance to her sex in preparation for entrance. Kim whimpered a little in anticipation.

"Control yourself girl," came a sharp voice from behind her.

The head boy's hard cock was driven right inside her in one long forceful stroke. Kim gasped. Her whole body was driven forward with the force of the penetration as she gripped tightly onto the corners of the desk. She felt her tits sliding against the neat piles of papers and scatter them underneath her as the young man forced himself into her. Oh shit, thought Kim, I'm going to get into trouble for that. She put that at the back of her mind as she felt the beautiful hard cock of that fit young man fill her. The head boy was driving into her with long relentless strokes. Strong manly hands gripped onto her hips to help him balance so he could penetrate her even more deeply with rough rapid movements. Kim's face was squashed against the desk looking at the wall so she could only imagine what a gloriously sexy scene it must have looked. She heard the crack of the ruler again, this time on the young man's back side as he fucked her.

"Come on boy, you can do better than that. Fuck her harder!"

The movement of his hips pressing against her back side became even harder and more urgent.

"I said fuck her boy," the headmistress ordered.

There was another hard crack on the boy's arse and in response to this his thrusts became, if possible, even harder and deeper. To Kim it was one glorious dirty fuck and she loved it. Already aroused by the build up and sense of anticipation she soon felt her climax welling up inside her cunt. Her body bucked and twisted as she came sliding the school reports across the desk and scattering a few onto the floor. She was too caught in the ecstasy of the moment of orgasm to worry about the consequences. The boy continued pounding into her until his beautiful hard member tensed and emptied its load into her sopping cunt. Kim was flustered and breathing heavily with her breasts squashed against the polished wood, still gripping onto the corners of the desk, her legs spread and trickles of spunk running down her thigh.

50

"Very good Mr Everard, that's all I need for now. You may leave," she said ordering him out dismissively.

Kim heard a shuffling as he pulled up his boxer shorts and then steps as he walked across the floor of the study before finally closing the door behind him. Kim felt a pang of regret that he had been dismissed. She was still on the desk panting and breathless. There was no time for her to recover though. Rough hands pulled at her pig-tails and forced her head up with a sharp and painful jolt. The angry face of the headmistress peered into hers.

"What do you call this Miss Kim?" she scolded, gesturing at the school reports, scattered and disordered across the desk. She bent down to pick one up from the floor and rolled it up.

"All my hard work messed up by a disobedient little school girl. Can't you show any discipline girl? You're going to pay for this Miss Kim. Oh, you're really going to pay for this."

"But it wasn't my fault," complained Kim, "the surface was so slippery and what can you expect when you've nine inches of hard cock thrust inside you and, besides, I couldn't help coming."

"You insolent little bitch! Still answering back I see."

She struck Kim across the face with the rolled up school report. Kim recoiled with the shock and pain. She really hadn't expected that.

"And another thing girl. You got too much pleasure out of that."

"Well, he was a bit hot," muttered Kim and immediately regretted that slipping out.

"You're really going to pay. Haven't you learnt anything at the 'Nemesisland Academy for Submissive Girls'. That was a treat for the boy. The head boy has special privileges and one of them is getting the chance to fuck some of the girls of the Academy. It was for his pleasure, and for my amusement to see one of my girls submit to a good hard fucking, not for your pleasure. You've a lot to learn."

"Yes ma'am," muttered Kim quietly, finally showing a little bit of contrition.

"Get up now girl."

Kim lifted her aching body up, relieved that she had finally been released from being spread-eagled on the desk. She heard steps going to the side of the room where a long row of canes was hanging. Kim dreaded what was going to happen next. She was now really worried at how much she'd angered the headmistress by answering back and messing up her school reports.

She watched as the headmistress took off her academic gown and mortar board, hung them on a coat stand in the corner of the study and rolled up her sleeves. She looked a formidable figure in her crisp white blouse that showed the contours of her ample bosom perfectly and her tight black skirt and shapely legs. She stepped over to the rack of canes hanging from the wall and ran her hand gently across them as if weighing up which one she would use. She picked one off the rack and started to swish it through the air as she judged the weight and balance of it.

"No, that one doesn't feel quite right," she muttered to herself and then louder, conscious that Kim was watching and listening, "I have so many and it's so hard to choose. There's a cane for every occasion and it's important to choose the right one. And I need to teach you a lesson so I want one that's really going to sting girl."

Kim gulped in fear and anticipation. The headmistress selected another cane, nestled it in her hand and swished it through the air in a criss-cross pattern.

"Hmm, that still doesn't feel quite right."

She put it back on the rack and chose another one. Through all this deliberate process of selecting the right cane the tension was building up in Kim and a sense of trepidation coursed through her veins.

"Ah yes, my favourite rattan cane," the headmistress muttered approvingly as she held another cane between her hands and flexed it, "yes, there's a nice bit of flexibility there, that should sting nicely."

She stepped forward. Kim felt extremely vulnerable, conscious that her rosy bottom was naked and exposed and inviting the inevitable punishment. The headmistress ran the cane gently across Kim's bottom. A tingle of sexual tension zinged through Kim's brain. The headmistress tapped her arse smartly with the tip of the cane. It stung but Kim knew this was only a taster for what was to come.

"So, girl, what sort of punishment do you think matches your heinous behaviour?"

Kim gave some consideration to this question before replying. Traditionally, you think of six thought Kim; that ought to be enough. Six whacks of the cane and perhaps I will be out of here.

"Six of the best, if it pleases you ma'am."

The headmistress laughed out loud, "Six of the best. Six! You consider yourself quite the wit don't you Miss Kim? Girl, don't you know where you are. 'The Nemesis Academy for Submissive Girls'. Six is hardly a punishment at all – it's only a tickle. Thirty more like," and then she added maliciously, "and your impertinence at suggesting such a lenient punishment has just got you more."

Kim gasped. She'd only ever experienced some light slapping on her back-side in the parlour. How would she survive thirty lashes from a cane?

"Get yourself into position girl. I want your arms outstretched and your palms flat against the wall." Kim did as she was told, "Now lower your arms and present your back-side to me."

Kim nervously stuck out her arse. It was still glowing and tingling from the slapping she had received earlier. Her heart was racing. She could hear the swishing of the cane behind her as the headmistress tested it and the tension she felt went right down to the pit of her stomach. She had a real sense of trepidation about what was going to follow.

"Are you ready for your punishment girl?"

"Yes ma'am."

The headmistress hitched up Kim's skirt, pulling it up over her back to expose her lovely round bottom and create a nice target for her to aim for.

"Yes what, girl?"

"Yes, thank you ma'am," Kim corrected herself.

Kim took a sharp intake of breath to prepare. She heard the whooshing sound of cane slicing through air and a crack as it landed hard on her bottom. Her body and arms were forced against the wall with the power of the stroke.

"Ow!" Kim screamed out.

She couldn't help it. The headmistress had shown no mercy. It was a really hard stroke to start with and it hurt, it hurt and stung really badly.

"Miss Kim, this is the 'Academy for Submissive Girls'. Girls are expected to receive their punishments obediently and silently. All I need to hear from you is the counting of the strokes. Do you understand girl?"

"Yes ma'am," Kim whimpered but her arse was stinging already and she silently wondered how she could take the thirty strokes let alone hold her squeals of pain back.

The next nine strokes weren't quite as severe as the first one as Kim obediently counted them out, "...8...9...10."

"So girl, tell me, what is two plus three."

Kim considered what to say carefully but was close to tears, "What would you have me say? It's five, ma'am. It must be five."

The swishing sound of the cane slashed through the air before it landed with a crack on Kim's bottom. The shock of pain took her breath away, "...11," she groaned through the tears welling up in her eyes. The headmistress continued with another four strokes.

"Now, let's try again girl, what's two plus three?"

"Seven, ma'am. It's seven!" Kim blurted out.

"Girl it's not as simple as that for you. It's no good shouting out what you think I want to hear. You must believe it. I don't think you really believed that answer."

Whack, "...16," whack, "...17," whack, "...18," whack, "...19," whack, "...20."

"Let's have another try shall we girl?" the headmistress taunted, "what is two plus three?"

"Seven. Please ma'am it's seven, it really is seven!"

The cane swished through the air and another five strokes crashed onto Kim's arse with a wicked crack.

"How many?"

"Seven. It really is seven ma'am. Truly, I believe it's seven ma'am. Honestly!"

"Now that's better girl, isn't it? There's a bit more conviction to your answer now."

"Thank you ma'am," Kim gasped through the pain.

"Now that leaves another five and a further ten for asking for such a lenient punishment."

Another ten! Oh my god, that's harsh, thought Kim, though she daren't say anything. She resolved to keep quiet and accept her punishment.

"I'll excuse you from counting the last ten Miss Kim so you can really focus on the pain of the strokes."

"Thank you ma'am. That's very good of you ma'am."

"And it's good to hear a bit of respect and contrition form you now girl. Perhaps you've learnt your lesson."

The strokes of the cane came reining down on Kim's back-side, whack, "...26," whack, "...27," whack, "...28," whack, "...29," whack, "...30."

Kim's arse was aching now. She could feel the soreness and bruising where the cane had slashed across her soft flesh and the deep red welts forming across her pale skin. She had reached a plateau where she could absorb the pain of each fresh hit. She had almost reached a point where she was embracing and welcoming each new stroke. The final ten, she thought. Please give them to me. I want them. Let me have them, let me feel the pain...and the strange inexplicable pleasure that comes with it.

Kim was not going to be disappointed. The cane hissed and slashed. It zipped through the air with such force and landed on Kim's arse with a loud crack. The last ten strokes were the hardest and most severe of them all. But, Kim did not flinch and she did not squeal or scream. She absorbed every biting slash and welcomed it. She deserved it. She deserved to be punished. And yes...two plus three was seven! She believed that now. She believed in the logic of Nemesisland sums.

"Thank you ma'am. Thank you for punishing me ma'am."

She could hear the headmistress's breathing, heavy with the exertion of the final punishment. She stayed in position, her palms still resting against the wall, her arse swollen with red stripes across it.

"Finally girl, you've learnt your lesson. This experience will help you in your journey through the rest of Nemesisland Miss Kim. I hope the lesson has sunk in. I don't want to see you in my study again. Get up. You're dismissed now girl."

Kim straightened her body and flexed her muscles to get some movement back into them. She could feel her arse throbbing. Her head was in a whirl and she had a strange floating feeling. She also felt close to tears with the hurt and humiliation but she held them back. She bent down and pulled up her navy blue knickers, straightened her skirt and waddled towards the door unable to disguise the effects of her brutal beating. She heard the headmistress's final command as she dismissed her with the same perfunctory indifference as she'd told the head boy to go.

"And leave your school uniform outside the door."

8: The Black Cat's Tale Part 1

Kim had left her school uniform behind as she had been ordered and been cast back into Nemesisland, finding herself back in the corridor where she had encountered the black cat. Her back-side was throbbing and covered in red welt marks and darkening bruises from the corporal punishment she had received at the hands of the headmistress. Kim slumped against the wire mesh of the cat's cage, her bosom heaving with the hurt and humiliation that had been inflicted on her. The cat called Nano seemed quite knowledgeable and had helped her before; maybe he could give her some more advice.

"Kim, are you OK?" the black cat asked kindly.

"No, not really," replied Kim, nearly in tears. "I'm so confused. I was having a lovely time at the tea party and then it all went out of control when I got some questions wrong. Now, I've been beaten and humiliated by the headmistress in the school room. The Red Queen told me I could leave at any time; that I'm not a prisoner here. Part of me wants to go but she has such a hold over me and she keeps hinting that she knows something about me."

"I understand Kim, Nemesisland is not an easy place to be," consoled the black cat. "You'll find yourself swinging from one set of emotions to another. As you've seen the mistress is very capricious and will keep you on your toes not knowing what to expect next."

"You seem to know a great deal about Nemesisland. Do you know why she wanted me so much and what her plans really are for me?"

"Oh no, nobody knows that. Nobody here ever quite knows what to expect. She'll always spring some surprise on you. You may think you know what she plans but then she'll do something completely different."

"Hmm," said Kim, "then perhaps you can help me with something else. When I first met her, the Red Queen said something very strange, she said, 'she's just as lovely as I remember her.' Tell me black cat, do you know what she meant by that?"

Kim looked into the black cat's eyes and saw a change immediately come over him. He looked crestfallen and very sad.

"Please tell me," she said, "I can tell you know something."

"Oh yes, Kim, but it's a very sad tale."

"You must tell me," ordered Kim crossly, "you can't say that and not tell me."

"Kim, I believe you were chosen by the mistress in her guise as the Goddess Nemesis. I don't know what for exactly, I'm a mere slave to her and don't possess that kind of knowledge, I don't think even Duchess always knows that. But, I do know you were one of thirteen girls chosen as some kind of initiate to be trained by her to serve or to become something very honoured and important."

"What!" exclaimed Kim, "I'm really confused now. Do you mean in this world, in Nemesisland, or in the world I've come from? In the real world or in a dream world?"

"Don't make the mistake of thinking that Nemesisland isn't real Kim. But no, I don't know for sure. As I've said, I never know what her purpose is."

"But I don't understand. If I was chosen by her as you say, then what happened?"

Kim saw tears welling up in the black cat's eyes. She had never seen a cat cry before.

"Why are you so sad? Why should my fate affect you so much?"

"It's a long story Kim," the black cat sniffed, "and I had an important part to play in it."

"What do you mean? You must tell me. I don't care what it is that happened, I just need to know. I won't be angry with you."

"Oh, but you might be Kim, once I tell you."

"Can it be so bad?" asked Kim.

"I'll guess I'll have to let you be the judge of that. There are some things you need to understand first Kim. You need to know that Mistress Nemesis, amongst her many guises, is a pagan goddess, the spiritual ancestor of her Greek namesake, and is in communion with other pagan goddesses. Now, this sisterhood of goddesses have now, and in history, had enemies in the new religions. Remember that at one time the female was greatly revered as a divine figure and you will see that reflected in every culture over history. Now, wherever the new religions emerged and made alliance with the powerful Roman emperors or the Arab Caliphs they suppressed the old religions. Edicts were issued to outlaw pagan practises and as these churches became institutionalised so these religions set about the task of suppressing, or absorbing, the old pagan beliefs to eradicate the power of the feminine. They even suppressed their own teachings that did not fit with this thinking, destroying or hiding texts that might contradict their male dominated version of their faith."

"The Dead Sea scrolls!" gasped Kim.

"Yes, that's right, the Gospels of Mary Magdalene, Thomas and Judas, all hidden for centuries."

"Yeah, I've read the 'Da Vinci Code," laughed Kim, "I'm afraid that's where any of my knowledge of these things comes from."

"Well, the pagan goddesses are still battling against the new faiths that seek to remove the power of the divine female and the Red Queen, Goddess Nemesis herself, is at the forefront of that conflict. You need to know this background Kim to understand what happened. I mentioned that the goddesses had selected thirteen initiates who they were seeking to train. Now, the church of the Knights Templar, supporters of the new religion, seeing the power of the pagan goddesses growing and the threat from a band of them, seized the initiative by capturing these thirteen acolytes. That is as much as I know and this is the point where I come into the tale."

"Sorry black cat; but let me get this straight. I really don't get this, are you saying I was one of those girls?"

"Yes, Kim, that's right, I am."

Kim laughed, "But that's absurd, how can that be? Surely I would know or remember something?"

"I'm sorry Kim, I can't explain that. Somehow your memory of these events much have been wiped out of your mind."

Even as Kim was listening to the black cat a chill shuddered through her. She had such fragmented memories and had always felt that a whole chunk of her life was a haze of distorted and unconnected thoughts. It had always worried her, so much so that she often wondered if she had suffered from a kind of temporary amnesia. It was almost as if what she was hearing was helping her make some sense of her past. Kim was gripped now and encouraged the black cat to continue his story.

"Now Goddess Nemesis set a mission for me. She sent me to a marble temple in Constantinople, which used to be a place of devotion to the goddesses but which had been captured by the Knights Templar. It was here that the thirteen acolytes were being held. Goddess Nemesis described the layout of the temple to me, gave precise instructions and provided certain symbols and tools to aid me with the quest to seek out the thirteen girls and return them all, in tact, to the goddesses."

"Tell me, I want to know everything Nano, don't leave anything out." Kim urged.

The black cat eagerly took up Kim's request as he assumed the role of a skald, a travelling story teller, and began his magical tale.

"I had been directed to the hills outside Constantinople. When I looked back, in the distance, I could see the huge dome and pointed minarets of the Church of Hagia Sophia. In front of me, as Goddess Nemesis described, was a pure white marble temple. The setting sun cast its light over the wall basking it in an orange glow. I walked warily the couple of hundred yards towards the marble wall.

I stood before a sheer golden gate, a single sheet of pure gold dazzling in the twilight sun. There was no lock, no hinge, no blemish and no sign of how it would be possible to enter. I had been told the temple was protected by a guardian who would help me, so I waited. As the sun sank in the east and darkness descended the walls of the marble temple became illuminated by the luminous glow of a full moon. I felt in my bones the deep spirituality of this moment, a sense of impending change and foreboding came over me. I was conscious of a presence and beside me a large wolf with a shaggy red coat appeared. It turned its head towards me and fixed its yellow eyes on me.

"I am the Wolf Goddess and I have been charged as guardian to protect this sacred site. I am also a goddess of the moon and my powers wax and wane with the shifting phases of the moon. I am at my most powerful at the time of the full moon, which is why you have been sent on this mission at this time. You will need my aid to pass through the first set of gates into the courtyard beyond."

The Wolf Goddess strode up to the golden gate. Her howl would have brought down the very gates of hell but at the sound of her call some deep magic of the goddesses of old was invoked. The gates did not open, but their physical form dissipated into a golden mist.

The Wolf Goddess turned to me, "Slave Nano, my power can only hold the gate open for so long. Go now. May the goddesses give you courage and strength. Much rests on completing your mission. Do not fail."

As I passed through the golden dust there was a sensation like light tentacles touching me and a feeling of euphoria washed over me. On the other side I found myself in a courtyard illuminated by the bright light of the full moon. Across from me was the silver gate and set in its centre was a pentagon shaped hole for a key just as the Goddess Nemesis had described to me. At some time, long ago, this must have been a courtyard garden for the goddesses that inhabited the temple, but now it had been left to ruin.

My instructions were straightforward; find the five sided key made from the lapis lazuli stone and insert it into the key hole. This sounded easy, but where in this tangled mass of vegetation was I going to find the stone? My eyes scanned over the remains of the courtyard garden. To search though the dense foliage of overgrown herbs and wild flowers could take days. My eyes were drawn to a stunning display of black berries from a bush of belladonna, deadly nightshade; beautiful, but deadly, just like the goddesses themselves. I carefully plucked many bunches of the deadly black berries and put them in my bag.

It struck me that the marble walls of the courtyard garden were decorated with a frieze of scenes depicting goddesses from different parts of the world. I had a stroke of inspiration. I had learnt that in Egyptian times lapis lazuli had been placed in burial chambers to assist the spirit to ascend to heaven. I scoured for a scene that depicted ancient Egypt and soon found one; an Egyptian goddess or high priestess standing over a sarcophagus, her hands upraised. My instincts had proved sound. Sure enough, I saw a rock embedded in the marble in the goddess's eye; a blue stone flecked with delicate strands of green and gold in the shape of a pentagon. I fought my way through the tangled undergrowth to the silver door and placed the stone in the hole where it fitted perfectly and immediately the invisible and ingenious mechanism sprung into action, The piece of lapis lazuli rotated five times in the key hole and then I heard a loud click. Gently, and apprehensively, I pushed the door open and passed through the silver gate.

I was now inside the temple itself. I had stepped through into a corridor that stretched out before me to the left and right for perhaps thirty or forty yards until it curved away. The corridor, lit by flames in chalice shaped beacons mounted on the wall, was eerily silent. Before me was the crystal door, just as it had been described to me; it was translucent and looking through it was like gazing into a mist.

I found the silver hook in the marble wall from which I was told I should collect a piece of amethyst. It was a rough uncut stone, its delicate light purple crystals glinted in the light of the beacons. I was aware of the significance and power of the stone and that it had powerful properties. I had been told that the crystal door could only be opened with the power of the mind by somebody with a pure heart and that the amethyst stone would aid me.

I got myself into a position of supplication,face down on the floor with my head facing the crystal gate. I laid still and silent for what seemed like an age. Occasionally I felt my mind and concentration waiver but I pulled myself back, knowing that any interruption to my devotion would break the spell needed to release the gate. How long was I laid on the floor? It was hard to say, after a certain point time seemed to have no meaning – an hour, two, perhaps three.

Eventually, after a long period of mediation I heard a click and then a slow grinding sound as the crystal gate raised itself. As the gate slid up I leapt into action. I knew that I only had thirteen seconds (one for each enslaved girl) before the gate closed on me. I grasped my bag and leapt across the threshold of the gate.

I passed through into the next room, a windowless marble ante chamber. Facing me was the black quartz gate, smooth, shining and flawless. In the centre of the chamber was a marble table and on it a goblet and glass flask with a skull etched on it with a label attached to it that read 'Drink Me'. I began to understand the layout of the temple better. I had passed through a highly protected ceremonial entrance leading to this final gate and, beyond that, an inner temple. The disciples of the new religion had never been able to solve the mysteries of the four gates and had never been able to penetrate this part of the marble palace. I was close to my goal now.

But first I needed to find a way through the gate. I took up the two pieces of crystal, which Goddess Nemesis had told me to seek out, from the ground and put them together; they locked perfectly into one another but the gate did not move. My heart sank. I switched my focus to the black quartz table, the silver goblet and the bottle of poison. It had to have some purpose. What if it were not poison but something crucial to the completion of the quest and placed there as a trick to see if the person being tested had the courage to drink from it? I made my choice. I took up the glass flask, removed the stopper, poured the fluid out into the goblet and drank it.

As soon as I had gulped the last drop I realised I might have made a fatal mistake. I felt nauseous, my head began to spin and I slipped into a terrible dark nightmare. I felt myself in free fall, descending into some forgotten netherworld. Then, I saw hands reaching out to me. I heard the anguished calls of forgotten slaves. I realised that I had descended into the in between world of deprived slaves. I could see the faces of the rejected slaves swirling before me, their eyes and mouths screwed up in an agonised visage of loss and rejection, and hear their pitiful wails and groans.

I did not know how long I was lost in this vision. I remembered recovering my consciousness, physically exhausted, dizzy and nauseous. I knew I had to seize the moment. I stood before the black quartz gate, took a deep breath and held the two crystals together. Silently, secretly, the black gate slid down into the ground. I had three seconds. One…two…three. I quickly stepped through and turned round quickly to see the black gate slide back up again.

I heard laughs and voices. I quickly hid behind a marble pillar to take stock. I had entered what must be the inner sanctum of the temple of the goddesses. The place had been desecrated by the supporters of the new religion, but it was clear what a magnificent place it must have been. I was in a huge square hall within which there was a large circle of marble pillars supporting a vaulted ceiling covered in flaking gold leaf. The chamber was painted with brightly coloured frescoes depicting the goddesses in their animal forms but although these were now faded and flaking I could imagine what a wondrous place this must have been.

As I glanced around the pillar into the centre of the chamber I saw them; the objects of my mission, the thirteen young acolytes. They were all naked, chained up by their wrists and ankles, spread-eagled between two marble pillars in a semicircle within the inner chamber. The signs of their ordeal were evident, as they all had bruises and cuts, but despite that their beauty and luminous presence was still evident.

Kim interrupted, "Was I one of them me Nano? I need to know."

"Yes, Kim. As soon as I saw you earlier through the wire mesh I recognised you. That was why I looked so fearful as if my past deeds had come back to haunt me. But there is more to tell."

"Sorry to interrupt, do go on."

Then, I saw a sight that sickened me. It was you, Kim, though I didn't know who you were at the time, laid out on the floor being held down by guards dressed in tabards with the red cross of the Knights Templar. You were being desecrated and entered by one of their priests dressed in vestments and wearing a gold cross. I heard your gentle pleas being ignored as the heretic forced himself into you to the sound of the laughs and taunts of the other men. There must have been nearly twenty guards there, each waiting for their turn to abuse and torment you.

Kim looked on aghast, "Oh my god, that's disgusting. You're telling me those guards just fucked and abused me."

"I'm sorry Kim, but yes. I didn't hang around to watch, I had to work on my own plans for trying to get you out, but I don't think there can be any doubt about it."

"Shit, how degrading. But I still don't get it. Such a horrible traumatic experience yet I can't remember a thing? I don't know what to think."

"I can't explain it Kim. Maybe it was so awful you wiped it from your mind. Perhaps it was wiped from your memory deliberately to help you cope and survive. I honestly don't know. I can only say what I saw."

Kim looked thoughtful, "this is all so weird. I find it hard to believe all this stuff happened to me without me remembering anything. But, you must carry on with your tale."

The black cat continued, "There was no way I could overcome them on my own. I turned back round to hide myself behind the marble pillar and to reflect on my next course of action. The only advantage I had was secrecy; none of the guards would have realised their defences had been breached. It would be foolhardy to take them all in a frontal assault so a more cunning strategy was needed.

I took the hard choice to leave the thirteen acolytes for now and put my plan into effect. I sneaked from behind the pillars and into a passage that led me away form the inner sanctum. I was looking for the refectory where the food for the whole temple was prepared. I strode into the kitchen and the men working at the long trestle table looked up at me. "My name is Nano. I have been summoned here to help in the kitchens." One of the men, presumably the head chef gazed at me suspiciously. "I'm the head chef and I haven't asked for any help here. Well, we can always do with more hands, I suppose you can come and help prepare lunch".

I was set the task of chopping vegetables and cuts of meat for a stew that was being made for lunch. This work was perfect for my purpose. I waited until all the other men had stopped for a break and had their backs turned, went into my bag and secretly pulled out the black berries I had picked from the courtyard garden in the moonlight. Deadly nightshade, named with good reason, is one of the most toxic plants on the earth. I emptied hundreds of the berries into the cast iron stew pot. I hoped there were enough there to wreak the devastation I needed to complete my task. I went to join the other men for a drink and let the deadly broth simmer.

After a short while a group of the Knights Templar guards came into the kitchen. "Hey, you men, what are you lounging about for. We've had a hard morning fucking young girls and we're all starving. When's lunch going to be ready?" The stew was dished out and bowls sent out to the other parts of the temple. The men hungrily ate their food, one of them commented, "I don't know what the cooks put in the broth today – it was delicious, but I tell you what, Its made me feel really strange." "Yeah, I know what you mean," replied another, "I feel all dizzy and I've awful stomach cramps."

He groaned, collapsing on all fours onto the floor and grasping his stomach. Another guard had fallen onto the floor in a fit of convulsions until he stiffened and went quiet. It was soon silent as finally they all succumbed to the poison. The belladonna had done its deadly work. I could only hope that the stew had been taken by everybody in the temple and that this sight was being repeated all over the marble palace.

I sought out the keys for the shackles of the young acolytes from the guard room and proceeded cautiously through the passages to the ceremonial chamber in the centre of the temple. All along the way I saw dead guards strewn on the marble floors. An eerie silence permeated the whole temple and there was no sign of any life. I soon reached the inner sanctum again. I stood in the chamber before the thirteen girls chained to the pillars. I felt a rush of excitement as I sensed victory was in my grasp and that the release of the young women was in hand.

Then, I heard a voice from behind me. I turned around. An old man in a monk's habit with a large silver cross hanging from his neck was hunched on the floor against the wall. His face was impenetrable from underneath his hood. Then, he looked up and his eyes, stunningly bright and alert for a man of his age, caught mine. If this was the only heretic from the new religion remaining in the temple then even I should have no difficulty in overwhelming him and completing my task. Or, so I thought, until his weasel words started to echo across the chamber.

"Congratulations, my young friend – you have done well. I applaud your courage and cunning in overwhelming the foot soldiers of Christ. Your mistress has chosen her protagonist wisely and prepared him well. I have never known the gold, silver, crystal and quartz gates to be penetrated before, yet you have managed to pass through all four. You must have subtle powers behind you."

His voice was clear, slow and seductive. I found myself being drawn in. The old man stood up awkwardly clasping a wood staff to help support him and shuffled towards me never once turning his sharp gaze away from me. He grasped my arm for support.

"I bear you no ill will, my friend. You have justly earned the moment of your triumph. But listen to me, my son, don't you see what I can offer you – all of these thirteen girls could be yours to use how you desire. It is in your power to have them, I will not stand in your way if you wish to take them. Look at them. They are still helpless, they would do anything for you if you released them."

I was aware I was being lured into a trap, but the voice of the old man was so calmly seductive that everything he said seemed to make sense. His silky tones were bewitching me. My mind was in conflict, torn between resistance and his seductive temptation. He grasped my face with his hand and turned it around the semi-circle of marble columns making me gaze at each of the thirteen naked girls chained to the pillars. They were all gagged and none were able to call out any warnings to me or to break the spell of the aged monk's voice.

"Look upon them, my son. All of that soft naked flesh could be yours. Thirteen girls chosen for their beauty, presence and spirituality to be trained to serve the goddesses and they could be yours. They may have been used over zealously by my disciples but imagine them restored, bathed in rose water, their delectable bodies perfumed with the finest scents from the orient. Just think, as they touch your face with their soft hands, as they caress your body, as their gentle fingers arouse your sexual feelings. Feel the touch of their scented hair as it brushes against your naked body whilst they run their hands all over you. Until, finally, their fingers gently brush against your thigh, then your balls and then ultimately touch your cock. What man could resist such attention?"

My training at the hands of Goddess Nemesis, the years of devoted servitude to her and the worship of the sacred feminine, was being put to the test. I could feel the stirrings in my loins, the gentle swelling in my cock. I knew that if I allowed myself to get an erection I would be defeated. I strained every sinew of my body and mind to hold back the emerging tumescence in my cock.

"Don't resist now. Listen to what will befall you. Feel your cock erect and hard. Imagine as the soft lips of a young acolyte envelops your cock, feel the silky texture of her saliva around you and the gentle movement as her mouth takes in the shaft of your hard cock and runs up and down your erection bringing you just to the point of your climax. Then, imagine, as she pulls her mouth away, leans back and spreads her legs wide for you, as you kneel down and then enter her. How long will you last? How long before the final explosion of orgasm erupts inside her? Then, the deed is done – you would have impregnated a trainee goddess with your seed and she will be yours. All thirteen of them could be yours; every day and every night they would be there for you to take your pleasure."

The task was on a knife edge. I was battling with myself to control my body, to try and break free from the hypnotic and seductive words of the old monk. I remembered the advice that had been given me, use the tools that have been given. Amethyst. It is the Goddess Nemesis's birth stone. It has mystical qualities – it brings good fortune, it cleanses, it brings about a chaste frame of mind...it protects against seduction! I thrust my hand into my bag and clasp it around the piece of uncut crystal. Instantaneously I started to think more clearly. I could feel the cleansing properties releasing me from the spell of the old monk. "No, old man, I will not yield to temptation," I pronounced.

I pulled myself away from his grasp, turned and pushed him hard. He fell back, his head crashed against the marble floor and he was soon nestled in a pool of his blood. The final obstacle to the completion of my mission had been removed.

I quickly set about the work of releasing the girls. Then, a strange thing suddenly occurred to me. I did a quick count; one of the young acolytes was missing. There were only twelve! Having thought my task was nearly at an end I realised my duty was now to search the remainder of the temple for the missing girl. I gathered all of the girls up and let them through the black quartz gate one at a time. I had got to the last girl, the twelfth, which was you Kim. I remember that you had been chained up for so long and had been so badly treated that you were in a daze. Then I felt cold steel pressed against my neck and I heard a female voice whisper in my ear, "The last one is mine. You may have poisoned all the soldiers and priests and released eleven of us, but your victory will not be complete, servant of the goddesses."

I was shocked. The smell of a sweet perfume filled my nose. I felt long hair against the side of my face and the curves of a female body pressed against my back as her hold tightened and the knife was held against my throat. "Yes, I'm the missing thirteenth girl. But, I've chosen another path, I've decided to join the physical and sexual world. I've given my body up to satisfy the lusts of the disciples of the new religion. In return I have been given a favoured status, I have been pampered and offered rich clothes and fine jewellery to wear. Come over the the Knights Templar who may reward you if you repent by rejecting your mistress and emptying your seed into me. Make this choice, abject slave of the goddesses, or the only alternative is death."

How many more twists will my mission take? I pondered my next course of action quickly but carefully. I felt the knife pressing on my throat and even now I could feel warm drops of blood on my neck. I gasped for breath. "Oh fair and beautiful maiden, I am undone and your words are so full of wisdom. The very end of this mission has finally revealed my true self. Long have I desired to have girls to satisfy my sexual desires. The temptations placed before me by the old monk were not lost on me. My sexual urges have been aroused. Now that I can hear your words, smell your sweet scent and feel your breasts pressed against me I realise that I would like nothing more than to have your naked body held against mine". She replied, "Oh yes, I can feel that you desire me. There may be hope for you yet". I continued, "Let me admire your beautiful body, let me see your young pert breasts. Just talking and imagining is arousing me. Whether you decide to kill me or take me with you let me satisfy my sexual needs now on the floor of this temple now". "So you want to take me, penetrate and impregnate me now, on the marble floor of this shrine to the goddesses?" she asked, I replied, "Oh, yes, young mistress, more than anything else."

She relaxed her grip slightly and pulled the knife away from my neck. I seized my opportunity, pushing her backwards with all of my strength. The force of the movement sent us both crashing onto the marble floor and the knife spinning away. I had played a treacherous and dangerous game, enticing the young girl into believing I might follow her to create one small opening that I could exploit.

I confronted her, "Don't you understand that by going with the disciples of the new religion you are betraying your sex, that you will subject yourself to a life of abuse just to satisfy the lusts of your male tormentors. Your rich clothes and jewellery are just meaningless vanity and will count for nothing. Come back, follow me back through the gates where I can re-unite you with the goddesses". I pleaded with her desperately. She faced up to me, her eyes wild with hatred and anger. She made a leap for the knife, her speed, suppleness and agility taking me by surprise as she twisted round and thrust the dagger into my side. I collapsed in pain onto the floor with a deep and bloody wound.

"You're wrong, when I return the followers of the new religion will hold me in high honour. Not only that but I will take this other girl back with me so they can impregnate her." With that parting exclamation she grasped your hand Kim and dragged you running out of the inner sanctum and out of my reach. My last desperate plea to her had failed. I was crestfallen. I had rescued eleven of the girls but I felt a bitter sense of failure that during that last encounter I had lost the battle to persuade the fallen acolyte and that she had escaped with you Kim.".

"I'm sorry Kim, I failed you. It was my fault you weren't rescued."

"But what happened next? What happened after I was taken away? Do you know?"

"Yes Kim, my story does continue. There are several more twists to it."

A voice echoed down the corridor.

"Nurse Kim, are you ready yet? I'm waiting for you and I have a patient here."

"But the rest of the story!" Kim gasped in exasperation.

"No Kim, you'll have to go to her. We'll both be in big trouble if you don't."

9: Nurse Sally

"Girl, aren't you ready yet? Come on hurry along, I've got a patient waiting."

Kim scurried down a brightly lit corridor opposite the under stair cage where the black cat was kept towards the voice summoning her impatiently. On this occasion the dark haired figure, The Red Queen, Mistress Nemesis, the Hatter, the Headmistress, whatever she cared to call herself was waiting for her at the end of the corridor dressed in a white pvc nurse's uniform, her arms crossed and the toe of an high heeled shoe tapping the floor.

"I'm very sorry, madam," Kim gasped.

"You should address me as Nurse Sally or just Nurse."

"I'm sorry Nurse Sally."

"I expect the highest standards of discipline here, Student Nurse Kim. This is very lax of you arriving at the clinic late like this. Now, your student nurse's uniform is here."

"I'm sorry Nurse Sally, I'll put my uniform on straight away."

Kim hurriedly picked up a red pvc nurse's uniform and struggled hurriedly into it, zipping up the front so that her cleavage was bursting out of the tight shiny material. She also had a pair of black tights and black high heeled shoes like Nurse Sally's. Finally she perched a red cap with white cross on her head. They were like an inverse reflection of each other, Nurse Sally in a white uniform with a red cross on her chest and Kim in red with a white cross.

"That's better girl, now hurry up, I've a patient ready to be treated."

Kim smoothed the stiff shiny material of her dress and followed Nurse Sally towards a door, which had a brass plaque with the following inscription engraved on it: 'Clinic for Corrective Therapy,' and underneath, 'Proprietor: Nurse Sally, Dip. Nursing (Nemesisland College of Nursing)'. Oh dear, thought Kim, what strange new adventure am I embarking on now.

Kim followed Nurse Sally into the clinic. The first thing that struck her was the sweet, almost sickly, smell; that distinctive medical smell that Kim remembered from hospital visits, a mixture of TCP and disinfectant. The second thing that hit Kim was the overpowering brightness that dazzled her. The final thing Kim took in was an overwhelming impression of shiny metal implements. There was a metal rack with medical instruments, stainless steel bowls, bottles of sterilising fluid, rolls of bandages and spotless white towels.

It was a small room dominated by a white treatment table on the black and white tiled floor and on it was one of Nurse Sally's patients, one of Nemesisland's slaves, thought Kim. His body was covered in a long white operating gown and his legs were lifted into wooden stirrups where they had been spread and tied with white ropes so his genitals were exposed and ready for inspection. He was tied down to the examination bench with white leather straps. His head had been wrapped in bandages, except for his eyes and his mouth, which was filled with a gruesome looking metal dental cage.

"Now, Mr Dugdale, you're very lucky today because I have a student nurse, Kim, with me today to help. She's going to assist me with some of the procedures. She's studying for her diploma in nursing and I'm training her in some of my special corrective treatments. She may only be a student nurse but I expect you to treat her with the same respect that you would me."

"Nnnngg," grunted the patient, his mouth so stretched by the dental gag he couldn't utter anything else. I expect, considered Kim, if he objected to being treated by a student nurse there was really nothing he could do about it.

"Now, you know why you are here, don't you Mr Dugdale. You've been referred by Mistress Nemesis for some unsatisfactory behaviour, haven't you? Some of your responses haven't been appropriately submissive, have they? She tells me you've been getting sexual excitement from some of your punishments, is that true Mr Dugdale?"

"Yynnnggg."

Nurse Sally turned to Kim and spoke in a matronly tone of voice like a senior member of staff consulting with her junior colleague discussing the patient as if he wasn't even there.

"His is typical of the kind of case that gets referred to my clinic, Student Nurse Kim. You see many of the men here in Nemesisland lack self control. It has to be punished into them and sometimes, when they don't respond to that, they must be sent to me for more extreme corrective treatment. You see this one here," she said pointing to the man splayed out on the examination table, "he's been getting erections in Mistress Nemesis's presence. Now, that is totally unacceptable. He's been referred here so I can find the source of his problem. At my clinic I test responses to different stimuli and try to correct their behaviour."

"Yes, I think I understand," Kim responded.

"Now, the first thing a student nurse has to do is check the medical records. There should be a consent form in the file over there," she said, pointing.

Kim opened up the file. The first document inside was a form. She glanced over it, 'I, Mr Dick Dugdale of Pig and Pepper House, Nemesisland consent to whatever treatments the Clinic for Corrective Therapy advise, however invasive they may be, and acknowledge that such treatments are necessary to rectify inappropriate behaviour'. There was a signature at the bottom.

"Yes, these look in order Nurse Sally, there's a completed consent form in here."

"Excellent, then we can proceed. Now, whilst I'm preparing and sterilising my implements I want you to do some tasks for me. First, you can use some of the cotton buds and the mouthwash to clean the inside of his mouth and then I want you to shave the hairs off his balls and from around his arse hole until they are smooth and clean. There's a bowl and water, a razor and some spray on lather," she explained pointing to where everything was. "Is that clear Kim?"

"Yes Nurse Sally."

As she had been told, Kim started by dipping a cotton bud in some mouth-wash. It felt very strange at first but Kim soon set about her tasks studiously pushing the bud into his mouth between the shiny dental brace and rubbing the inside of his cheek and tongue. She could not help but lean over him as she did this task and was conscious of her cleavage, squeezed into the tight pvc nurse's uniform, hanging over him. He's getting a real eye-full thought Kim as she felt her tits jiggling as she rubbed his tongue with the cotton bud. Kim, glanced down to see that the sight of Kim's bust was turning him on; his cock was getting erect.

"Nurse Sally, I think your patient has a problem," said Kim, thinking she should draw her attention to his behaviour.

"Well done, Student Nurse Kim, that's very observant of you. You've done well to report that to me. You see the difficulties we have with some of our patients." She turned to the patient and admonished him, "Mr Dugdale, do you see the problems you have. The Student Nurse is not here for your sexual gratification, is she?"

"Nnnngggg."

"You know you shouldn't be getting excited at the sight of Student Nurse Kim's breasts, that's totally unacceptable. I can see why your mistress has sent you here. That's incorrigible behaviour."

Nurse Sally turned round to the tray of shiny metal implements she had been arranging and picked something up. When she turned back Kim looked on aghast. She was holding a pin-wheel, a metal implement with tiny sharp points on the end of a wheel.

"This should do the trick," said Nurse Sally, "here just feel it Kim."

She offered the tool to Kim who carefully put her finger on the end of one of the sharp spokes. Oh my god, thought Kim; that gives a painful prick on a finger, what it must be feel like on a something as sensitive as a penis I can't imagine. Nurse Sally leant over him and dug the sharp pins into the slave's hard cock and rolled the wheel up the shaft.

"Nnnngggg," grunted the slave.

Kim's eyes watered for him as Nurse Sally ran onto the tip of his cock and across the little hole at its end.

"Nnnnggg."

"Student Nurse, this will be good training for you. You have a go," she said, handing the gleaming metal implement over to Kim.

Kim took the tool into her hand and repeated what she had seen Nurse Sally do, pushing the metal prongs onto the wheel into his cock and running it up the shaft. His erection had not started to wilt yet.

"You'll need to press harder for this one," advised Nurse Sally, "his is a serious case. Don't show him any mercy."

Kim did as she was told and dug the metal wheel hard and deep into the shaft of his cock.

"Aaahhh."

"Yes, that's better," said Nurse Sally.

Kim ran the wheel up to the tip of his cock and pressed hard running it back and forth across the most sensitive part of his member. His body jerked up and down with the pain but he remained securely tied by the straps. The procedure had the desired effect as his cock had started going soft.

"Well done Kim, that's much better. You can shave him now then I can carry on with my treatments."

Kim set about shaving the hairs around the slave's cock. She squirted some of the foam from the aerosol onto his cock and balls to create a lather. Then, with studied concentration, she set to work with the razor running gently around the base of his cock, over his balls and either side of the cracks in his arse, every so often dunking it into the hot water to clean the soap and hairs off. When she had finished she admired her handiwork. She rubbed her fingers across his smooth skin. Nurse Sally joined in, rubbing her hand around his balls to test how smooth the skin was and how good a job Kim had done. Finally, she took the soft cock in her hand.

"That's a good job nurse. Now look here," she said squeezing the end of his cock, "you can see why he needs treatment can't you? See, he's leaking, isn't he. You know that's not permitted, don't you Mr Dugdale?"

"Urrr."

"Now, Student Nurse Kim, this is where the procedures get, how should I say, more invasive. You need to follow all my instructions carefully and watch everything I do. But, before then you need to put these on."

Nurse Sally handed Kim some thin blue surgical gloves and a face mask. They both put these on. What a sight we must look, thought Kim, as they both stood over him, their mouths covered and two sets of eyes pouring over him with their hands held before them. His breathing was heavy.

"Nurse Sally, he looks rather anxious."

"And so he should be Nurse Kim. First of all I want to test his response to some anal penetration to see if that heightens his sexual desire."

Nurse Sally turned back to her tray of instruments. She held up a hideous looking piece of metal that gleamed in the bright lights of the clinic. Kim had seen one before. It was a speculum and she knew exactly where it was going.

"Now, Kim, I'd like you to prepare him for me. There's some lubricant there," she said pointing to a shelf, "you need to put a generous amount on your fingers and then work them up into his hole to lubricate him. You can stretch his hole a bit with your fingers too whilst you are up there."

"Yes, Nurse Sally."

Kim had never done anything like this before; all the time she had worked in the parlour she had never received a request for anal play. But, she did as she was told, squeezed some lube onto her gloved fingers and rubbed it along the crack of his arse and then, finding the hole, eased a finger up into it. The slave groaned from behind his metal gag. Kim rotated her finger around as it still felt tense until gradually the muscles began to relax. Then she inserted another finger in and pushed both fingers up and down in a rocking motion until he groaned in response. Kim had to admit she was enjoying this. It felt empowering to take control and invade a man's most intimate orifices without him being able to do anything about it.

"Very good Student Nurse Kim, I can see you are going to have a natural talent for some of my procedures. Have you loosened him up for me?"

"Yes Nurse Sally, I have."

"Good, now let me take over from here."

She stood over the slave, the gruesome metal object in hand. She inserted the penis shaped part of the object deep inside him to its fullest length. His body twisted and strained against the white leather straps holding him onto the treatment table.

"Nnnnggg, Nnnngggg," he groaned, his head thrashing from side to side.

"Now, come, come Mister Dugdale," said Nurse Sally, "you must take your treatment. You cannot return to Nemesisland, you cannot go back to your mistress unless you accept your medicine willingly. Besides, this is only the start. There's worse to come as I'm sure you realise."

The slave nodded in acknowledgement. The implement having been fully inserted Nurse Sally worked the spring that extended the mechanism in the metal penis that stretched his arse. Kim looked on in wide-eyed in amazement. She had never experienced medical play before and what she saw was a revelation to her. How can he take that?, she wondered, as the metal object opened wider and wider and the slave strained and strained against strap and buckle, his screams muffled by the metal gag in his mouth. Kim gazed on in astonishment as she could stare right up into his anus.

"Do you see your problem, Mr Dugdale," Nurse Sally scolded, "even under this extreme stress you are still getting excited. Look at his penis Nurse Kim, it's only starting to get hard again and, see, those tell-tale little globs of pre-cum on the tip of his cock. I'm sorry but you have to take some more Mr Dugdale but before I do that I'm going to get the Student Nurse to carry out another treatment at the same time. Girl, go to my tray, you'll find a pair of forceps there. Bring them back with you."

Kim obediently went behind Nurse Sally's back, gaped at the array of instruments, and picked out the forceps; long metal handles with sharp points at their ends. The shiny metal felt good in her hands. She returned to her position by Nurse Sally's side; the pair of them making for a nightmare masked fetish vision in red and white. Kim noted the look of sadistic concentration in the eyes of Nurse Sally.

"Good. Now Student Nurse Kim, I want you to squeeze his balls with the metal prongs whilst I extend him further." Her gaze fixed onto the slave, "Are you ready Mr Dugdale? You know you need this treatment don't you?"

Kim fixed the tips of the forceps onto the sac of his balls and then squeezed hard just at the same time as Nurse Sally extended the speculum just a tiny bit further. He's in a hopeless plight, thought Kim; he was completely in their hands with no escape from the tight bondage of the leather straps. His muffled screams of agony echoed against the clinical white walls. Really, how delicious, thought Kim as she released the handle of the forceps only to move them into another position and squeeze them tight again. Nurse Sally anticipated Kim's movement and eased the speculum just another fraction wider. The two fetish nurses worked in tandem to continue their torment of the slave.

"That's better," Nurse Sally finally said. "You see how the treatment has put a stop to any erection developing. Now, Student Nurse Kim, I hope you're learning from this little demonstration. I must admit I'm impressed with your skill in these procedures."

"Thank you," Kim replied, "it really is most enlightening for me Nurse Sally."

"The next treatment will be challenging for him I think. It's a procedure he's never had before and it will be scary, but I'm afraid his behaviour merits this corrective treatment."

Kim dreaded to think what it might be if it was more extreme than having a piece of metal put up your back-side and having it stretched.

"Nurse Kim, go to the tray with my implements and fetch me the black box."

"Yes, Nurse Sally."

Kim went to fetch the box as she had been told; her curiosity aroused as to what its contents might be, and handed it to Nurse Sally who opened it. Inside, resting in red velvet, were eight sleek silver rods with a curve at one end.

"Do you know what these are?"

Kim nodded her headed, "No."

"These are sounds. Do you know what they are for?"

Kim nodded her head again. Her eyes widened in amazement and shock as it dawned on her what Nurse Sally was going to do with them. Surely not, she thought. Kim had never seen anything like them before. Surely, she's not going to do that with them. Kim watched in awe as the Nurse Sally, with a look of intense concentration, fed one of the metal rods into the hole in the slave's penis and gently eased it down his urethra. Kim noticed her technique; how she allowed the metal rods to do the work for her without pushing them. She also glanced across at the man strapped to the treatment bench to gauge his reaction. It must surely be agony, thought Kim, yet, although his breathing was heavy, there was no attempt to scream in pain, only a dreamy glazed look in his eye. Nurse Sally had inserted the whole length of the metal rod down his cock so a small piece of the sounds protruded from the hole in his cock.

"Touch it," encouraged Nurse Sally, "feel how deeply it's penetrated him."

Kim reached out tentatively and touched the tip of his cock with one finger of her surgical glove. She ran it down the length of his penis feeling the hard metal inside him until she could touch the furthermost point where the metal curved. It was an amazing feeling to see what this person could do and what the slave would submit to under her ministering hands.

74

"Wow, it's fascinating," said Kim, "I never would have thought somebody could take that.

"Oh, my girl, you'd be surprised what these men can take to please their mistress, or their Nurse," laughed Nurse Sally. "OK, Student Nurse, it's your turn now."

"What," gasped Kim, "you want me to do that? Is it safe for me?"

Nurse Sally was pulling the sounds out, "Oh yes, you've watched what I've done and I'll be next to you to guide you. Besides, Mr Dugdale, you have to accept your treatments from the Student Nurse as well as me, don't you?"

Nurse Sally handed Kim the next sounds from the box, which was a slightly thicker gauge from the earlier one. Kim was tense; she could feel beads of sweat forming on her brow as she breathed heavily through her face mask. She took a deep breath to calm herself and then set about her task. She slipped the cold shiny metal into the end of his cock and felt it getting sucked in. She had seen how Nurse Sally had worked, easing the metal deeper with gentle nudges, not trying to force it and letting the weight of the rod and gravity do most of the work for her. Before she knew it the rod was half-way down the slave's cock.

"Well done, Student Nurse, that's good," Nurse Sally encouraged.

Kim concentrated, occasionally turning her head to watch the man's reaction; some deep breaths, some little groans but he did not seem distressed. It was as if he had drifted off into his own little dream world as he surrendered himself to the ministrations of these two fetish nurses. Kim herself felt heady and excited at the power she had over him. Finally, she had done it; the rod was as deep inside the penis as it was going to go. Kim touched the sounds at the end of its curve to test the depth of its final resting place and pushed her finger against the metal. The slave let out a contented groan. That is awesome, thought Kim. She cast a glance across at Nurse Sally who was watching her reaction and beamed a wide smile at her. Kim smiled back and let out a little laugh. She left the rod embedded in the cock for a few minutes and admired her handiwork before pulling it out.

"There you are Mr Dugdale, that's your treatment over for today. I trust that when you return to Mistress Nemesis you won't suffer from the same weaknesses again. If I see you back here I can find some particularly vicious treatments for an untamed cock. Now, thank Student Nurse Kim."

"Thnng oo," the slave mouthed through the metal mouth gag.

"It's a pleasure," said Kim, "and if I see you here again there are another six sounds in that box, all thicker than what you've had in you today. I'll take great pleasure in inserting those up your cock."

Nurse Sally had gone back to her instrument table and was writing something. Perhaps it's a prescription, she thought, or her case notes. Nurse Sally turned around and ceremoniously handed Kim a sheet of light brown paper. Kim held it in her hand and gazed down at it. It had an initial 'N' at the top decorated with medical instruments around it. It was a certificate. At the top it read 'Nemesisland College of Nursing' and then, 'This is to certify that Student Nurse Kim has attended a course in corrective therapy administered by qualified instructor Nurse Sally and has passed Level 1 Medical Treatments.' Kim was really quite proud of herself. How cool, she thought, I don't ever remember getting a certificate for anything before.

"Gosh, thanks," said Kim, a beaming smile across her face.

"Well done Student Nurse Kim," said Nurse Sally. "You've excelled today. You've performed very well, I'm pleased with you. I'll report that back to Mistress Nemesis. Now you're probably needed somewhere else now so I'll tidy up here and let you get along. Leave your nurse's uniform at the door."

"Yes Nurse Sally, thank you very much for instructing me," Kim replied as she departed the clinical whiteness of the medical room.

10: The Purple Caterpillar

"You've been talking to the girl have you Slave Nano? And what have you told her?"

"Mistress, I started to tell her the story of how she got here."

The black cat cowered before the commanding figure before him, his head hanging forlornly. He knew instantly from her stance and the tone of her voice he had displeased her, that his decision to start recounting his tale to Kim was a mistake and that he would have to pay for it. A purple clad figure balanced on high heels towered over him, her eyes flashing with anger. Her purple streaked hair bobbed before him as she set about reprimanding him. Her voice echoed around the corridor with a latent menace the black cat recognised and which he knew bode ill for him.

"So, she understands the part you have played in her past. Having seen the girl, now fallen from the grace of my presence and tutelage and put away in a massage parlour to be debauched by worthless males who only care for their own sexual needs, I hope you are suitably contrite about your failings that have contributed to her fate."

"Yes Mistress Nemesis, I felt sorry for her. She seemed so confused and sad and when she started asking questions it was obvious I knew something about her past so it was difficult not to tell her something."

"So, you took it upon yourself to tell the tale of how she came here without consulting your mistress?"

"Yes Mistress Nemesis, I'm very sorry."

"Did you not think that I would want to choose when to let the girl have that information?"

"Of course Mistress I can see that. I thought I was helping. I can see I've made a grave mistake. I'm really sorry."

"It's me, and only me, who decides what is for the best in Nemesisland. After all this time in my servitude haven't you understood that yet? The problem is you are thinking for yourself slave. You have surrendered control to me; you don't need to do that any more. It's dangerous for you Slave Nano because there are so many snares you can get trapped in. And there's another thing Nano. I think you like the sound of your own voice too much. You wanted to tell the girl your tale; I believe you think it gives you some importance in my world. It wouldn't surprise me if you felt sexually excited by the girl Nano and you know how perilous that is for you. Well, let me tell you slave, I'll soon disabuse you of any illusions you might have about your place in Nemesisland."

"Honestly Mistress, I don't think that's it. I just felt sorry for her. I wasn't thinking. I realise now I shouldn't have said anything without your permission Mistress."

"Yes, and I'll make sure you learn your lesson. You are lucky on one count, slave, I'm not concerned that the girl Kim has started to learn something about herself. She still has a long way to go before she will truly submit to me and understanding something of her strange past might help her on that path. The time is ripe for her to learn these things. I will create a situation where you are together again and, now, I give you permission to complete the tale when there is an opportune moment. But, that has no bearing on the punishment you will face for acting without my authority. I don't lock you away just for you to sit there chatting to my other servants in Nemesisland, do I?

"No you don't Mistress Nemesis, I'm very sorry."

"I've had enough of you now Nano. Vicky Duchess, take him away and lock him up in the cage. I've already thought of a fitting way to deal with him. I'll stay here and wait for the girl to come out of the clinic."

The Duchess attached a lead to the collar and led the black cat away as his mistress had commanded. Mistress Nemesis perched herself on top of toadstool shaped stool of bright yellow with red spots that Vicky Duchess had set down for her. She waited in silent contemplation for the arrival of Kim.

I want this girl for my slave girl, she reflected. Seeing her again makes me realise why I chose her to have a place in my world in the first place and, despite being so used in the brothel, she still has something special about her. She's got many of the qualities I desire to see in a slave girl and she can be trained in the rest. It's not just that she is lovely, her golden hair, voluptuous curves and ample breasts make her a fitting complement to my obsidian blackness. I can see it, she imagined, slaves will be captivated by her, she can be used to lure them into her world with the promise of erotic delights, she can tantalise them, until they see that she is unattainable and the only path is submission to me. But, it's not just her alluring and sensual looks, she has more than that. She is willing and ripe to be moulded to my needs. She is playful and imaginative and will go further for me than merely obeying orders parrot fashion; her behaviour in the pit and at the tea party has demonstrated that. She wasn't just following a command, she entered into the role, she became the other

78

person that I created for her and revelled in it. She became a character in Nemesisland.

And yet, Mistress Nemesis considered, she still has a lot to learn before she can truly submit. I have to take her further. She must be made to face her innermost darkest desires and admit to them and then follow the path that has been laid out for of her own free will. I desire her though. Oh yes, I want her in my world and I will have her. It will require all of my skill to take her with me though. I have to push her boundaries further and further without breaking her and losing her. She has to submit to me knowingly and willingly. She smiled to herself. Oh yes, it's a challenge, but I know I will win her over in the end and I will enjoy every moment of the journey. I will push her, I will take her with me, until she realises who she really is and all resistance collapses until she offers herself to me and she is mine; my slave girl.

Mistress Nemesis was lost in her reverie when she heard movement from the corridor. Kim had emerged from Nurse Sally's clinic. Kim was buzzing. The heady experience of carrying out the medical treatments, the feeling of control over the patient and his helpless submission at her hands had made her light headed. And it was most strange, she had also got a sense of satisfaction from being told she had performed well. She had stripped off and left her nurse's uniform on a chair outside the door of the clinic as she had been told and was now anxious to get back to the cage with the black cat to hear the rest of his tale.

As she hurried down the brightly lit corridor towards the gloomy passage where the under-stair cage was she had a slight twinge of disappointment to see the cage was empty, its door left swinging open and its entrance guarded by another figure. Kim had now ceased to be surprised at how this mysterious figure who controlled this world could appear in different guises as before her was Nurse Sally, who she had left behind in the clinic and could not possibly have passed her in the corridor, let alone have got changed so quickly, dressed in a very different costume.

The dim light of the passage way was still strong enough to reflect off the shiny purple pvc cat-suit she was wearing. The penetrating blue eyes, framed by the black purple streaked hair, fixed onto her. At her gaze Kim's heart jumped a beat and this disturbing need, this yearning desire to give herself up to her that she had experienced when she first met the Red Queen, washed over her in luxuriant waves of submissive feeling. Bizarrely, the purple figure was sat on a chair that was shaped and coloured like a toadstool. Suddenly Kim realised seeing the figure clad entirely in skin tight purple and she couldn't help but blurt out.

"A purple caterpillar!"

Without ever surrendering her haughty presence of power and control the purple figure allowed herself the slightest of smiles at Kim's exclamation of recognition.

"Yes girl, that's right, the purple caterpillar."

"I've just come from Nurse Sally's clinic and look I've got a certificate," Kim said holding out the scroll.

"Yes that's very good Kim," the purple caterpillar's smile broadening as Kim's infectious enthusiasm, even naivety, touched her.

"Where's the black cat?" asked Kim.

"Oh, he has displeased me and will be dealt with later, in my own time. But, come and sit down here at my feet, girl."

Kim felt fearful for the black cat. It was clear his mistress was angry with him over something and she could only think it was for telling her the tale. Kim so wanted to hear how it finished and feared that now the cat had been put away she would never find out what happened to her. But Kim did as she was told and sat down on the cold floor at the purple caterpillar's stiletto heeled feet. The caterpillar adjusted her choker, a piece of purple silk with a black jewel set in it, looked down kindly at her and gently started to touch Kim's hair with her elbow-length purple gloves. Kim got a warm tingly feeling from this attention like a cat curled up in its owners lap. The purple caterpillar bent down and whispered slowly and firmly in her ear.

"So, tell me girl, who...are...*you*?"

Kim was taken aback at the directness of the question. She recalled the scene in Alice in Wonderland, the caterpillar sat on the mushroom smoking on a hookah pipe interrogating a bewildered Alice who had just been turned into so many different sizes. She empathised with the Alice character.

"I don't know," said Kim quietly, "or at least I thought I knew this morning but then so many things have happened to me since then that I don't really know any more. I got up this morning for another day's work at the parlour. I don't mind it and I'm good at it, at least believe I am, and the money's alright but I don't believe it's me. I socialise a bit, sometimes with the other girls, but most of the time when I get home I'm just knackered and watch the telly. Sometimes I don't feel like it's me. Sometimes it's like I'm out of my body watching somebody else do all that. And then I got whisked away here and I don't know who I am or where I am. I don't even know if this is real or if it's a dream. And people keep hinting things about my past and the black cat has told me the strangest story and I don't know whether to believe it or not. And yet, somehow, in some strange kind of way I feel right here, that it's the other world that's false."

The purple caterpillar's eyes flashed and her dark eyebrows raised quizzically.

"You feel you belong here, don't you?"

"Yes," replied Kim, "yes, oddly enough I do."

"And how have you found Nemesisland?"

"What can I say? Strange, bizarre! Sometimes I feel put upon as though I'm being treated cruelly, other times I've had great fun. Really, I don't know what to make of it. But, it's kind of you to ask."

The purple caterpillar was still stroking Kim, gently touching her hair, her cheeks, her shoulders, occasionally moving down to brush her tits. The feel of the shiny material on her bare flesh was sensuous and all the sensations of the physical attention she was being given lured Kim into a warm glow and yes, she really did feel that she belonged. But, at those last few words she detected a change in mood. The purple caterpillar spoke, her voice now firmer and more authoritative. She had assumed the tone Kim remembered from the Red Queen.

"But you see Kim, here's the thing, I'm not asking you to be kind. Don't you see, sometimes you need to be treated cruelly to understand, that is part of my world. It will not always be fun for you here Kim. You still have a lot to learn before you truly belong. But, if that's what you feel, if that's where you want to be, then Kim that's up to you to let me take you there."

Kim looked into her eyes mesmerised by her haunting tones and listened to her tantalisingly portentous words.

"I do not keep anybody here against their will; I have already told you that girl. Whatever happens, wherever you are taken in my domain, however hard you are pushed, you must desire it for yourself Kim. As you proceed on your journey through Nemesisland it will not be easy, it will get harder and darker for you Kim when you enter the chambers upstairs beyond the iron gate. Do you want to go there Kim? Do you really want that?"

Kim's heart was throbbing with a mixture of fear, anticipation and desire. She needed to hear the rest of the story and the only way to do that was if she stayed in Nemesisland. But, it was more than that. Despite the thinly veiled threats of the dark challenges that await her, despite, or perhaps because of, the fear of the unknown, in some inexplicable way she trusted the dominant figure before her – the purple caterpillar, the Red Queen, the Headmistress, Nurse Sally…Mistress Nemesis and whatever name she called herself and whatever persona she adopted. The pause and the silence was electrifying as the two figures, one curled submissively on the floor and the other, a fetish fantasy vision in purple, towering over her, played out a tense psychological drama. Kim knew she faced a moment of choice. There was only one answer she could give.

Her voice was breathless but emphatic.

"Yes. Yes, I want to follow you. Take me into the rest of your realm."

The purple caterpillar smiled contentedly and nodded. She realised it was a tense moment and, though she never doubted her ability to get inside Kim's head and control her, she still felt a surge of relief when she heard Kim make the decision she wanted to hear. She is mine and I want her back, she thought. I want her in my world. I want her as my slave girl. I will have her and she will submit to me completely and willingly.

"Get onto your knees before me girl," ordered the purple caterpillar.

Her voice was imperious and commanding now. The spell had been broken, a fateful decision made and consummated with this one order and Kim's submissive compliance with it as she got down onto her knees.

For her part, strangely, Kim felt a great weight had been lifted from her. She had initially felt indignant at having been taken away from her world and locked away but then she had been intrigued by the Red Queen's offer to become part of Nemesisland. She had at times enjoyed it but on other occasions had felt treated cruelly. She was powerless to resist the seductive control of the powerful female figure before her. She believed she understood what was expected of her. She realised that part of the deal she had made with the simple words "Yes, I want to follow you" involved submitting herself into her hands.

The purple caterpillar stood up from her toadstool seat and looked down on her submissive girl. Kim looked up at her adoringly haunted by the mysterious control she had over her. Kim had been captivated by her voice and by her dominant presence but looking up at her now as she knelt before her she could she what a commanding physical presence she was. She was taller than Kim and dark and mysterious whilst Kim was softer and more rounded. From her position on her knees Kim could see how the figure hugging shiny pvc clung to the elegant curve of her hips. She had a stunning statuesque figure that you just wanted to worship. Oh my god, thought Kim, if I feel that kind of attraction what must her male servants feel when they serve her.

"Kiss my shoes girl."

Kim bent down and touched the black leather of her shoes with her lips. She needed no other commands. Her head was in a whirl but she knew exactly what she had to do and, inexplicably, it felt wonderful. She gently kissed the leather of the shoes and then moved onto the straps that buckled around the purple caterpillar's elegant ankles. She licked the leather and the buckles luxuriating in the glorious submissive feeling that welled up inside her.

"That's good girl, now my cat-suit."

The hem of the leg of the purple pvc was just above the ankle strap of the shoes. She kissed it and licked it slowly and sensuously, wanting to make the moment and the tingling feeling inside her crotch last forever. She could feel the line of her slim but muscular legs. The caterpillar's legs were long but Kim didn't care, she wanted to touch every inch of shiny material with her lips. She worked her way up the purple caterpillar's firm thighs holding onto the smooth purple pvc with her hands to support herself. As she got to the top she was conscious of her crotch at Kim's eye level and yearned to touch the purple caterpillar's sex underneath the pvc. But, she had other ideas as she turned around and gently stuck her back-side out into Kim's face inviting her to kiss her pvc clad arse. Kim eagerly accepted the offer, kissing and licking the rounded shiny offering that had been presented to her enthusiastically.

Once every inch of material had been touched by Kim's lips the voluptuous rear of the purple caterpillar turned away and Kim was once again on her knees, facing her, looking up into the hauntingly beautiful features and dazzling blue eyes. The caterpillar was now nestling a flogger in her hands. It was black with a horse's head at one end and had a spade shaped patch of leather at the other. The horse's head was offered to Kim and she kissed it. The commands were wordless because no words were needed. The end with the leather flogger was presented to Kim and she kissed that too. Kim knew what was going to happen next but she would not dare have called for the purple caterpillar to stop, had no desire for her to stop. Kim just wanted to offer herself. The black leather flogger was run gently across Kim's cheek, over her shoulders and across her tits that were now throbbing with desire and need. The smell and the touch of the leather and the sense of anticipation were overpowering. Do it, thought Kim. Please, strike me. Please let me feel it. She wanted it, she needed, it more than anything else she had desired in her life.

Finally, after an agonising wait, the flogger whipped down onto her breasts. Kim gasped and moaned. It was painful, of course it was painful, but it was like no other pain she had experienced before. It was mingled with a surge of erotic pleasure that crashed through her brain right down to her cunt. Each stroke was like a tsunami of sensation and emotion. Kim had always been curious about what went on in the head of her clients who had asked to be dominated, what need it fulfilled in them and now, in this bizarre place, at the hands of this powerful dominatrix, she understood.

The purple caterpillar took up a position behind Kim and with a firm hand on the nape of her neck pushed her down so that she was on all fours. She knelt over Kim, strands of her fragrant black hair caressing her back. Kim breathed in her scent, sweet and exotic. She nestled her back side onto the small of Kim's back as if she was being ridden like a horse and she felt the chilly stiffness of the pvc on her skin.

"Do you want it Kim?" she whispered in her ear.

"Yes," Kim gasped.

"Do you really want it?"

"Yes, please, yes," Kim pleaded.

The flogger snapped smartly on her arse. She felt the soft rosy flesh redden and glow with every touch as they alternated between gentle taps and sweeping hard strokes. She walked the tightrope between pleasure and pain, one moment teetering over the edge towards one and the next being pulled back to the other. It was exotic and exciting and all Kim could do was surrender to it. She gasped and moaned but made no pleas for the strokes to stop. Eventually, the purple figure leant over her so that her face was pressed against Kim's and she could feel the soft touch of her hair against her face. She said nothing. Kim needed no words of encouragement or praise; she understood. The purple figure turned her head and planted one gentle kiss with her red painted lips onto Kim's cheek. Kim expelled a short gasp at the tenderness and kindness of that moment following, as it did, the savage beating that her sore arse had just endured. The figure lifted itself off of Kim's body hot and sweating from the strain of supporting its weight and the pain of the punishment that had been inflicted. Kim was brought to her feet again.

The purple caterpillar ran her gloved fingers through Kim's dishevelled hair and sensuously across her cheek.

"Are you ready to go beyond the gate?"

Kim's head was spinning; it was an effort to get anything past her lips.

"Mmmm," was all she could utter.

The purple caterpillar put a collar on her, tightening the soft leather around her neck and attaching a lead to it.

"Come with me."

Kim followed obediently until she faced the forbidding iron-gate the black cat had pointed out to her earlier. She stared upon the large iron 'N' welded onto it and looked through the grill onto the staircase beyond it. The purple caterpillar unlatched it and the door swung open with the sound of iron scraping on iron. There was a slight flicker of hesitation as Kim reflected on the step she was taking. What am I doing taking another plunge into the unknown? What other dark dreams will be stirred up on the other side? What hold does this formidable woman have over me? But, they were merely final twinges of doubt. There was never any question in Kim's mind that she would not follow to whatever faced her on the other side.

Kim passed through the iron-gate.

11: The Black Butterfly

After Kim had passed through the iron-gate the purple caterpillar turned around to face her. She held a blindfold in her hand and slipped it over Kim's head, the elastic holding it firm against her eyes. The thick material plunged Kim into darkness.

"You're now entering the heart of the Red Queen's domain. Earlier I asked you who you were; this is where you will be tested and find out. But, I've warned you Kim, there'll be many challenges you'll have to face. I will lead you blindfolded through the parts of Nemesisland that cannot be revealed to you yet. Be careful on the stairs."

Kim was led up the stairs. Aware that she was still feeling very heady she took each step slowly until she was at the top when another hand gently took hold of her elbow to guide her. The atmosphere had a density to it like a presage of impending crisis. She was led through a passage into another room where there was a slight chill to the air. She felt the touch of leather on her wrists and ankles, the tightening of straps around them and then the pulling of arms and legs as she was spread-eagled on a wooden board against the wall. More straps were pulled around her body, across her breasts and her thighs so that she was pinned back tightly, barely able to move at all.

"You will stay there a little while until the mistress is ready," said a voice that Kim recognised as the Duchess or Vicky.

Kim felt herself stretched out and exposed. Deprived of sight Kim strained to exercise all of her other senses. She knew the Red Queen and the Duchess had withdrawn and she was alone; she had no sense of anybody else being in this room. She felt a profound darkness around her; no hint of light bled behind her blindfold. She also had a sense of space and of a slight chill in the air. It was not uncomfortable and the feeling of cold was hardly a physical sensation at all, more a mental state. She smelt leather, not just from the straps that secured her, but all around her, and also cold iron. Then there was the lingering aroma of the Red Queen or Mistress Nemesis, exotic with a hint of the heavy scent of patchouli. It was a dungeon. The black cat had hinted at it and Kim knew in her heart that's where she was. She felt a sense of strangeness and fear but this was mixed with one of acceptance and, more than that, a sense of belonging. I will embrace this world I'm in, thought Kim, and wait patiently to face my fate, whatever that might be.

The purple caterpillar had retired to transform herself into a chrysalis so that she could emerge changed into another guise. Vicky, no longer dressed as the Red Queen's Duchess was in another costume consisting of black tights and a white pvc basque.

"How is she madam? Has she offered herself up to you?"

"She's close Vicky, very close. I think I have her. I can feel it. But, she still has the longest and hardest part of her journey to go so I won't get complacent or let my guard down."

"She's lovely madam. She looked so pale and soft and vulnerable spread out on your bondage board."

"Patience Vicky. I know how much you want to play with her. You'll get your chance in time. But for now you must help me prepare."

Vicky helped tighten the black pvc bodice whilst Mistress Nemesis puffed up thick layers of black lace on its sleeves and on her dress. Her hair, no longer smooth and shiny, was full-bodied and tumbled in black waves down her shoulders. Her eye-make up was thick and dark, her lips painted with black lip-stick. The purple caterpillar had transformed herself into a black fetish butterfly.

"Give me my gloves."

"Here you are madam," said Vicky passing her a pair of long black lace gloves. "You look perfect madam."

"Thank you Vicky, now we can begin the next stage of Kim's journey."

The mistress led the way back to the dungeon with Vicky following her. Kim heard the click of heels on the stone floor and instinctively looked up even though she could see nothing. She felt the brush of light material against her skin, the presence of a body close to her and the smell of exotic scent.

"I think I will have her gagged for this Vicky."

Kim let out a murmur of protest.

"What's up girl! Do you dare to resist me?" the voice was harsh and angry.

"No, really no."

"That's better girl. You know you have given yourself up to me, you have surrendered control and you must accept the consequences."

"Mmm, yes, I know," Kim nodded resigning herself to the fate she had chosen.

Vicky passed his mistress a ball gag, which she nestled in her hands.

"Open your mouth wide girl."

She inserted the red rubber ball into Kim's mouth, which closed around it, before tightening the strap at the back of her head so it was fitted firmly inside. Kim's mouth was full. The taste of rubber filled it and was mingled with a slight antiseptic taste from whatever the ball had been cleaned with. Already floating from her earlier physical exertion and having been stretched out and strapped to the wall Kim faced a new test of endurance. She felt the build up of saliva around the rubber ball as she tried to swallow. Kim could breathe easily enough but found she had to adjust the rhythm of her breathing to take in long deep breaths of air, the oxygen filling her lungs and going straight to her head making her feel even more woozy. Her head dropped and lolled around as she drew in the heady drafts of air. Then she heard the noise. She heard a buzzing noise. The buzzing of electricity. It was unmistakable. Kim was scared now. What was going to happen to her?

She felt the first shock as something brushed against her thigh with the touch of a hundred tiny pin pricks as the current buzzed through her. She let out a scream of shock and surprise, which only came out as a muffled grunt as she bit down onto the hard rubber ball. The device buzzed again as it touched her other thigh and Kim's whole body bucked and strained against the leather straps. She heard a squeal of sadistic laughter.

"Poor Kim, does it tingle a little bit?" the voice taunted her. "Vicky, I think we'll have the blindfold off now so the girl can join in the fun."

Kim felt the blindfold being pulled up from over her eyes. Directly in her face was the instrument of her torment and the figure wielding it, the purple caterpillar transformed into a butterfly with wings of black lace, a twisted smile of pleasure and a sadistic glean in her eye. Kim recognised the object immediately; it was a violet wand and the strands that carried its current were waving threateningly in front of her. The subtle persuasive tones of the caterpillar were replaced with mirth and taunts.

"See how she squirms Vicky. Shall we make her dance again?"

She needed no reply or encouragement from her assistant to carry on. The flexible prongs of the electric rod brushed against one of Kim's tits. There was a crackle and a blue spark that lit up the dungeon gloom as the tool inflicted its mischievous torment. Kim spluttered and gasped into the ball gag as her breasts jerked and wobbled in reaction to the tingling pain that shot through her. She took in a deep breath before the implement brushed against her other tit. The black butterfly was in hysterics at Kim's predicament.

"See how she squirms Vicky," she said as she brushed the violet wand across Kim's breasts again and purple and blue sparks cracked over her naked flesh.

"The sparks look wonderful madam, just like firework night."

"Yes Vicky, brilliant, just like bonfire night," her wide excited eyes and thick black eye shadow gripping Kim's gaze, "and now all we need is a bonfire. Perhaps we could light a fire underneath you and as we watch the flames flicker up we can have a display of purple sparks."

"Nnngg," muttered Kim through the gag. Surely she wasn't serious?

"Oh yes, yes, I think I'll light a little bonfire underneath you and you can light up my dungeon Kim."

Kim's pupils widened in terror. Oh my god, she thought, I think she really is serious.

The black butterfly turned away and gathered up a gothic cast iron candlestick mounted with two short thick candles. She placed it at the base of the wooden frame Kim was strapped to and lit the wicks with another already lighted candle. Kim could strain her head far enough to see the candelabra between her legs and the wicks flicker with a bright yellow flame. Shit, thought Kim, she really meant it, she really has turned me into a bonfire. At first Kim felt nothing but soon, as the flames flared and built up their strength and as the heat rose she could feel the waves of hot air waft up her thigh, onto her cunt lips and up her back-side.

"It's bonfire night Vicky," the black butterfly laughed hysterically, "now let's have some more fireworks."

The violet wand brushed across Kim's mid-riff just above the patch of fair public hair. Purple light sparked from the strands. The fumes of electricity and smell of melting wax penetrated Kim's nostrils. The wand brushed gently against her cunt lips and Kim thrashed wildly in shock and pain, straining against the leather straps. And when the sharp pinching pain of the electric current was removed Kim still had to contend with the throbbing heat of the candle flames as it rose up around her. Kim drew in deep drafts of air from around the rubber ball. Compose yourself, she told herself, this is a trial, endure it. She doesn't mean to do me any real harm, does she? She playing with me, testing me...at least I hope so!

There was a crackle and more purple sparks and Kim's nakedness pulled against her restraints. Sadistic laughter rang out across the dungeon.

"She looks fantastic madam."

"Yes she does, doesn't she Vicky," replied the black butterfly in delight. "Move that mirror around Vicky so she can see herself reflected in it."

Vicky dragged a full length mirror directly opposite Kim and then the black butterfly and her assistant took up a position either side of her. Kim looked across. Wow. I've got to say I look amazing, thought Kim. She could see herself clearly in the candle-lit gloom spread-eagled against the wall, a pattern of black leather straps across her pale skin and then between her legs the gothic iron candlestick. The inside of her legs and her crotch glowed red from the flames of the candles. Then, on either side of her were the butterfly, a vision of puffs of black lace and shiny pvc that reflected in the candlelight. On the other side of her was the black butterfly's transvestite assistant, equally stunning and sinister in her kinky black tights, white pvc basque and painted white face mask.

"Do you see yourself girl, do you she how wonderful you look? My own little bonfire night display, lit up for my entertainment."

"Mmmm," Kim nodded.

It was true. She admired her glowing shape in the mirror. It was scary and exotic and exciting and, yes, it was true, she looked fantastic. More purple sparks. More sadistic laughter. Kim had learnt to anticipate the prickles of the electric sparks but her body still twitched and strained, much to the amusement of her tormentors and, watching herself in the mirror, Kim could see the funny side, spread-eagled with a red rubber ball in her mouth, her body squirming in pain in response to the purple flecks of the violet wand.

"That was fun, I enjoyed that girl," chuckled the black butterfly as she snuffed out the candles and started to undo ball gag. "You make a good firework display."

"Thank you," replied Kim, "I got to quite enjoy it in the end."

"Enjoy it?" The blue eyes flashed, "but it's irrelevant if you enjoy it, you're here for my pleasure and amusement."

"Yes, of course, I know," replied Kim in response to the gentle reprimand from her mistress.

The black lips spread into a smile, "And I certainly found that entertaining. Are you OK Kim?" she added.

Kim took a few seconds to reflect on her experience and flex her aching limbs and muscles but then said, "Yeah, yeah. I was really scared at one point, but yeah I'm good."

"You should feel scared Kim. You can only learn trust if you are exposed to fear. You'd better have something to drink," said the black butterfly, handing Kim a bottle of water. "And besides this is only the beginning. I want you to keep your strength up for your next test."

"There's more?"

"Oh yes, that was only a little introduction to my dungeon world. I've much more planned for you yet Kim. You still have to prove yourself fit to serve me."

12: The Walrus and The Carpenter

"Oh yes," said the black butterfly, "I've much more planned for you. You have to learn to submit to me completely to find yourself, you do understand that don't you Kim? You have to accept that you can be offered up to other of my slaves as well Kim. Your experience working in the parlour should prepare you well for the next part of your journey."

Kim didn't like the sound of that. She looked around her. She had been so focused on the black butterfly, the purple sparks and her own endurance that her surroundings only merged into a gloomy blur in the background. Now that she had been untied she could take them in. It was as Kim had guessed, she was in a dungeon. She looked down the length of the room. The walls were lined with an array of ropes, masks, hoods, floggers, whips and canes. As she glanced down she saw the wooden box that housed the violet wand. There was large equipment too, a long table or rack, a whipping bench and bondage chair. Her eyes darted around quickly taking in the space and calculating which pieces of equipment she might end up on.

"Vicky, help Kim get dressed."

Vicky handed Kim a pale blue dress. It was another 'Alice' dress thought Kim, but this one was not a fetish latex one like she wore at the Hatter's tea party, this frock was made of fresh smelling neatly pressed cotton. Vicky helped her pull it over her head and do up the buttons down its front before putting on a crisp white apron over it and pulling on a pair of white lace-topped hold-ups. Vicky took great pleasure in brushing the tangled knots out of Kim's hair.

"Very good, she looks excellent Vicky. A picture of youthful innocence."

Vicky laughed, "Well, we'll have to do something about that won't we madam?"

Kim didn't like the sound of that.

"Oh yes, we'll definitely have to do something about that," she laughed.

The black butterfly and Vicky took an elbow each and guided Kim to one of the pieces of equipment in the dungeon. It was a plank of wood suspended from the ceiling by four chains, one at each corner.

"Get down on there girl," she ordered.

Kim lay down onto the wooden board, gripping onto the chains to support herself.

"Move down a bit."

Kim shuffled down so that her crotch was practically hanging over the end. Vicky took an arm and raised it up against the chain and began to tie her wrist to the chain with some white rope. The black butterfly did the same with the other arm and then they repeated the process with her ankles, which were tied to the chains at the other end until she was firmly strapped onto the suspension bench.

"Is she secure Vicky?"

"Yes madam."

The black butterfly gently rocked the swing. Kim had started to recover her composure but now, tied up in this swing, the feeling of helplessness and the gentle rocking motion made that heady submissive feeling return. Her mistress stood at one end looking down at her.

"You can bring them in now Vicky," she said. "You look so sweet lying there Kim, not a fetish Alice, but a real Alice in a nice cotton dress. But you know Kim, not everything in my domain is as it seems. And you know, in my world there are those with appetites, insatiable appetites."

Kim looked up into her eyes, but behind her were two other shadowy figures. As the black butterfly moved to one side she could see them more clearly. They were odd figures. One was thin and gaunt and wore nothing but a blue cap and blue jerkin. The other was huge and round with a massive ginger handle-bar moustache and was naked except for an oily waist-coat. Oh no, what next, thought Kim, it was the walrus and the carpenter.

"Have fun boys," the black butterfly called out as she left Kim to the attentions of the two story book characters. Oh shit, thought Kim, what's going to happen to me now?

"She looks tasty," announced the walrus.

"Yes, very tasty," echoed the carpenter.

"Do you think she'll come and play with us?"

"It doesn't look as though she has any choice walrus. She has offered her up for us," replied the carpenter, who started massaging Kim's tits through the crisp cotton pinafore dress.

"I think we should have some fun," said the carpenter as his fingers disappeared under the dress to explore Kim's cunt.

"Oh, definitely yes."

The walrus's fat fingers were running down Kim's mound seeking out her hole as the carpenter unbuttoned the top of the dress to expose her lovely breasts for more attention and started to rub and kneed her nipples. Kim began to purr with the attention. She couldn't help it, it was an instinctive reaction. She might have felt violated but she didn't. She had too much experience for that and besides, she had so let herself go into the spirit of Nemesisland that nothing really shocked her any more. She gasped. The walrus had found her sex and slipped a finger inside it and was massaging the inside of her cunt with a twisting motion. Shit, thought Kim, that feels good. Her cunt was sopping wet. It just responded instantly to stimulation in that way. Kim put it down to the years working in the massage parlour where she had to be in a constant state of readiness. Kim groaned. Another finger had been thrust into her cunt and the carpenter was tweaking her tender nipples between thumb and finger. The walrus pulled out his fingers and held them to his nose.

"She smells of oysters," he announced.

"Oh, that's our favourite," said the carpenter.

Oysters, thought Kim, what a cheek!

"Here, have a taste of her," said the walrus stretching his hand out to the carpenter.

He hungrily sucked Kim's cunt juices off the walrus's fingers.

"Very tasty. I've always said, you can't beat the smell and taste of oysters. Are you going to eat her up?"

"Oh yeah," said the walrus.

"Well don't eat her all up. Save some of her juices for me. I know how greedy you are."

"Me, greedy? You're just as greedy."

The carpenter didn't argue with his companion.

"I bet her tits taste good, especially her nipples. They'll be nice and salty. I can feel the sweat on her breasts and smell her odour walrus. Come and have a taste."

The walrus and the carpenter took one breast each, licking and sucking on them as Kim moaned with pleasure. Their eager tongues flicked over her swollen and aroused nipples making her cunt juices flow even more. Then one of them took a nipple between his teeth and squeezed. Kim squirmed on the suspension bench and squealed with sharp pain and the lingering feeling of pleasure that followed it. Her tits were getting all sorts of attention; long strokes of the tongue, little nibbles here and there, the odd bite on her nipple. She was tied up and there was nothing Kim could do about it but soak up the sensations. If she was honest with herself it was all the more exciting and sexy because she was restrained and exposed. As the walrus had said, she had been offered up by the Red Queen as a plaything to two characters in her world.

Inevitably, they soon turned their attention to her crotch. It was as the Red Queen had said; their appetites really were insatiable. The walrus went first, burying his thick ginger whiskers into Kim's pubic hair and probing her cunt with his tongue before finding the bud of her clit and flicking it with fast movements which sent Kim wild.

"Don't be greedy," said the carpenter, "I want a taste now. Does she taste good?"

"Oh yeah," replied the walrus, "best oysters I've ever tasted. Best eaten neat, you won't need any bread and butter with her juices. You'd only spoil the flavour."

The carpenter got down onto Kim's mound and eagerly began to eat her up. He also explored her now throbbing clit with his tongue. Kim was moaning with pleasure and bucking against the restraints that tied her against the bench as she felt the climax welling up insider her. The walrus and the carpenter took it in turns to flick her clit until she let out a screech of pleasure as she came, her body stretching and shaking against her restraints and the swing swaying in time to the motions of her body.

"I think she quite enjoyed that," said the carpenter.

"I think she's a little out of breath," commented the walrus.

"And we've only just begun."

They had both been turned on by handling Kim's lovely breasts and sucking on her cunt juices and had raging erections that needed release. Kim didn't need much imagination to know what would happen next.

The walrus took up a position again at the bottom of the swing. During the exhilaration of her orgasm she hadn't noticed that her wrists and ankles were aching where the ropes and strained against them. She was still stretched out and vulnerable on the suspension swing but braced herself for being taken by the insatiable walrus and carpenter.

Her cunt was suspended at just the right height for the walrus to enter her from a standing position. She could see his throbbing cock, as red as his ruddy face and nose, sticking out from a bush of ginger pubic hair. The hard cock slipped into her cunt, wet from the juices of her own climax. He started fucking her with hard pounding motions, which made the swing rock back and forth in time to thrusts of the walrus.

"Oh yeah, please fuck me," groaned Kim as the hard cock filled her.

Kim's experience in the brothel meant she was a pro and she could feign pleasure and orgasm at the drop of a hat if she needed to but right now she really wanted it. It must have been something to do with wanting to be play out her role in this strange world but she was aching for it and welcomed the hard cock into her. The sensuality of the bondage and the hypnotic rocking motions of the swing all contributed to her desire. She looked down to watch the rotund, almost grotesque, figure of the walrus humping her.

Meanwhile, the carpenter had taken up a position at the head of the swing. His erect cock was thin and long, just like him. He took hold of her face and turned it towards him. Kim could see the glistening pre-cum on the end of his cock and stretched out her tongue to lick it off setting off a little ripple of pleasure through the carpenter. He threaded his thin member between her lips and Kim eagerly took it into her mouth and sucked on it. She wrapped her tongue around its tip to great effect as she heard him groan. Kim had loads of practise at this and she knew she was an expert. Oral was definitely one of her specialities at the parlour. She knew where to put her tongue and how to judge the pace of her sucking motion to perfection. She allowed the carpenter to thread his cock in and out of her mouth as she sucked on it and added licks and darting motions with her tongue whilst the walrus pounded into her with energetic grunts.

What a state I'm in, reflected Kim, tied down, a cock in my cunt, another cock in my mouth and loving every minute of it. Her whole body and mouth seemed to move back and forth in one simultaneous motion. Then she felt the walrus's hips clench and muscles tighten. He let out a loud moan of pleasure as Kim felt the spurt of hot spunk enter her.

"Don't be greedy walrus, it's my turn now," called the carpenter as he slid his cock out of Kim's mouth.

They changed positions. Kim welcomed the carpenter's long cock into her. The tension had built up in her sex again and she desperately needed another orgasm. The walrus came to the head of the suspension frame and offered up his cock to Kim. Its tip was glistening with a combination of Kim's juices and his own spunk. The cock was going soft but Kim thought her skilled tongue might bring him to another erection. He smelt of sweat and musky sex. She took his cock in her mouth and tasted the salty slippery taste of spunk and cunt juices. Hmm, delicious, thought Kim, I love this, love the taste of dirty sex in my mouth. She rolled her tongue around the walrus's cock and felt a jump of response in her mouth.

The carpenter was fucking her hard with long strokes making sure his cock penetrated deep into her sex. With each thrust Kim could feel him grinding against her clit and the tension building up inside her. God, I need some release again, thought Kim as she used the motion of the swing to rocked her own hips back and forth to help bring her to climax. She released the walrus's cock from her mouth and let out a loud ecstatic scream. Her wrists and ankles remained bound but her body shook in euphoric motions.

"Shit, oh shit that's good," she groaned.

Her body was hot with sweat and the recently cool starched cotton dress was now sopping with wet patches and traces of come. She felt like a sexy, slutty Alice now.

To Kim's surprise the carpenter withdrew his cock after Kim's orgasm had subsided. He had other plans. The walrus pulled back the top of Kim's dress to expose the beautiful fleshy orbs of her breasts. The carpenter stood over her and started masturbating. He was already close to coming from his frantic fucking so it didn't take long before a stream of hot sticky spunk spurted over Kim's tits. Kim revelled in the disgusting slimy warmth of come over her breasts.

The both leaned over her and reached out their tongues, the walrus's fat and wide, the carpenter's long and thin, and voraciously licked up the carpenter's come from her breasts. Kim could feel the rough texture of their tongues licking up the slimy spunk. It was so sexy and rude that Kim thought she might even come again. Soon her tits had been cleaned of every glistening white globule of spunk.

"It was kind of you to come," said the carpenter.

Kim laughed, "Thank you," she said, "not that I had much choice in the matter, being all tied up."

"Yes, I weep for you," the walrus said, "I deeply sympathize."

"And you are so very nice!" said the carpenter.

"Well thank you," replied Kim, trying to get into the spirit of Nemesisland, "it's been a pleasure to fuck with you."

The walrus and the carpenter left the dungeon leaving poor Kim still tied on the suspension bench. Fortunately Vicky returned after just a few minutes to untie her and get her down.

"So what did you make of the walrus and the carpenter?" asked Vicky.

"Well," said Kim, "I think I liked the walrus best because he was a little bit sorry about me being tied up."

"But he fucked you for longer than the carpenter though," said Vicky.

"Oh yes, that was mean!" Kim said indignantly. "Then I like the carpenter best."

"But he fucked you as much as he could."

"Well, this is a puzzler," reflected Kim. "They were both equally sex-mad insatiable fuckers then!"

Kim checked herself as she heard the noise of the dungeon door opening. It was the Red Queen again still dressed as the black butterfly.

"Very good Kim. I think the walrus and carpenter were very impressed by your enthusiasm and how you entered into the spirit of Nemesisland."

"Thank you," replied Kim.

"They're very lucky servants to get an opportunity like that. You look as though you've had a good time with them Kim."

Kim looked a state as Vicky helped her off with the Alice dress. She looked hot and dishevelled, her fair hair was in tangles and there was a far-away glazed look in her eye.

"Yes, I'm exhausted," said Kim.

"Well yes Kim I think perhaps you deserve a bit of a sit down now."

13: The Black Cat's Tale Part 2

Kim was led through into another smaller room. The first thing that caught her eye in one corner of the room was an arrangement of two cages a small one underneath with a larger one on top of it. Kim saw a black shadow in the lower cage and the outline of the black cat squeezed into a tight space its ankles and wrists chained to the bars of the cage. Her heart jumped; perhaps now she will finally get to hear the final part of the black cat's tale and what happened to her after she was taken away from the temple in Constantinople.

The black figure knelt down to address her slave. One black laced glove threaded itself through the bars of the cage, gripped the black cat's nipple and tweaked it fiercely.

"Yes, I've brought you some company Nano. But, listen to me, I don't expect you to get excited just because you can look up and see the girl's crotch right over your head."

"No, of course not mistress."

She turned to Kim, "I'm going to lock you away for a bit now and give you a break girl. If you notice any lascivious behaviour in that creature," she said pointing to the cat, "then I want you to report it to me."

The black butterfly opened the door of the second cage and beckoned Kim in before closing it behind her and padlocking the door. She settled down into a corner of the cage and rested her back-side on the cool iron bars. Unlike the cat, she had not been tethered and was in the larger of the two cages and so had some room to move around.

"I shall leave you both here for a bit as I've other business in Nemesisland and need to prepare myself."

She turned her back on them and strode out of the room, a bustle of black lace being the last sight of her before she closed the door behind her. Kim was alone with the black cat again.

"What is this place?" she asked, straining her eyes to peer into each dark corner.

"This is the mistress's grey room, her isolation room. This is where she puts her servants when she wants them out of the way, sometimes as a punishment to keep them away from her presence and sometimes for them to wait so they can prepare themselves for some other ordeal. Look, over

97

there is her isolation box. I've been in there. It's a very dark and forbidding place."

"Oh, I see," said Kim, "and do you think she's preparing me for some ordeal."

"I expect so Kim. But tell me, how are things for you in Nemesisland?"

"Oh, I've had several more encounters. I helped the nurse and got a certificate, you know. I've also entered into a kind of pact with the mistress I think. I accepted the challenge to come up here and submit to her."

"It's the only way Kim. I did that many years ago. If that's where your heart is there is no choice but to let yourself become a character in Nemesisland. Once you do that you'll begin to find your true place."

"Yes I think I'm beginning to understand that," replied Kim. "But tell me, you must continue your tale. I need to know what happened after I got taken away from the temple in Constantinople?"

"Well, when I returned to Nemesisland, the mistress was most displeased with me. It was true, I had rescued eleven of the acolytes, but the thirteenth girl had been killed by the Knights Templar guards and the one that took you away was actually an illusion created by them to tempt and trick me. Not only that, each of the initiates had been chosen by a goddess. The thirteenth novice was Goddess Hecate's and the twelfth, you Kim, had been selected by Goddess Nemesis herself. So, you can imagine how angry she was with me for letting you get taken away. She had provided me with tools to heal my wound and, of course, I should have continued my pursuit through the shrine to rescue you."

Kim was startled at this new revelation, "So, this Mistress Nemesis, the Red Queen, whatever you call her, had chosen me?"

"Yes Kim, I think that's right. You were her novice."

Kim pondered this new revelation.

"Is that why she's so interested in me? Is that why she's brought me here, to Nemesisland?"

"I don't know her mind Kim, but yes, I would imagine so. She must still feel some affinity with you; it seems that her fate and yours are intertwined. I'm sorry Kim. Can you forgive me for failing you?"

"I don't know what I think," replied Kim. "I don't think I blame you. It's all so strange that I can't find it in me to hold a grudge against you black cat. But tell me, there's more, what happened next."

"Truly Kim I was inconsolable with how I had been tricked, the bitter knowledge of my defeat and what that meant for Goddess Nemesis; to lose her chosen acolyte. I was, as you can imagine, severely punished for my failure. But she offered me a chance to redeem myself by sending me on a second mission to free you. The stakes were higher now because, remember, you had been impregnated with the seed of the Knights Templar priest. I don't fully understand, but it was considered that this union of a Knight's Templar priest and the chosen novice of a goddess would produce a male child that would be a potent threat to the goddesses. It was imperative to prevent this child being born and that was my mission."

"Goddess Nemesis provided me with guidance on how to carry out the mission. She told me that, first of all, I would have to seek out a special jewel, the diamond of Sekhmet, which is very precious to the goddesses and vital to the success of the quest. She handed me a bunch of yellow flowers, "This is St John's Wort," she said, "a herb that stimulates and revives and helps to counter madness and dark thoughts. It will be of use to you Nano." Also, I still possessed the magical talismans from my previous mission; the amethyst, the lapis lazuli stone and the two crystals."

"Tell me what happened, Nano. Continue the story."

The black cat continued his tale.

"Goddess Nemesis told me to go to the Temple of La Villedieu-Le-Maurepas, a Knight's Templar Chapel at Elancourt in the suburbs west of Paris. She told me that this was where you were being held in secret. When I got there it was hard to believe my eyes; the scene in front of me was so idyllic. I was looking onto a 14th century honey coloured stone chapel and outbuildings, a delightful tree lined duck pond and a black stone statue of a knight of the Knights Templar, all this bathed in the warmth of the August sun. It was hard to believe that somewhere, hidden deep underground in the bowels of the crypt, there were secret passage ways and a chamber where you were being held captive.

I was dressed as inconspicuously as possible – a T-shirt, jeans and trainers, clutching a copy of the Michelin guide to France, just another cultural tourist come to immerse himself in the history and mythology of the Knights Templar like thousands before me. On my back I had a rucksack containing the tools I needed to assist me and a change of clothes for you.

Inside the chapel there was a plaque explaining the history and mythology of the Knights Templar. A part of this account caught my eye and I read it carefully. "It is believed that the knights of the Knights Templar brought back to France many relics found in the churches of Jerusalem during their occupation of that city during the crusades. They allegedly returned with relics such as fragments of the true cross, sacred swords and icons. Most famously it is said that they returned with the holy grail, the chalice that caught Christ's blood as he died on the cross and this has long been a subject for speculation in history and literature. It is also claimed that the Knights Templar brought back to France a magnificent diamond, taken from the temple to Sekhmet on the banks of the Nile and then hidden in the church of Jerusalem. There is no evidence that this is the case and neither grail nor diamond have ever been found". So this must be the precious item that Goddess Nemesis ordered me to find and recover for the goddesses.

I sat down on one of the pews and scoured the walls of the chapel for any evidence of doors or secret entrances. Then I heard a voice I recognised. It was the seductive voice of the Knight's Templar priest I had encountered in Constantinople. So, I had not killed him after all, only knocked him unconscious. He was with a younger man, presumably a lesser member of their order. My heart jumped a beat. I slid down into the seat of the pew and pretended to be intently reading the guide to the chapel that I had picked up at the entrance. I risked one fleeting glance at the man's face to confirm my suspicions.

I followed them cautiously down the aisles of the chapel. They went into the chancel and then through a small wooden door at the far end of the temple. I waited a short time and surreptitiously eased open the door, peering through the narrow gap I had opened. I saw them, perhaps twenty yards ahead, as they passed through a stone door fashioned out of the walls, which closed behind them. I had found the entrance into the hidden chambers of the temple but now faced the same dilemma posed by the shrine in Constantinople. I saw a pentagon shaped blemish in the smooth stone wall. I pulled out the lapis lazuli key stone I had brought with me from my previous mission and placed it gently in the hole. The traces of the lines of a door appeared in the stone and I gently pushed open the door and cautiously peered out. In front of me was a winding staircase that led deep into the bowels of the chapel. I could hear voices ahead of me and followed them until I got close enough to overhear the conversation.

The old man explained, "The girl must be kept safe and protected. The birth of the child in her womb must proceed without any risk. This male child, the product of a powerful priest of our order and the novice of a goddess will be a special one with great powers that will be of use to us. She must remain hidden in the depths of this temple where she is safe and none of the spies of the goddesses will find her."

I followed the two men to a small chapel or sanctuary at the heart of the crypt. The shrine was open and I entered through a gap between two stone pillars. From a distance I caught a glimpse of the glass tomb where you were imprisoned. I had seen enough to be sure this was the place I must return to. But, my first task was to find the diamond that Goddess Nemesis had told me of, which was crucial to the successful completion of my mission.

The crypt was not large and I hoped it would not be too difficult to orientate myself. It was a dark and hidden place for keeping the secrets of the Knights Templar. The chapel was in the centre and around it a network of corridors and chambers. I quickly searched the labyrinth of passages in the crypt for what I hoped to find, some kind of secret chamber where the relics of the order were stored. Then I suddenly noticed the familiar pentagon shaped flaw in the stone work. Once again the lapis lazuli key stone fitted and fine traces of lines forming the outline of a door appeared. The stone door pushed open, I passed through and gently closed it behind me.

The sight that befell me there was astounding. It was a windowless stone chamber, impossible to enter without the key stone, crammed full of ancient relics from the new religion, presumably plundered from the sepulchre of Jerusalem during the crusades and taken by the Knights Templar and hidden in this dark and secret place only accessible to the highest members of their order. It did not look in particularly good order and I feared how much time I would have to spend rummaging through these treasures before I found the object that I had been summoned to find. There were numerous crosses, some simple crude wooden ones, others elaborately crafted and decorated with jewels. There were various shields and swords, some depicting the cross of the Knights Templar, others curved scimitars with Arabic writing on their blades captured from Saladin the magnificent during the sieges of Jerusalem. There were scores of Byzantine icons depicting the crucifixion or the madonna and child, all illuminated in glittering gold leaf.

Then my eyes alighted on what I was seeking. It was set in a wooden case with a glass lid and nestled in aged and faded red velvet. But the lustre and magnificence of the object it contained was immediately apparent to me. A huge diamond, the jewel of Amon Ra, taken from the shrine to the Goddess Sekhmet to Jerusalem and then by the Knights Templar to France. I carefully lifted the glazed lid and took the diamond from its resting place. I felt the enormity of the moment. This stone, a relic from the goddesses of the ancient world was nestling in my hands. I was overawed at the power enshrined in this gem. It seemed like sacrilege to handle it with such lack of respect, but I had little choice but to put it in my jeans pocket.

I left the chamber of the relics and traced my steps back to the chapel. This was an underground shrine with an open pillared entrance and at its centre was a silver lined glass box mounted on a wrought iron frame. I immediately recognized the young acolyte, you Kim, the 12th girl who had been taken from me in the marble palace in Constantinople. You were laid out naked and entombed in the glass case. You looked different. Before you were confused and damaged but now, the bruises and scars from the abuse you had suffered had healed. You radiated a serene calm and beauty. Your locks of fair hair were spread over your naked breasts and your hands were resting on the bump containing the unborn child of a Knights Templar master. You were full with child. It could have been a vision from a fairy tale of a golden princess waiting to be awakened by a prince who had completed a dangerous quest to find her. But, I knew differently. I knew what dark dreams must be running through your head; nightmares of the abuse you had suffered, of your enforced impregnation and the object in her womb that would unleash terror and fear in the world of the goddesses if it was allowed to be born.

I knew that time was of the essence. Once again I was faced with a dilemma. Should I smash open the glass tomb and risk attracting guards with the noise or even risk shards of glass injuring you? I knew Goddess Nemesis had specifically directed me to collect the diamond first, not just for its beauty and splendour and so it could be returned to its rightful place, but also because it had a practical use. I knew the diamond was capable of cutting through the glass; and this was no ordinary diamond. I put the diamond to the glass and, true to its reputation, the hard stone sliced through the glazed panel. I worked quickly and carefully until I was able to lift a whole side panel out of its silver frame. Then I had another tool, the gift given to me by my mistress, the herb St John's Wort, which revives and brings to life. I took some, crushed the leaves between the fingers of my hand, and held it under your nose. The pungent scent filled the air. Your breathing became deeper and then, suddenly, your eyes flickered open.

You stirred and turning towards me, spoke, "My dreams have been dark. I have visions of a powerful force wielding great power against me. Are you one of my tormentors?" I replied, "No, young acolyte of the Goddess Nemesis. I am Nano. I have been sent by your mistress and mentor to rescue you from the captivity of the Knights Templar." I knelt down beside you. "You may remember me from the marble temple in Constantinople. I must offer my abject apologies to you for deserting you and leaving you in that place. I have been given this chance to atone for my mistakes, but I must offer my deepest regret for anything you have suffered as a consequence of my failings."

You replied, "Nano, if you can help me escape from here I may find it in my heart to forgive you. But, there's no time now for regret, you must work quickly. I know it's a terrible deed you must do but it's necessary to prevent the even greater evil that I have foreseen in my dreams and visions. You have been given the tools to carry this out?" I replied, "Yes, young novice, I have." I got one of the pieces of crystal and held it tight against your pregnant stomach.

It glowed red and started to burn your skin as its power spread and penetrated into your womb. I could see you struggling against the pain, your face creased up in agony trying desperately not to scream out. I held some more of the St John's Wort herb for you to breathe in and that seemed to ease both the pain and your mental anguish. The magical crystal did its work and the potency of its invisible rays suffocated the unborn foetus and expelled it from your womb. Your body strained and stretched as if indeed you were really giving birth as the foetus of the male child mess was pushed out of you. I could do nothing more than look on in sympathy at your suffering and administer drafts of the healing herb to help you.

I emptied the bloodied mess into the glass cage where you had lately been lying to demonstrate to our enemies that the powerful heir to their order had been destroyed. I had no qualms about my actions, I had to do what was necessary in the interests of the goddesses. My instructions were perfectly clear and the dangers had been confirmed by your dreams and visions Kim; this child could not be allowed to survive.

Kim was transfixed by the unravelling of the black cat's tale.

"Is this all true, Nano? Or is it a nightmare within a dream?"

"Oh, yes, it's true. Have you never seen the mark on your stomach Kim and wondered where it came from? It's the burn from the crystal."

Kim was aghast as she ran her fingers across her stomach. There was a rough hexagon shaped red blemish on her skin with a darker red point in it's centre. Of course she had seen it before, had thought that it might be a birth mark though, it was true, she never remembered having it as a child. Surely not? Surely this bizarre tale about her couldn't be true; it had to be an illusion. Dream or not, she had to hear the end of the tale.

"Don't stop Nano. Carry on, finish your story," she ordered.

"After the child had been aborted by the magical powers of the crystal you were left pale and shaken but also aware of the urgency of our position. You were soon up and dressed in the T-shirt and skirt that I had brought for you to escape in. "We cannot delay any longer, Nano, we must escape before the guardians of the temple find out that their defences have been penetrated. There is a door in the rear of this shrine, which I remember being the shortest route back to the surface".

I nodded and followed you. We entered into a passage and then turned into another, wending our way through the secret labyrinth of corridors. Then we entered a long chamber lined with mirrored glass. As we ran down the mirrored corridor I saw fleeting images of the pair of us fleeing. As we neared the end of the chamber I heard a peal of laughter. It was the old man, the priest now changed into the ceremonial dress of the Knights Templar. He called out, mocking me, "Don't think that flight from here will be so easy slave of the goddesses."

I turned around to see how close the pursuit was and saw the old man and a group of guards framed in the entrance to the mirrored chamber. "You have already been tricked by illusions once. What choices will you make now?" At first I didn't understand what he meant. Then a shock of realisation struck me like a thunderbolt. You had disappeared from my side, miraculously sucked into the mirrored chamber. Before me, lining the long corridor, were an infinity of Kims, images all wearing the same T-shirt and skirt I had dressed you in. I had been tricked again. Some foul power had sucked you away and turned you into an illusion locked into the mirrored chamber. The myriad images of you stretched out before me their arms outreached. They started to call out to me. "Take me Nano", "I am the true novice, take me", "Don't believe her, she's an illusion, I'm the true one." The murmuring of imploring demands, as the voices called out from behind the mirrored walls, deafened me.

The high priest's laugh echoed above the muffled cries of the figures trapped in the mirror. "Fooled by illusion again, slave, when will you learn. Now will you make the right choice or will you give up and submit to me or, even worse, will you face the wrath of your own mistress when you return empty handed or with an illusion created by us?"

I stood still, my head spinning with the taunts of the priest and the cries of the girls. I tried to remain calm. I grasped the piece of amethyst that was in my pocket to help clarify my thoughts. Kim had kept hold of one of the pieces of crystal. The devotees of the new religion were cunning and skilful but even they could not reproduce the powers of the crystal. I stood quietly in the centre of the chamber and held out the crystal in the palm of my hand, closed my eyes and entrusted to my own instincts. I opened my eyes again. There, amidst the swirling images calling out to be released, there was one, with her arm stretched, the other part of the crystal in her hand. The power of the two crystals was working to bring them together. You were pushing gently against the glass which began to yield and bend until you were able to pass your hand through. I grasped it and pulled you out of the mirror.

"Quickly, we must get out of this place," I urged. We raced to the end of the passage. Our pursuers followed us and entered into the far end of the chamber. We needed something to buy us some time. We would not be able to outrun the Knights Templar guards. I had to think of something to delay them. I took my crystal and threw it hard against the mirrored roof of the chamber and caught it again as it fell down. I waited and stared at the mirrored walls in hopeful anticipation. A crack opened up on the mirrored ceiling. It spread slowly and little by little ran down the length of the corridor and then down the sides of the chamber. And then the glass shattered into thousands of tiny shards that poured down like a deadly rain over the guards that had crossed the threshold of the mirrored chamber in pursuit. I shouted to you, "Run, run now, as fast as you can."

I didn't wait to watch the explosions of shattered glass as the mirrored chamber imploded in on itself. In the distance as we dashed through the corridors of the crypt I could hear the shattering of glass and the shouts of panic from the guards. I recognised one passage from my earlier exploration of the crypt. At the end I could see the winding staircase I had descended earlier that would lead us up into the chapel. From the inside we simply pushed open the stone door and burst out of the next door into the chapel. A few tourists turned around to see what the commotion was about but quickly went back to their tour of the church.

We emerged onto the steps at the entrance of the temple. The August sun still shone on the site but the atmosphere of the place was altogether different; the idyllic vision I had encountered earlier had been supplanted by a feeling of menace. Sitting on the steps was a woman, as if she had been expecting us and was waiting for us. She stood up, turned to me and started to speak. "It seems that you are in need of some assistance Nano" she said. "How do I know that I can trust you?" I asked. "What choice do you have? You will need to get the girl away before the guardians of temple catch up with you and she is recaptured and all your efforts would have been in vain." I considered carefully and then turned to the woman and said, "Yes, I accept your offer of aid."

At those words the body of the woman gradually started to change shape. I had never before witnessed anything like this miraculous transformation. Her arms changed into wings, her legs into sharp talons, her nose into a curved beak, all before my very eyes. Soon, the metamorphosis was complete and standing next to me was a magnificent giant golden eagle. She turned her beaked head towards me. "I am Goddess Cihuacōātl, the winged eagle goddess of the Aztecs. My aid has been sought to assist the young novice's return to the realm of the goddesses. Quickly, put her on my back."

I helped you onto the back of the eagle and then she spread her giant wings and launched herself into the air. As she swooped up, with you clinging to her feathered back, she circled the chapel three times and then sped off into the distance. Soon she was a mere speck in the distant blue sky as she sped away."

"I don't understand," Kim said, "so I was rescued. I did escape. What happened after that?"

"Ah, but there's a twist to the tale. I did have another encounter with the priest and the Knights Templar guards and did eventually escape the chapel, but that's another story. I returned to Nemesisland believing my mission had been an unqualified success. It's true that I had successfully removed the threat from the unborn child and for that the goddesses were pleased. But Goddess Nemesis was angry with me. She said that again I had been fooled by a trick. The eagle was not truly one of the goddesses but another illusion created by the Knights Templar.

"And this is the nub of my tale, Kim. Now that the child you were carrying had been destroyed you had been desecrated in their eyes and were of no use to them. The eagle carried you back to the other world. Knowing that you had been Goddess Nemesis's chosen novice they placed you in a brothel in Manchester to spite her and eradicated all memory of your recent past. That Kim is how you came to be working in the parlour. You can see the part I have played in it. On two occasions it was my failings that let you fall into the hands of those who would harm you. Now I have completed my tale you can see why I was so struck with fear and remorse when I first recognised you in Nemesisland."

There was a silence as Kim absorbed the subtleties of the tale and the enormity of its impact on her and Nano reflected on the choices he had made that influenced Kim's fate. It was Kim that broke the silence.

"I don't know what to think. If that's the end of the tale then I think I'm more confused than before. The idea that I'm was some kind of chosen novice for something seems so weird and then there's the shape-shifting creatures. It's a magical story but surely none of it can be true?"

"Do you not believe that such things are possible?"

They both looked up. Silently their mistress had slipped back into the grey chamber.

106

14: The Pagan Priestess

"There are many strange and inexplicable powers."

She had changed now and was wearing a dress with a purple satin underskirt covered in black lace-like material and a bodice in woven colours of black and purple, all in a pagan style. Her costume was completed by a headdress of white stones with one pendant gem resting on her forehead. She looked magnificent and stunningly beautiful as Kim and the black cat both looked up in awe of her. She was the perfect figure of a pagan priestess prepared for the conduct of some arcane ritual.

"The pain and pleasure that you feel in this world, is that not real?"

"Oh yes, definitely," laughed Kim.

"Then do you still believe you are in a dream?"

"I don't know. I want to believe, but some of it is so strange."

"Everything the black cat has told you is true. His account of your life is what actually happened even if your inability to comprehend it, or spells cast on you, have buried the memories deep into your subconscious. Delve deep into yourself Kim and you will discover this. Your fates are woven together and intertwined with my own. Vicky, take the black cat and prepare him. I need to speak to Kim about her next trial."

Vicky came forward and unlocked the wrist and ankle cuffs, un-padlocked the doors and led the black cat away.

"So Kim, you've heard the cat's tale, you've heard the part he has played in your downfall. His actions and his failings at critical moments are the reason why you ended up in that brothel Kim. Do you not think there should be some retribution to pay?"

"I don't know. He did rescue me in the end, in a fashion and, having heard his tale, I believe he meant well. I don't believe he intended me any harm."

"You still have much to learn about my world. It's your right to extract vengeance. I want you to torture him. You should want him to suffer for you."

"But, I don't bear him any grudge for what he's done and besides I rather like him to be honest."

"This slave of mine, Nano, he is a loyal and devoted servant and he has served me for many years now. But, when he transgresses, when he fails me or when a task is not completed to my satisfaction then he must be punished. It has nothing to do with not liking or holding grudges. This is about justice and retribution, about devotion and service. He wronged you and he must pay. I expect you to administer his punishment Kim. Trust me; he will thank you for it in the end, he will understand why you need to do it."

"Is that what you want me to do?"

"What do you want to do Kim? Retribution must come from within you. In my world you must learn to submit to me when I require but you must also be able to administer punishment when it is deserved. And it is deserved isn't it?"

"Well, you're right; he did leave me behind in the Temple in Constantinople."

"Yes Kim."

"And he didn't see that the eagle that took me away was a trick and illusion, even though he had been warned to look out for such things."

"Exactly Kim."

"So really, he does deserve to be punished."

"I shall take pleasure in watching over you as you do it. I shall be a pagan priestess and you will be my acolyte."

"Like it should have been, you mean?"

Their eyes met knowingly.

"Yes Kim, how it should have been."

Mistress had brought some clothes for Kim to get changed in. There was a purple and black silk corset, a short black lace skirt, black tights and gloves. The pagan priestess put a white mask on Kim, its face painted with purple lips curled up into a sinister smile. Then she put a silver sickle moon disk over her neck and Kim noticed that she was wearing a full silver disc; two pagan figures symbolising the new and full moons. Finally, Kim was handed a headdress made of purple and black feathers, which she perched on top of her head.

"You know how you must conduct yourself Kim? You must permit no mercy. Your retribution must be severe."

"Yes, I understand," Kim replied.

The pagan priestess and her assistant returned to the dungeon. Vicky was waiting also dressed in purple and black. The black cat had already been blindfolded and laid out onto the rack, his ankles in leg spreaders and his arms stretched out and wrists secured to the rack.

"First, let's secure him to the rack a bit more tightly. Cats are slippery creatures; we don't want him escaping from his bonds. Vicky, fetch me some ropes. Kim, you can help me."

Vicky handed the mistress several coils of rope.

Kim looked on fascinated as the pagan priestess set to work. She tossed the end of the ropes to Kim who had taken up a position on the other side of the rack and she threaded them through metal hooks set into the edge of the rack and passed them back again until eventually the black cat was tied down in an elaborate network of ropes and knots. Kim admired the skilful work and the artistry of the finished design with a large knot on the cat's chest and an array of ropes coming out of it like the rays of a sun. The cat remained silent on the rack only expelling little gasps of breath when the ropes were tightened and they dug into his flesh. He looked strange laid out there, thought Kim. This human body covered in sleek black fur and whiskers and pointed ears and his black and white tail that stuck out from underneath him onto the heavy wood of the rack. In contrast to this was the pure white of the ropes and the pattern they formed over his black fur.

"He's prepared for you now Kim," said the pagan priestess, "everything in this dungeon is at your disposal," she continued her hand sweeping across the length of the room to show the plethora of instruments of torment that lined its walls.

Kim looked down at the black cat. She paused to think. Where should I start, she thought? There's too many things to choose from. I know, first of all, I want him to see me dressed like a pagan witch so I can look into his eyes and make him know why he needs to be punished. Kim stepped up to his head and started to slowly pull the blindfold from over his eyes. The pagan priestess and Vicky, anticipating what Kim was going to do, had moved into position so that they were also leaning over him. Kim smiled. When the blindfold was lifted he would see all three of them in their purple and black gothic splendour. As his sight was restored the cat let out a moan. It must be scary, thought Kim, to be poured over by three mystical pagan magicians, the haunting dark beauty of the priestess and the sinister, faceless white masks of her two assistants, knowing that you are about to be the protagonist in a bizarre ritual of punishment and revenge.

"Nano. Black cat. Slave to the pagan priestess Nemesis, servant of the Red Queen; you have been brought before me to face a reckoning."

Kim was well impressed with herself. Her friendly enquiring voice she used to encourage the cat to tell his tale had been dispatched and replaced with a ringing dominant tone. Kim took control and made it crystal clear from her first words that she was in charge.

"I appear before you now, restored as the acolyte of my mistress, the pagan priestess of Nemesis, the goddess of fate and retribution, to extract my vengeance on you for failings against my person. I appear to you as

Nyx, goddess of the night, Nemesis's daughter, and, like her, wielder of pain and suffering."

That was inspired, Kim congratulated herself. She had dragged that up from a late night chat with one of the girls who worked in the parlour for a short while. She was a classics student at the university who was trying to earn some extra money and one night had gone through a whole list of classical goddess's names with her. I was obviously meant to have that conversation just for this moment. The pagan priestess, who had withdrawn into the shadows, looked on admiringly at Kim's ingenuity.

"Do you understand the charges that are laid against you Nano? That you failed in the mission set for you to rescue me from the captivity of the Knights Templar in the temple at Constantinople and that you surrendered me back into their hands because you had been tricked by the illusion of the eagle goddess created by them. Do you acknowledge the consequences of your actions? That the chosen acolyte of the Goddess Nemesis was subjected to abuse and made to work in a brothel."

Kim was absorbed into her role now. But, it was more than a role. She believed the tale of the black cat, she believed she had been chosen, she believed that she had been wronged and had suffered because of it and believed that vengeance was due to her. The black cat could see all of this in her eyes and was mesmerised by this new version of Kim that was before him, the avenging pagan witch of the night. And he feared what would happen to him.

"Do you have anything to say in your defence?"

"No, there's nothing I can say. Everything you accuse me of is true. I'd only say in my defence that I did try my best; that I never meant you any harm and I'm truly repentant at my failings."

"That may be so, but that's not sufficient for you to escape my retribution. Do you accept whatever punishment I deliver?"

"Yes Goddess Nyx, I surrender myself up to you."

"Be assured that my punishment will be extreme and severe."

Now Kim had to decide which amongst the array of implements at her disposal she would use. She scanned the shelves and hooks that lined the dungeon wall. There was so much to choose from and some, like some of the electrical toys, she wasn't sure how to use or get the best out of. And then she had to judge how far she should go. Her hand strayed towards the plastic clothes pegs for some cock and ball torture, casting a glance across to the pagan priestess, then moved her hand across to some of the nastier metal clamps and got an approving look from her. She gathered up some floggers and candles as well. These were all things she would have like to have tried in the brothel if she had got a willing client.

110

She bent over the prostrate and helpless cat. She teased him by rubbing his pointed ears and stroking his long whiskers and taunted him by dangling the metal clips in front of his eyes. She played with his nipples a little bit, tweaking them to make them stand firm and upright and then she leant across him and took a nipple between her teeth and bit on it sharply. The cat groaned in pain. Yes, Kim reflected, she was going to enjoy this. It was a shame about the poor black cat, who had really been rather helpful to Kim whilst she had been in Nemesisland, but he deserved it and he would have to suffer for her. She opened up one of the metal clamps and ran her finger across its teeth. Oh yes, she thought, these nasty little brutes were really going to hurt. She released the spring on them and let the clamp close on the black cat's nipple. A squeal of pain was expelled from his lips. She put another clamp on his other nipple and got the same reaction. Then Kim turned her attention to his cock and balls as she squeezed another three clamps onto the sac of his balls and, lastly, the piece de resistance, the final wicked piece of metal on the tip of his cock. Oh yes, that one made him squirm laughed Kim to herself.

Nano lay splayed out onto the rack. It was a shame, thought Kim, not to use this impressive instrument of torture to its fullest. After all it had such wicked potential. There was a double torment that she could inflict here both through the stretching of the cat's limbs but also the effect this would have on the clamps on his nipples as his chest stretched back.

"Are you ready to suffer for me?" she whispered in his ear.

"Yes, yes. Please make me suffer for you," came the breathless response.

Kim stood at the side of his head clutching the wheel that stretched the victim's arms. She turned it once. There was plenty of slack to be taken up before the cat's arms were fully stretched but she could see that even that movement had sent a tingle of pain shuddering through the metal clamps. She turned the wheel again.

"Aaahh."

Hmm, that hit the spot, thought Kim. She leant over his chest took the two clamps on his nipples into her hand, pulled them up and down and then gave them a little twist.

"Oohhh."

She continued to rock and twist the metal clamps and watch her helpless victim squirm in agony.

"Suffer for me. Accept my just retribution."

"Yes, yes, thank you Kim. Thank you Goddess Nyx. Thank you for punishing me."

She took the wheel of the rack in her hand again and rotated it one more time until his arms were fully stretched and the teeth of the metal clamps

111

dug deeper into his nipples. Kim decided to leave him like that for a while and pay attention to his cock and balls.

Kim decided that the nature of the ritual required a test and a trial by fire, in keeping with the arcane pagan ambience created in the dungeon, was the most apt. She took up five large church candles and put one at each corner of the rack by the black cat's bound hands and feet and the fifth between his legs and lit each of them with an already lit candle. She squeezed the two metal clamps on his nipples to make sure that he wasn't getting too comfortable in his bondage and heard the groans of pain pass his lips. The she took up some night lights set in their metal bases and, lighting them, she placed one on his chest and another on his midriff. She bent over him, her green eyes staring at him through the slits in the sinister white mask, her wavy fair hair brushing sensuously against his face. She held the lighted candle before his terrified, awe-struck eyes.

"I will have my retribution on you. You will be made to suffer for me, you will feel the heat of the hot wax on you, the soft lick of flame against your skin. Goddess Nyx has decreed that you will be punished by a trial of fire so that all your faults can be expunged from you."

"Yes, Goddess Nyx," came the whispered reply.

Kim was amazed at herself. She did not know where all of this came from, how she got the inspiration of using the candles in this way or where she had acquired this ritualistic language of punishment and ceremony but all she knew was that it came to her very naturally, as if this were a role she were born to play. The pagan priestess looked on approvingly in the shadows, content to let her little protégé explore the full depths of her imagination.

"And you must keep still and silent whilst you suffer or the flame and the wax will spill onto you. Are you sure you can you do that?"

"Yes, Goddess Nyx."

"There's one last flame you must hold for me."

She took up another night light and lit it.

"Open wide for me." The black cat's mouth opened. "Now take it between your teeth."

His teeth closed down on the light and gripped it tightly.

"Can you hold that for me?"

There was a guttural noise in the affirmative from the back of the black cat's throat.

"Then I shall begin."

Kim stepped back to admire her handiwork. The cat laid splayed out on the rack, his black fur illuminated in the dungeon gloom by the flickering red light of the candles spread around him and on him. The flames danced around him in a mesmerising ritual. He lay still and silent, holding his body taught, waiting in fear and anticipation for what will follow. Kim pictured his mental control and anguish as he sought to compose himself knowing that he would be put to the test and knowing the agonising consequences of any lose of control.

Kim removed the metal clamp from the end of his penis and held a lighted candle high over his cock, gently tipping it so that drops of molten wax fell onto its exposed red tip. She sensed his body tense and flutter as the intense pain of the hot wax on the most sensitive part of his body hit him. Kim had some idea of what it might feel like as this was something she had tried with a female friend of hers in the parlour just as an experiment and as a drunken dare. She had experienced and understood the sharp intensity and sensuousness that hot wax induced. She continued, this time holding the flame closer to his cock and then drizzling the hot globules onto his balls as well. The pain was more intense and Kim could see the night light nestled on his mid-riff waver slightly but still his control held. Kim went further, allowing the pool of wax to build up before bringing the candle closer and then closer again to his throbbing genitals until the dancing flame was nearly touch them, gradually increasing the level of pain. By now the wax had started to harden over the tip of his cock.

Kim decided to pay attention to other parts of his body. She drizzled hot wax over his thighs and then onto his torso drawing a large figure eight on his body interweaved around the ropes and the night lights resting on his chest and mid-riff. The black cat withstood the torment well. Perhaps, Kim thought, she needed to increase the intensity of her punishment again and she knew exactly how to do that. Her hand reached over to one of the fierce metal clamps that still gripped his nipples, she squeezed its end to release the pressure. As the blood and sensation rushed back into the tips of his nipples a surge of pain went through the black cat's body. His eyes closed tight and Kim could hear a controlled gasp of pain emit from the mouth still holding the night light firmly in its teeth. She released the second clamp. She toyed with him, gently brushing the raw red tips of his nipples with her finger knowing they would be so sensitive to touch. Then she leant over him holding his gaze so he dare not turn away from her eyes. She held the candle over his chest all the while looking at him.

"Now, accept my retribution," she said as drops of hot wax fell on his already sore nipples.

She could see he was suffering. She could she he was using all his mental strength to control himself. There were the subtlest ripples of movement and slightest gasp from his lips but Kim knew this only masked the agony he must be feeling for her. And she felt wonderful, wielding that power over him, making him suffer for her.

Kim wanted to inflict one final act of pain and retribution before the black cat's penance was complete. She moved the candle down to the side of his body and held the flame close to the skin, as close as she dare without it touching. She watched his flesh glow red in the candle light and sensed him endure the pain of the burning candle so close to his body. When she pulled the candle away she had left a nice red mark on him.

Kim stepped back and announced, "I am satisfied that I have extracted my vengeance for your failings and that your atonement for them is complete."

She removed the night-lights, first from his mouth and then from his body and then blew out the church candles that surrounded him.

The pagan priestess, Nemesis, and her assistant emerged from the shadows in the corner of the dungeon where they had been watching Kim conduct her ceremony.

"That was wonderful Kim. It gave me great pleasure to see how you acquitted yourself and conducted that punishment."

"Oh, thanks," said Kim, "I just felt the part. I don't know where some of that stuff came from to be honest."

"She was magnificent," ventured Vicky, "she has been watching you and learning from you madam. She was a natural. It was as if she were born to it."

"But she is Vicky, she is," Mistress Nemesis replied enigmatically. "Can you not see now why I chose her to be my acolyte? Kim, can you not recognise how the tales you have heard about your strange past must be true?"

"Yes I do. I think I do. It's hard to explain, I felt important doing that. It's as if I felt special in some way that I've never felt before."

The pagan priestess brushed a finger against her cheek and planted a gentle kiss on her lips.

"But you are, my dear, believe me, you are."

Kim felt this odd exchange left many questions unanswered but decided it was the wrong time to pursue them. Instead, she turned her attention to the black cat, still bound onto the rack in a submissive daze.

"Will you turn him back into real person now do you think?" asked Kim.

The pagan priestess stepped over to human animal secured tight in the criss-cross pattern of white ropes and stroked his ears and whiskers and sensuously ran her long painted fingernails down his black fur.

"I think that might be possible. He has taken his punishment at your hands well. Tell me, slave, are you repentant?"

"Yes, truly I am Goddess Nemesis. Kim's punishment was just. It was fair of her to extract retribution for my failures."

"Yes, it was a delicious and entertaining piece of torment. Nano, I'm satisfied you've atoned for your faults and can be welcomed back into my dungeon in your human form soon. But I want you to remain in the guise of the black cat for the ball I'm preparing."

"There's going to be a ball?" asked Kim excitedly.

"Oh yes, and I expect it to be in your honour, but not yet. There are still some trials you have to face and more that you have to learn. You have to show true and complete submission to my will before there can be any celebration."

Kim wasn't sure she liked the sound of that. What more could the pagan priestess expect of her?

15: The Duchess

Kim was left with her own thoughts for a while as the pagan priestess and her maid left the dungeon with her slave, Nano or the black cat as Kim thought of him. Kim's head was a whirlwind of thoughts and emotions. She still hadn't really had time to absorb fully the significance of the second part of the black cat's tale. It wasn't that she didn't believe it or didn't want to believe it; it's just that it sounded so weird and, if that had all happened to her, it must have been eradicated from her memory as she had no recollection of it.

In some ways this was no surprise to her. There had always appeared to be gaps in her life; things she couldn't make sense of or didn't feel right about. She had felt disconnected all the way through her childhood and her difficult adolescent years, which all seemed like an unreal blur. She kind of wanted to believe the tale, however strange. She felt it gave her a kind of purpose and direction she'd never had in her life. To think she was chosen in some way was encouraging and to believe she really did have those adventures in underground labyrinths was exciting.

But then she took a reality check. It seemed so unlikely that she had been taken to temples in Constantinople or Knights Templar chapels in France. Then there was the strange part of the tale about the phantom impregnation. And yet, there was that red mark on her stomach and she just remembered it being there without any explanation when she started working in the parlour.

Kim sighed. And now there was talk of more trials. What did the Red Queen want with her? Why was she so interested in her? Kim couldn't quite put her finger on it, but she was being treated differently from any other character in Nemesisland. She was the focus of the Red Queen's attention and, just beneath the surface of her implacable dominance, Kim sensed an anxiety in her. She really did want Kim to submit to her. It wasn't just a game, thought Kim; she really did want her in this world, but for what remained shrouded in mystery for Kim.

Vicky had returned now, dressed again as the Duchess, in black and red pvc with her black heart shaped apron and white mask. Now, the Duchess interested Kim too. She had a special position in Nemesisland as the Red Queen's maid and as Mistress Nemesis's companion; the mysterious transvestite lady in waiting who always appeared masked. Kim had watched Vicky, or the Duchess, carefully. The Red Queen's eyes could switch from harsh glare to delighted amusement in a flash but underneath the mask Kim could see there was a kindness and generosity in the Duchess's eyes. Well, thought Kim, you'd have to have some special qualities to so consistently serve the whims of the Red Queen all the time. Also, Kim could see the Duchess was attracted to her. She remembered the gentle touches she had received at his hands when she first arrived in Nemesisland, could see the aroused looks he gave her from behind the mask when he looked at her body, whether naked or dressed in some costume.

The Duchess laid a white piece of material out on the rack before turning to Kim.

"The Red Queen would like you to wear something else for your next trial so you'd better take off your pagan dress now Kim."

Kim obediently did as she was told and pulled the dress over her head so that she was left just wearing the black satin knickers and bra that were underneath it. She caught a glimpse of the Duchess watching her and appreciatively admiring her voluptuous body as she did so. Her ample breasts squeezed out of the cups of the bra. Kim had great tits, she knew that, and a great arse and a beautifully rounded sexy body, which she knew she used to great effect. Kim wondered if she could use her feminine wiles on the Duchess, who was obviously drawn to her. The Red Queen was too powerful and inscrutable to get information from and the black cat had probably told her all that he knew through his tales, but she must have shared some confidences with her maid, the Duchess.

"So, Duchess, what are the Red Queen's plans for me next?" Kim asked.

Vicky looked alarmed at being asked such a direct question and answered, "I don't know what her plans are. She plans everything in Nemesisland very carefully but I don't understand anything of her wider purpose. I'm only a maid. I only serve her. I've only been asked to pass on the next instructions for you."

Kim was afraid she'd put the Duchess off with such a direct assault, perhaps she would need to be more subtle.

"Yes, Duchess, but you're her maid, she must have dropped some hints, she must have said something about me."

The Duchess looked distinctly uncomfortable, "No, honestly Kim, nothing really just the odd cryptic comment, which amounts to nothing more than you know already."

"You don't know why she's brought me here?"

"I only know she said something about wanting a slave girl."

Ah, perhaps I'm getting somewhere now thought Kim.

117

"Yes, but why me? What's so special about me?"

"Really, I don't know, only what you've heard from the tales you've been told."

Kim advanced towards him. She locked onto the eyes behind the mask and could see them struggling with her emotions. She wants to help, thought Kim, I can see that, but she won't betray her mistress. Kim pulled herself close to her and brushed the dark hair of her wig. The look behind the mask was took on an anxious expression now.

"She won't be back yet, will she? Only, you see Duchess, I think there's something I can offer you if you answer my questions," Kim said, reaching her hand down and lifting up the Duchess's pvc skirt just a little so her hand could reach the layers of petticoats underneath. There was confusion and panic in the Duchess's eyes now.

"I bet you'd like to play with me, wouldn't you. I could see it in your eyes from the first moment in Nemesisland."

There was no reply. She was obviously in no position to deny it. Her hands went further up her petticoats until Kim felt some lacy knickers and, within them, a very erect cock. No question she was turned on by Kim and her little game. Most likely she's not allowed to get aroused, thought Kim, which would explain her discomfort at the predicament Kim was consciously putting her in.

Kim slipped her hand into the Duchess's knickers to grasp his erect cock. She let out a gasp of shock...and pleasure.

"I can't Kim. I'll get into trouble with the Red Queen for this. And honestly Kim, I don't know much."

"Much! So you know something," said Kim triumphantly, pulling on the Duchess's cock.

She pulled her body closer to the Duchess's so that her ample tits were pressed hard against the transvestite maid's false ones. She pulled the lacy knickers down and the hard cock sprang out from its restraint and then rang her thumb along its tip.

"Oh, but you're leaking, Duchess, the Red Queen will already be mad at you for that, why not really give her something to be mad about," Kim taunted.

"Kim, please, no. I shouldn't be doing this."

Kim moved some layers of petticoats away, gripped the cock firmly in her hand and started rubbing vigorously. The poor Duchess was torn between her ardent desire for sexual pleasure and release from Kim and her duty to serve her mistress.

"I promise you Kim, I don't know much."

"Tell me what you know," urged Kim, "and I'll make you come. Come on, you know you want it. Take hold of my tits, I can see you've been aching to do that."

"Oh Kim, you look so lovely," said the Duchess as she caved in and lifted up her hands to take Kim's soft fleshy orbs into her grasp.

"Tell me," whispered Kim.

Vicky's breathing was heavy as Kim continued to masturbate her cock under the petticoats. She slowed the pace of her rubbing a bit to let her take in some breath.

"Honestly Kim, there's not much to tell. She said she wanted a slave girl. She talked of a girl in a massage parlour in Manchester. She said something about her life being connected with this girl."

Kim stopped rubbing the Duchess's cock.

"Connected? What did she mean by that?"

"Honestly Kim, I don't know. I promise you I don't know any more. She doesn't give so much away, even to me. That's all I know."

Kim was inclined to believe her. She didn't think the Duchess knew how they were connected. She kind of knew there was some link between them because the stories related she had been chosen as an acolyte by Mistress Nemesis. But why? Why her and not any other girl working in the parlour? There had to be something else.

Kim had a wicked smile on her face now. So, she thought, what should she do with the Duchess now? She had been brought to the edge of climax before Kim pulled back. Should she finish him off or leave him in frustrated limbo she wondered? She was obviously desperate for it and, it was naughty of Kim, but she quite liked the idea of giving him some release and pleasure knowing that she would probably face some retribution from the Red Queen for her behaviour. Kim's smile broadened. She would do better than wanking him off.

She put her lips to the Duchess's mask and pushed her tongue past it into her mouth searching out for hers. The Duchess kissed her through the mask with desperate desire. She had her where she wanted, thought Kim. All that experience in the parlour meant she knew how to play men, even this exotic transvestite slut, she thought. Kim pulled her lips away.

"Do you want to come Duchess."

"Oh, please, yes please Kim," the Duchess groaned.

"Even though you'll get punished if she finds out."

"Yes Kim, even if she finds out."

Kim sunk to her knees. She lifted up layers of lacy material and buried her head into the Duchess's crotch. She took her balls in her mouth and sucked them and nipped them with her teeth as the Duchess moaned in ecstasy. Then Kim buried her cock into her mouth sucking urgently on it, pulling at it with her lips, flicking its tip with her tongue. She'd never come across a man yet who could resist her oral and she was determined to give the Duchess a good time. After all Kim suspected she would pay for it in some way. If anyone could have seen them, she thought, with her head bobbing up and down hidden underneath the long pvc skirt and petticoats. She could feel the veins on her cock throbbing with anticipation and knew her climax was imminent. She paused for a moment, hesitating for some more gentle flicks with her tongue, which she know men found delightful, before going at it with renewed vigour to bring her relief. She felt the Duchess's hips bucking with the final throes of pleasure and then the sticky salty come squirt into her mouth. The Duchess groaned loudly in pleasure.

"Oh Kim. That's wonderful Kim. Thank you Kim."

Kim's head emerged from underneath all the petticoats. The Duchess had a far- away look in her eyes.

"There, and you haven't even got any tell-tale spunk stains on your petticoats," Kim reassured, licking her lips of the last traces of come.

"Oh, but I'll be in big trouble now."

"How? I won't split on you," said Kim.

"But she'll know Kim. She knows everything that happens in Nemesisland."

"Well, I hope it's worth it,"

"Oh yes it is Kim, thank you."

Kim was pleased with herself. She hadn't really got any more information from the Duchess but she'd had a lot of fun trying. Although it was a wicked thought, she kind of felt she had won a small victory by seducing the Red Queen's maid.

"Come on Kim, she'll be back soon. Take your bra and knickers off and put these clothes on quick."

Kim pulled a white cotton dress over her head. It was very plain and simple but the Duchess added a beautiful gold belt with a buckle in the shape of a scarab beetle. What a strange object thought Kim, though nothing surprised her much now.

"I'm sorry Kim, but my mistress wants you locked in one of the cages until she's ready."

Kim shrugged her shoulders. She'd got used to being tied up and locked away by now. The Duchess led her back into the other dungeon room where she had been put away with the black cat and put metal cuffs on her wrists and ankles, which he padlocked to the bars.

"She likes you Kim," the Duchess smiled, "I can tell that. She really warms to you and she wants you here in Nemesisland, I know it. Honestly

Kim I don't know what for, but she really wants you. You must trust her though Kim. I don't know what her purpose is, but she will have one."

"Thanks Vicky," said Kim, "thanks very much; that's kind of you to tell me that."

The Duchess nodded in appreciation of Kim's generosity and left the dungeon to return to her mistress.

16: The Egyptian Goddess

Vicky had left Kim in the cage whilst he went away to see if her mistress was ready. Kim speculated on what new test the Red Queen would come up with. She was finding it hard to think what it might be. She had already been subjected to torments that exceeded her imagination and couldn't think what new twists the ruler of Nemesisland would come up with. She sat back and ran little movies in her head of all the things she had done in this bizarre place and smiled. When she got back to the real world, back into the parlour she worked in, her clients were going to be in for some surprises.

She heard the rattle of the dungeon door as it opened and two figures emerged from behind it. What now thought Kim as she peered up at a Cleopatra-like presence. The Red Queen was transformed into an Egyptian goddess; this certainly wasn't in Alice in Wonderland, Kim considered. Her face was alabaster white and her hair, brushed impossibly smooth and straight, was as black as the dark winter nights on the Nile. Resting on her forehead was a golden headpiece in the shape of a scorpion, the claws reaching out above her, a symbol of dominance and menace. She was dressed in a flowing white gown embroidered with gold thread and resting on her lily white breasts was a pectoral of gold inlaid with carnelian and cut glass in dark and light blues. Most bizarrely of all was a pair of wings covered in gold leaf on her back, which spread out behind her so she looked like a magnificent winged goddess come to gather Kim up and transport her to another world.

If the Egyptian goddess looked ravishing in her exotic beauty, then Vicky exceeded her in bizarreness. Her chest was shaved smooth and oiled and all she wore was a richly decorated skirt except that on her head was a jackal mask with long snout and pointed ears. Kim's head was reeling with the possibilities. She had seen images from the tomb of Tutankhamen and the golden age of the pharaohs and their strange and exotic deities. Both were dressed for another ritual, but what could it be? Shit, thought Kim, as it suddenly struck her; ancient Egypt, pyramids, mummification. Surely not?

The Egyptian goddess made her stately progress to towards the cage with Vicky behind her, the heavy jackal mask bobbing up and down. Her piercing gaze looked through the bars of the cage.

"So, you have been having some fun with the Duchess have you? There's no point denying it, I see all."

"Yes mistress," Kim replied.

"That's very naughty of you Vicky," she said casting a sharp glance towards her, "there will be some reckoning to pay for that. Did she tempt you Kim, did she make you play with her. I know my maid can be wilful and naughty sometimes and likes to play with my slaves, especially any female ones."

"No mistress, honestly, she didn't. It was me that seduced her. I kind of wanted to do it."

"What, you think you can take my most trusted and loyal servants and play with them for your own amusement."

"Sorry mistress, I couldn't help it. His cock just looked so inviting I had to."

"Hmm. I think I can forgive you a little bit of fun, Kim. I like to see a slave girl with a bit of imagination. But Vicky, you should know better; there's no excuse for you," she reprimanded.

The jackal headed figure nodded forlornly.

"Open the cage and let her out," the Egyptian goddess ordered.

Vicky unlocked the padlocks and opened the door of the cage. Kim pulled herself out, fearful of what was going to follow. She stood in front of this Egyptian goddess. She was only a few inches taller than Kim but the combination of her statuesque figure and the claws of the headdress reaching out over her made it appear as if she towered over her. She held her hand out. Kim took it in hers and planted a kiss on it noticing the falcon shaped gold ring on one of her fingers. Kim pulled her mouth back and pursed her lips about to utter some statement of homage to her mistress in this new guise when a finger was put to her lips in a gesture beckoning her to be silent.

"Do you trust me Kim?"

"Yes, I do."

"Completely?"

"Yes."

"With your life?"

Kim gulped and hesitated slightly before nodding in affirmation. How could she say that she wondered? How could she make an expression of such extreme submission? And yet, there was no question she meant it.

"Good Kim, then your devotion will be put to the test. I hope you don't fail me," she added sharply.

Kim nodded. No, she didn't want to fail. She had pledged to surrender to her utterly.

"This is an important test, Kim," she said more kindly now. "You need to pass through a gateway. You need to be sacrificed and re-born as a character in Nemesisland in your own right, as my special slave girl and assistant. Do you understand?"

Kim nodded. Her heart was pounding? What on earth did she mean?

"Take my hand Kim."

She reached out her painted fingernails for Kim to grasp and led her to the middle of the room. She undid the lock on Kim's scarab belt and let it fall to the ground and then she took hold of the simple cotton tunic and pulled it over Kim's head so that she stood before her naked. She stroked her face and breasts gently sending a tingle down to Kim's sex. The she gestured for her to climb up onto a thin black wooden plank mounted on a frame at about waist height.

Kim let out a little squeak of fear or anticipation. The finger was put to her lips again.

"Don't say anything Kim. You must trust and believe. You see that the jackal-god Anubis, the deity of mummification and the after-life attends me. Lie in acceptance and let your goddess weigh your soul out for you and measure that it's worthy to join mine."

Kim laid perfectly still, her arms by her side and her legs straight and stiff feeling vulnerable in her nakedness on the narrow bench. She watched as the jackal-headed Duchess with her black snout and pointed ears approached carrying a long feather. She gently ran it across Kim's shoulders.

"An ostrich feather," commented the Egyptian goddess, "used to fan the pharaohs in ancient days, now used to pleasure and torment you, Kim."

It was certainly a sensual torment. The soft feather brushed against the peachy flesh of Kim's breasts and sent waves of pleasure through her body. The giant feather touched gently against Kim's white thighs and its gossamer touch sent the juices running through her sex. It felt so nice, so luxurious to lie there still and silent and soak up the erotic attention of the soft feather. The snout masked figure leant over her and pulled the feather back and forth across her soft skin; her arms, her shoulders, her belly, up her legs, across her aching mound. Kim tried to keep quiet but could not help but expel gasps of sensual pleasure as the feather did its work. Make the most of it, thought Kim, because I bet there's something else on the way. As the jackal headed figure continued its work with the feather the Egyptian goddess stood at her head, leant over her and gently brushed her hair with her hands, arranging her fair wavy locks. Her eyes looked into Kim's as the claws of the golden scorpion towered over her. Her touch was gentle and erotic as she ran a sharp fingernail along her cheek and her lips as the feather brushed over her cunt. Kim couldn't work out if this was

124

meant to be pleasure or torment and had gone beyond caring. The painted red lips parted and quiet breathless words came out.

"Your soul is heavy Kim. There is much you still don't know and a heavy burden you need to be released from."

Kim's head was reeling. What did she mean by that?

"That's enough pleasure for her now Anubis," said the Egyptian goddess to the jackal masked figure, "we must get down to the serious business of the sacrifice now."

Anubis put the ostrich feather down and passed the Egyptian goddess a giant roll of white cling film. She went down to Kim's feet and pulled some the cling film out with a ripping sound. She started at Kim's feet, wrapping the sticky substance around her toes and then around her ankles securing her tightly onto the board on which she laid. The quality of the cling film was unusual. It gripped tightly against Kim so she was afforded hardly any movement. She tried but could only get the slightest wiggle from her toes. The Egyptian goddess worked up the rest of her body, wrapping the stretchy material around her legs and pulling it tight and then passing it under the frame and back around again.

She had reached her thighs now and Kim felt her fingers against her soft flesh and the cold plastic pulling her against the board. It was a sensual sensation being pressed down and immobilised. She felt fingers brush her pubic hair and touch her mound, which sent a wave of ecstasy washing through her. She soon felt the cling film close around her sex. As the Egyptian goddess worked up her body pulling the cling film as tight as she could Kim felt strands of her long hair brush against her flesh and smelt her sweet and exotic scent. She worked especially hard to pull the cling film over Kim's tits and ensure that her soft mounds of flesh and her engorged nipples were wrapped tight.

She had reached Kim's neck. How far would she go?

"You trust me?"

"Mmm," Kim was in a sensual daze and could only mutter her approbation.

"Take this and make sure you hold it tightly between your teeth. Don't let it go."

She inserted a plastic tube into Kim's mouth. Kim's heart jumped a beat. What did this mean?

The cling film was wrapped around her neck and then twisted around the plastic tube to hold it firmly into place. Kim was wetting herself with fear and anticipation. She knew what was going to come next and, although part of her couldn't believe that she had allowed herself to be offered up for this mummification ritual, another part of her desperately wanted to surrender herself to it. It was this latter part that won over as she laid there quietly, submissively, yearning to be enveloped completely and give herself up.

"This is the gateway Kim, the path into another world for you. The jackal-headed god Anubis is here to ease your path through it," she said acknowledging the presence of Vicky in the mask. Kim drank in this moment before she was deprived of sight, perhaps of breath and life itself. Leaning over her was the imperious dark haired figure of the Egyptian goddess arraigned in golden jewellery and precious stones with her piercing blue eyes that penetrated right into her soul. Next to her was the snout headed figure of Anubis beckoning her on, inviting her to take a further step into this strange world she had committed herself to. She had one last chance to look down at herself, a bizarre figure mummified in white cling film. Kim thought she looked fantastic; very exotic and sexy in a bizarre way. She took one deep draft of air through her nose before the cling film wrapped around her face, over her eyes and ears until finally her head was covered. She tried to imagine what she looked like now, a cocoon of white with a plastic tube sticking out of her mouth.

Deprived of sight, sound and smell and with only the taste of the plastic tube in her mouth, she was totally immersed in the sensation of the thick white film clinging to her body. She drew in deep gasps of air through the tube, that very act making her head spin even more. The psychological sensation of surrender and submission was overpowering. She was immersed in her own body, the overwhelming feeling being that of the tight cling film holding her in. She felt herself drifting off and would have loved to have floated in this submissive nether-world for ever but then suddenly something yanked her back to a perverse kind of reality and an awareness there were still other people in the room, even though the sense of them seemed to be some distance away.

Hands touched her. She could feel them pressing against the cling film, rubbing themselves against her. She had no idea whose they were and she did not care; she could only feel the pressure of fingers pressing against her through the cling film. Who knows, perhaps some perverted servant in this place got their pleasure from such a sensation. She did not know. Kim was just one fire-ball of sensation wrapped in her cling film cocoon.

She felt her tits being rubbed and manipulated through the film. Anonymous hands plucked and tweaked at her nipples making them swell with tension. The sensation made her cunt wet. Then she felt something sharp against the outer layer she was wrapped in and a knife or pair of scissors cut into the cling film. She felt the cold metal against her flesh as it cut around her areola until a hole had been cut around it and it was exposed. Kim felt a shot of pain go through her as fingers squeezed her nipples. Her teeth closed around the plastic and gripped onto it as she breathed heavily through the tube. Her torment had not finished though as she felt a cold metal clamp close around the end of her swollen nipple. It was agonising. It would have been painful at any time but laid out helpless as she was and totally absorbed in the sensations of her own body the pain was amplified by her heightened sense of touch. She wanted to scream out but could only control her reactions by controlling her breath. After the initial shock of the nipple clamps being applied Kim was able to control herself and let the waves of pain spread over her.

She had just adjusted to her new predicament when she felt scissors pressing against her again, this time against her crotch. Somebody was carefully cutting a slit to open up the cling film and expose her cunt. God she was wet. The mixture of pain and pleasure and the combination of sensations had taken a grip on her. She felt an anonymous finger slide into her. She could not tell who it belonged to, whether it was the Egyptian goddess or the Anubis figure or some other character who had entered the dungeon that she was oblivious to. The finger worked its way up into her massaging her cunt walls before being pulled out. Then she felt something else; a dildo being inserted into her. Her cunt was sopping and Kim was ready for this kind of attention. It felt sensational as the hard object slid up her. A hand brushed against the nipple clamps to send a shock of pain and pleasure rippling through her.

Then, faintly, as if she was some disembodied spirit and the sound was coming from another place, she heard the buzzing. It was a vibrator and it had started to work its wonderful magic on her cunt. It buzzed for a short while and Kim bucked and twisted as hard as she could but she was held immobile by the tight cling film. She could only focus on the sensation of pleasure buzzing through her. Kim experienced the final twist to her torment. As she breathed heavily trying to control the writhing motions in her confinement and as she drew in one deep breath she sensed a finger closing over the end of the plastic tube. At the same time the speed of the vibrator was turned up a notch. What the fuck screamed Kim in her head. Trust her, was her only thought. Trust her echoed through her head as she desperately fought for breath whilst at the same time feeling waves of ecstasy in her cunt. The finger was lifted off the tube and Kim sucked in deep breath of fresh air. The vibrator buzzed louder and moved faster. The process was repeated a few times Kim had lost any sense of how many. By then Kim was right on the edge, desperate for normal breathes, desperate to come as the vibrator brought her to the point of climax. The finger was released and Kim was allowed to let out a muffled scream of ecstasy through the tube as euphoric waves of orgasm hit her. The physical sensation was extraordinary. It felt like her whole body was writhing in pleasure even though all the time it was restrained by the strict cocoon of cling film. She'd never had an orgasm like it. She was totally spent and her head was spinning with the combination of breath control and climax.

After the waves of orgasm had subsided she laid there quietly breathing heavily and deeply through the tube. The next sensation she felt was the scissor again, but this time they were cutting her free with long snips through the cling film. Kim shivered as she felt a rush of cold air against the sweat that had accumulated on her body underneath the cling film. The film was pulled apart and she wriggled her body to free herself from it. Finally, the cling film mask was removed from her head; her hair damp clinging to her forehead and cheek.

Looking over her was the Egyptian goddess with an enigmatic smile on her lips and the snout of the jackal head next to her. A hand reached out to her face and pulled her sweating and matted hair away gently from her forehead. Kim was euphoric and quite speechless.

"Well done Kim, you have passed through a severe test. How do you feel?"

She didn't know what to say, couldn't express the physical feelings or emotions coursing through her.

"Wow," she said, "I mean fucking wow!"

The serene ritual mask of the Egyptian goddess slipped as she allowed a smile to spread across her lips. She held her hand out to Kim and helped her up from the bench.

"Yes Kim, that was certainly an extreme experience and you handled it with great fortitude. You see, you trusted and when you do that you can drown in the sensations and when you do that the pain and pleasure meld together, don't they?"

"Shit yes," said Kim.

"It was an important test for you. You are my slave girl now Kim. You've demonstrated you can give up control to me."

Kim's head was still spinning with the overload of sensations as she rested her bottom against the wooden plank she had recently been strapped to. She was still unsteady on her feet and felt herself swaying. The Egyptian goddess gathered her up in her arms, holding onto her tightly. Kim felt safe gathered in her warm embrace the softness of her breasts underneath her cotton tunic pressing against her.

"You deserve a rest now. Vicky will look after you and then prepare you for your next trial."

"There's more!" gasped Kim.

"Oh yes, remember you've given yourself up to me now Kim. I can do whatever I want with you, can't I?"

"Yeah," replied Kim dreamily.

The eyebrows raised in a flash.

"Yeah, what?"

"Yes thank you mistress," Kim corrected herself.

"That's better Kim. I will see you again soon," she said ominously.

17: The Strap-on Mistress

Mistress Nemesis sat in her changing room preparing for Kim's next test. She was surrounded by her wardrobe of fetish clothing, row upon row of pvc dresses, tops and skirts in various colours, a collection of fetish boots and shoes, an array of wigs and a dressing table scattered with make-up. She had already changed but was sat in front of her dressing room mirror for a moment of quiet contemplation. She was dressed in her favourite black pvc cat-suit and knee high stiletto boots. The shiny material clung to her statuesque and shapely figure. She always felt dominant in this outfit. She knew only too well the effect this cat-suit had on her slaves. The shiny pvc stretched over her voluptuous bosom and hips made her feel alluring and powerful. The mere sight of it catapulted her slaves into a state of submission. She could see it in their eyes. She had put it on now for a reason. She wanted to feel at her most dominant and powerful for the act she must now inflict on her protégé, her special slave girl.

Mistress Nemesis reflected on Kim's progress through Nemesisland. She's done brilliantly. She's been everything I wanted and expected from her. I knew that given the chance her hidden but latent qualities would shine through, and they have. She's shown herself to be submissive when required but wickedly dominant when necessary. She's clever and imaginative and resourceful. She's respectful at the right time but wicked and fun when she needs to be. And she wants to submit. I can feel it. She's embraced Nemesisland. She's confused and bewildered at times and she knows there's something being hidden about her past and I'll need to address that, but not yet. There will be a time for that. I need her in my world. She's so close and I must have her. For me and my wider purpose but also for herself so she can find out who she is. I haven't made a mistake; everything I've heard of this girl is true. I can see into her soul and I know she's the girl I need. It's imperative I have her. I must have her submit to me, completely. This is the last act, the final test for her.

Mistress Nemesis took something down from the shelf above her dressing table. It was black, made of hard rubber, thick, long and fearsome looking. Larger and harder than any male cock, it was the ultimate tool of humiliation. It was the biggest most awesome strap-on she possessed.

I have to steel myself for this, she contemplated, as she handled the hard dark object in her hand. I know how special this girl is and what she means to me. I like her. However cruel I've needed to treat her I've great affection for her. But I must manifest my harsh side. I must take her through this final trial of submission; take her deepest taboo and make her face up to it so she can surrender herself completely. And then all can be revealed.

She took the leather belt and strapped it around her waist, tightening the harness so it sat snugly against her crotch. The black false cock protruded from her body. She could feel its hardness against her own sex and that made her feel empowered. She ran her red fingernails across its contours and felt its unforgiving hardness. She felt the power and dominance of it run through her. This would not be easy, for her or for Kim, but it had to be done. She got up from her dressing table chair and went into her dungeon.

Kim had already been prepared by Vicky. She was front down on her whipping bench, her wrists and ankles strapped to the bench and her naked body tied down with leather straps. She was helpless and vulnerable and Mistress Nemesis knew that what she faced would be a severe challenge for her. She stood in front of Kim the black strap on bobbing in front of her face. Kim was tied down so she couldn't look up; her whole attention was directed at the fearsome object around the Red Queen's waist.

"Do you see this girl?"

"Mmm, yes mistress," Kim muttered in a whispered whimper.

Mistress Nemesis could tell Kim knew where she intended to put the hard object. Kim realised it. She hoped that she intended to fuck her with the strap-on in the normal way, up her sopping cunt but somehow she knew instinctively that wasn't where it was going to go. It was the only part of her bound, battered and abused body that hadn't been used in Nemesisland and it was hardly likely it was going to escape attention.

"Do you know where this is going to go?" she asked in her cruellest tones; the question was rhetorical.

"Yes, mistress," Kim replied, oh yes she knew.

"This is going to go up your arse girl. I will force you to cross your last taboo Kim. You will submit to me whatever the pain, whatever the humiliation, do you understand?"

Kim whimpered and nodded. She had hated this when it had been forced on her before by an ex-boyfriend. Could she learn to receive it in Nemesisland? Kim was scared.

Mistress Nemesis grabbed Kim harshly by the hair and lifted her head up.

"Take it girl. Suck on it."

She pushed the object between Kim's lips as they parted. The huge false phallus filled Kim's mouth. The taste of the hard rubber filled her mouth and its smell, mingled with the aroma of Mistress Nemesis's perfume, wafted up her nostrils. At first she could hardly breathe and she had to take in deep drafts of air through her nose as she obediently did as she was told and sucked on it. Mistress was not going to show her any mercy. She pushed the rubber cock down her throat in deep strokes until at one point she started gagging. Kim was close to tears but she pulled herself back. Eventually Mistress Nemesis settled on a slow rhythmic movement that forced Kim to suck hard on the object.

Kim was relieved when the strap-one was pulled out of her mouth but it was only a brief respite as she knew what was going to follow. Mistress Nemesis said nothing. She marched beside Kim her stiletto heels clicking against the stone floor. She climbed up onto the whipping bench and knelt over Kim's back-side. Kim could feel the hard pvc against her the flesh of her arse and her thighs.

There was a slapping sound and Kim let out a howl of pain.

"Take it girl," the voice behind her reprimanded cruelly, "control yourself."

It was such a surprise. Kim wasn't expecting that, she was waiting for something very different. Mistress Nemesis slapped her hard with the open face of her hand five or six times. It was painful but this time Kim was ready for her.

"Vicky, pass me my riding crop."

Kim heard movement behind her and then the sharp whack of the leather loop of the crop against her back-side. Kim had to use all her inner strength not to let out a squeal of pain. She leaned right over Kim so that she could feel the pvc pressed against her and then the touch and smell of Mistress Nemesis's dark hair as it hung over her cheeks.

"You'll be my little pony, girl."

And she whacked Kim hard with the riding crop. She felt her arse glowing red with the harsh strokes.

"Vicky, fetch a ball gag and bridle and put it on her," ordered Mistress Nemesis.

Vicky did as she was told. She put a red ball gag into Kim's mouth and tightened the strap behind her head so it was kept firmly in place and then secured a metal bridle around her cheek and a pair of leather reins. Now, mistress climbed up onto her back and took hold of the reins. The weight of her pvc clad back-side pressed down onto Kim. The harsh strokes with the riding crop continued in earnest now.

"Come on take me for a ride girl."

Her back-side felt like it was on fire. The pain was now excruciating and Kim was sure there would be red welts on her arse from fierce strokes from the crop. There was no release from it; she was strapped down and could barely move and her cries and moans were muffled by the ball gag in her mouth. She could feel the movement of mistress on top of her, 'riding her' and the legs of her pvc cat suit squeezing her body. And yet, and this Kim couldn't explain logically, just like everything else in Nemesisland, she loved the sensations. She wanted it and her burning desire was to give herself up to whatever this powerful dominatrix threw at her.

At one side of the whipping bench there was a mirror and Kim was able to cock her head to one side. She had to admit it looked sensational. This pvc clad woman mounted on her, the riding crop in her hand. She would alternate the strokes of the whip with gentle strokes of Kim's sore and throbbing arse with her gloved hand and these felt like a heavenly interlude between the punishments. Eventually Mistress Nemesis's pony had been put through her paces and she passed the crop back to Vicky to hang back on the wall with the other floggers and whips.

"Vicky take the ball gag out," she ordered.

Vicky untied the strap and pulled the red rubber ball out. Kim exercised her jaw to relax it and get some movement back. She drew in long drafts of air through her mouth. The combination of physical punishment and restricted breathing had made her very woozy.

The cat-suited figure leant over her, once again Kim felt the cool shiny PVC pressing against her back. Her face was alongside Kim's. She could feel her warm breath against her check, smell the aroma of her red lipstick and the scent of her long black hair. It felt like submissive heaven.

"Do you trust me?"

The words were whispered in her ear firmly and urgently.

"Yes, I trust you."

"Do you trust me completely Kim?"

"Yes, I do," Kim whimpered.

And she meant it, she really did. She wanted nothing more than to give herself up to this powerful woman and be part of her world.

"Will you do anything for me Kim?"

"Yes, mistress, yes I will."

"Will you take it for me, will you take the strap-on Kim."

"Mmm, yeah."

Kim was fearful but she did trust her. In some strange inexplicable way she trusted her completely; Kim understood that she was looking out for her and there was some meaning to the rite of passage she was going through. This was different from when her boy-friend did it or when the psycho in the parlour tried to take her, completely different. This was an act of surrender and submission freely offered up and entered into.

She could see Vicky pass her some lube in the mirror out of the corner of her eye. She spread some generously over the black cock. Kim gulped. Would she really be able to take that thing inside of her. She felt a cold slippery feeling over her arse hole as she spread lube liberally over her with her pvc gloved hand.

At first she felt the object nudging at the flesh of her buttocks and then Mistress Nemesis use her hands to spread her bum cheeks so she could find the right spot. The black strap-on pushed against her hole as she felt her hips force it into her. She felt the muscles of her arse being pushed open by the thing and she tried desperately hard to receive it. She knew it wouldn't help to put up any resistance. Besides, she wanted it, she really wanted it. She felt the muscles being stretched and for a moment wondered whether she would be able to take it but then she felt the gnarled head of the false cock push into her anal passage and she knew she was there. She felt a sense of euphoria. The thing wasn't pushed into its full depth but it was nestled safely inside her and Kim knew she had probably gone through the worse now.

She glanced to one side and saw the stunning dark figure of Mistress Nemesis over her and the fearsome black strap-on, partly inserted into her arse. Kim had to admit it looked awesome. Having got the false cock comfortably inside Kim she started to fuck her, at first with long gentle strokes, sliding the strap-on inside her and gradually pushing it further and further into Kim's sex. Kim felt it filling her up as though her whole back-side was being stretched. It was a peculiar feeling, not painful as she remembered it from her first experience, but certainly challenging. It was on that boundary between pain and pleasure that Kim had experienced often in Nemesisland, a sensation she had grown to love. It was also wonderfully, gloriously submissive. The idea that another woman could take her in this way just turned Kim on immensely.

The momentum of the strokes started to increase and Kim could see reflected in the mirror the black strap-on going quickly inside her. Mistress Nemesis was holding onto Kim by the hips and pushing in and out hard. Kim could see she was working up a sweat herself and putting a huge effort into filling her. He long black hair was swinging back and forth with the movement. It was such a decadent and horny act, thought Kim, now a new convert to anal pleasure. The sensations in her arse were amazing, like every nerve ending inside her was alive and the juices in her cunt were flowing. Mistress Nemesis now leant over her so the full weight of her body was resting on Kim's and the movements became yet harder and faster.

Her body started to shake as the pvc clad body pressed down onto her, fucking her wildly. She expelled a squeak and groan and came. Kim could hardly believe that anal penetration could have that effect on her but it had. Mistress Nemesis did not stop though. She continued to pound into Kim as more waves of orgiastic pleasure spread over her.

Eventually she thread the strap-on out of Kim's back-side and dismounted from the whipping bench. Her breath was heavy and, unusually for her, she looked a bit dishevelled from the exertion she had put into fucking Kim's arse. She stood in front of her, her hands on her hips. Kim could hardly believe that the huge object had been right inside her, that her tiny arse-hole had taken such a thing.

Mistress Nemesis put a finger under her chin and lifted her head up so she could look into eyes. Her gaze was still fixed and harsh.

"Do you submit to me?"

"Yes," gasped Kim, "Yes, please, utterly."

With that response she turned away immediately and walked serenely out of the dungeon. Kim looked on in awe as she followed her beautifully rounded pvc clad rear out of the dungeon.

Mistress Nemesis closed the door of her dungeon behind her and exhaled a deep sigh. It was done she reflected; Kim has submitted to me. I had to treat her like that; had to keep up the role, however much I wanted to take her up in my arms afterwards and comfort her. She had given herself up completely and freely. I knew she would. Now the time for revelation and redress is close.

Kim didn't know how to react. Was that it? Was she just going to fuck her up the arse and walk away? Kim was confused, even hurt. Or was she over-reacting? Perhaps there was some other purpose to her actions? Kim had said she trusted her and she did. Kim had said she submitted to her and she did. There was always some new twist and turn in Nemesisland, maybe she had to be patient and see what the next one would be.

In the meantime Vicky was being especially kind and attentive towards her. She had undone her straps and helped her down from the whipping bench. That was nice of her as Kim was still a bit unsteady on her feet. She offered Kim a drink and said that Mistress Nemesis had said she should have a shower before being presented to her again for her next ordeal.

Another ordeal? Was there no end to the extremes of pleasure and torment in this place?

18: Goddess Nemesis's Tale

Vicky led Kim out of the dungeon and into another part of Nemesisland. She was naked except for a leather metal-studded collar and lead, which Vicky was holding onto, and also leather wrist and ankle cuffs linked by chains, which were just about long enough to enable her to walk albeit with some care and effort. They passed along a dark narrow corridor through another door onto a landing. It was an area she had not seen yet; this must have been the staircase I'd been led up earlier when I was blindfolded, thought Kim. Facing her was a set of wooden shutters and Kim could see through the intricate carved gaps in the door into the room beyond. Framed in the dark mahogany she caught a glimpse of the imperious figure of Mistress Nemesis, now dressed in pure white, sat on an ornate carved wooden throne. Kim sensed immediately this was a special place, which she was privileged to look into it. She felt like she was in an Arabian palace and she was a servant granted a furtive glance into a secret place, like a harem, waiting to be called to attend an exotic and powerful sultan.

Vicky pulled the wooden shutters to one side and invited Kim to enter pulling her on by her leather lead. Her bare feet stepped onto soft fibres. Kim looked down; there was no stone floor, like other parts of Nemesisland, but a black carpet and as she cast her eyes across the floor she could see this chamber was divided into two parts separated by a low wooden partition beyond which the floor was covered in black and white tiles in a chequer board pattern. Kim smiled to herself, how apt; a chess board. How fitting that this private domain should be arraigned to represent the games the Red Queen plays with her slaves and to symbolise how they are manipulated as part of an elaborate chess game controlled by this awesome figure. And, yes, I feel like a pawn, reflected Kim. I have been led on, square by square, inexorably to this place. What purpose have I been brought here for? Have I got to end of the board and am about to be elevated to a queen in my own right to sit alongside my mistress or am I still a pawn, destined to move from square to square for ever more at the behest of the Red Queen?

Kim's initial impressions from the furtive glance through the spaces in the wooden door were confirmed. There were links set into the ceiling and floor for suspending slaves, a line of floggers on the walls and opposite the Red Queen's throne a fearsome iron bondage chair but despite these trappings of bondage and sadism this was no dark and forbidding dungeon; It was a private and personal domain. It was well lit, with light flooding through some stained glass windows and its walls were white but decorated sumptuously in black and purple wall hangings and curtains. It was full of precious objects all of which must have had great personal meaning to their owner. It was a special place exuding an atmosphere of mystery and imagination.

On the low wooden partition was an incense burner in the shape of a winged Goddess Isis figure, which sent the exotic and intoxicating scent of frankincense across the chamber. The fumes spread out from the glass bowl mounted on the burner were almost opaque in their density. By some trick of her imagination Kim could see wisps of thick air form into the shape of a hand beckoning her further into Mistress Nemesis's mystical domain.

The piercing blue eyes looked up at her. The black raven, which Kim recognised from the massage parlour an age ago, was perched on the carved scroll that formed the arm rest of the throne. Its dark eyes flicked from its mistress to Kim and back again. Kim sensed the raven knew some reckoning was about to take place and she felt it herself. She had not been brought into this special place for nothing.

"Come forward Kim and kneel before me," the voice commanded.

Kim obeyed instinctively and stepped forward off the carpet onto the cold black and white tiles and walked across to the wooden throne to take her position on her knees in front of the imposing presence she had submitted herself up to. She looked up adoringly. In her heart Kim knew this was where she wanted to be, serving her.

She sat imperiously on her throne dressed in tight tunic made of the finest white Egyptian cotton and embellished with a belt of pure gold and golden bangles around her arm. The cool white material clung to her pale skin accentuating every curve of her body and her full rounded breasts which squeezed out of the dress like two pale half-moons. The impression conveyed was both cool and detached but extremely sensuous. Kim felt her heart pounding as she tried to control the feelings of attraction, even lust, for this magnificent figure. Goddess Nemesis had a flicker of a smile on her lips, almost as if she knew what Kim was thinking. On her sleek ebony hair was perched a diadem of gold decorated with winged figures depicting Nike the goddess of victory. In her right hand she held a golden goblet decorated with beautiful engravings of deer. Behind her throne there was a mirror in which Kim could see herself and the long straight hair of her mistress reflected. To one side of the mirror was a beautiful gilded wheel, which must have once belonged to a magnificent ceremonial chariot. Kim was awe struck.

"Servant Vicky, you may bring my celebration feast in now."

She gestured for Vicky to leave them before turning her attention back to Kim.

"You see me now transformed into another guise," she pronounced, her voice clear and formal. "I appear before you as the Greek Goddess Nemesis, my name-sake, whose mantle I have assumed. You have passed through many trials in your journey through Nemesisland and now the time for revelation and judgement is nearly here. Have you heard of the Greek word 'tyche' Kim?"

Kim nodded her head. She hadn't.

"'Tyche' is the ancient concept of fate of which I am the personification. It is my place to administer fate and judgement. I am a goddess of divine indignation and retribution against evil deeds and also of undeserved good fortune. Happiness and unhappiness are measured out by me so I can restore the balance of the fates. For my male slaves I am the wielder of fairness and I bring balance by correcting them and disciplining them. For you Kim, this is more subtle; for you, I restore the balance of the fates for one who has been wronged, but to do that I must have your complete subservience. Do you understand this Kim?"

"Yes mistress." Kim was not a little bemused by this speech, "I don't know much about 'tyche' or fate but I get this; I do know that in my heart I want to serve you. I've gone through a lot and understand your power and want to submit to you more than anything else."

Kim felt that with all her heart and soul. It was hard to explain despite all the strange things that had happened to her and psychological games played on her, but she really meant it.

Goddess Nemesis nodded quietly, acknowledging Kim's expression of subservience, "that is good Kim; your declaration is sufficient for me to proceed with my purpose."

"You want to be my slave girl, my special servant."

"Yes mistress, I do."

"You want to give yourself up totally to me."

"Yes, with all my heart."

"Yes, I believe you Kim. I see you have committed yourself to me. This is a cause for celebration. Ah, look, here's Vicky with a little feast for us. Will you join me in partaking of some offerings," she said with sly smile spreading across her lips.

"Yes, of course, I'd love to," enthused Kim. She was thrilled at being invited to join Goddess Nemesis in a celebration; how nice of her to ask her to eat with her.

"Don't move Kim, you must stay kneeling at my feet Kim."

Vicky had quietly returned to the chamber carrying a silver platter arraigned with food. Kim could see a flagon of wine, grapes, nuts, a bowl of yoghurt, honey, bread; simple but tasty morsels fit for presentation to a goddess and her acolyte Kim thought. Goddess Nemesis held out her curiously engraved golden goblet and Vicky poured some wine into it. The aroma of the wine with its hint of fruitiness wafted into Kim's nose. It smelt wonderful; what I'd do for a glass of chilled wine she thought expectantly, hoping that Vicky would produce another glass so she could join in this ritual celebration.

Goddess Nemesis put the gold goblet to her lips and sipped the golden fluid. Kim looked up at her as she swallowed. Her gaze fixed meaningfully onto Kim's and she stared straight at her as if she was looking into her very soul. She put the goblet to her lips and took another mouthful. She leant forward from her wooden throne so their noses were nearly touching and their eyes gazed intently into each other. Kim felt the intensity of the moment. Then, she turned to one side and spat the fluid out of her mouth onto the tiled floor. She said nothing. She kept Kim's gaze and merely lifted a finger and pointed at it. Kim knew what she had to do.

She smiled. Why had she believed she would be offered something as simple as a glass of wine? Why had she thought that her mistress, her goddess, would make her life as her slave as easy as that? No, Kim knew what she had to do but she didn't mind; she relished in the task. She got down onto her hands and knees and put her lips to the tiled floor and slurped up a pool of the wine. It was still cool but had lost its sharp chill. It still had the fresh sharp taste of citrus but mingled with that was a hint of Goddess Nemesis's lipstick. It felt wonderful. Kim wanted to drink up every drop that had been spat onto the floor and wallow in the sensuous submissive feeling of drawing in the fluid passed through the mouth of this goddess. Yes sure, it's humiliating, thought Kim, but wickedly and gloriously so. Her tongue licked the floor avidly, greedily sucking in every drop of the precious liquid until none remained. She looked up and saw that Goddess Nemesis had been watching her, appreciating the dedication and enthusiasm with which she had carried out the task.

She took another mouthful of wine and leant forward again. This time, as Kim stared up at her, instead of turning her head to one side she raised a hand and ran her red painted fingernail along Kim's soft lips. A tingle went straight down to her cunt. God, thought Kim; that felt so sensuous. The fingernail gently parted Kim's lips in a gesture which invited Kim to open her mouth. Oh my god, is she really going to, thought Kim. Her cunt was sopping in anticipation. And sure enough, Kim was right. Goddess Nemesis leant right over her until their mouths were nearly touching and Kim could practically taste her lipstick and then she pursed her lips and let a spurt of the clear crisp white wine, swilled and warmed up in her cheeks, flood into Kim's expectant mouth. Kim nearly came on the spot. She wanted it so much, it was such a glorious and sexy act; humiliation and reward all mixed together so Kim could hardly tell where one finished and the other began. Kim rather thought it was the latter but it didn't matter to her; she just wanted to suck the fluid in and draw it down into her own body so that part of her mistress was inside her.

Goddess Nemesis turned to Vicky again, who was standing patient and erect, in more ways than one as Kim could detect a hard-on bulging through her petticoats and maid's dress. She picked up a small bunch of grapes and plucked a couple off for herself and popped them into her mouth. Kim could see some of the juice from the grapes on her lips as mistress raised a finger and softly wiped it from her lips and then held it out for Kim to suck off. Kim's heart raced. She picked up a piece of bread from the silver platter, broke it into a few pieces, offered one to her black raven and aimlessly tossed the rest onto the floor scattering them over the black and white floor tiles.

She stared back at Kim, "I hope you're enjoying your little feast Kim. You didn't think you could yet sit alongside me as an equal and share my food and drink with you, did you? You're still only permitted to eat the cast-off's from my plate. Now, crawl on all fours and eat the bread from the floor."

Kim did as she was told and crawled with difficulty, struggling with the chains between her ankle and wrist cuffs that hampered her movement. She picked it up one piece of dried bread between her teeth, chewed it and then swallowed. She crawled on all fours to pick up each of the pieces that had been scattered over the tiles before returning to her mistress and kneeling obediently before her. Goddess Nemesis had picked another bunch of grapes and had picked one off and popped it into her mouth. She took another one but this time she dropped it nonchalantly onto the floor in front of Kim. Then she gently kicked off her golden sandals and, with a bare foot, crushed the grape against a black tile. Kim stared down at the squidgy green mess. Once again, she knew what she had to do and bent down to lick the mixture of pulp and juice off the floor. It tasted sweet, all the more so for having been crushed by her mistress's bare toes.

Kim looked up expectantly again. What a wonderful feast this was turning out to be, she thought.

Vicky passed Mistress Nemesis a golden bowl with yoghurt and honey and a sliver spoon. After taking a few mouthfuls, she leant forward and tipped the bowl emptying some of its contents over her own foot. Kim knew what she had to do. She bent over her feet and started to lick them clean, eating up the cool creamy yoghurt, working her tongue into every gap between her toes until they were clean.

Mistress Nemesis lifted her feet up and Vicky poured sticky golden honey all over the soles of her feet. She stood up, as statuesque figure towering over the girl crouched at her feet.

"Follow me Kim. You must follow my tracks and lick up every morsel of honey from the floor."

She took hold of the leather lead and led Kim behind. Her ankles and wrists were still chained together but had enough slack for her to crawl on all fours behind her mistress, her goddess. It was a slow and stately procession, as after each step Kim bent down to lick up each honeyed footprint off the black and white tiles. It should have been humiliating, indeed it was, but Kim felt exhilarated by this intensely submissive and erotic task. She licked up the golden nectar left imprinted by her mistress's foot eagerly not wanting to miss any drop of the sweet sticky honey infused with aromas and warmth of the soles of mistress's feet. They walked a circle around her throne in silence, save for the sound of Kim's eager licking as she followed in the footsteps of Goddess Nemesis.

When they had completed their circuit she took up her place on her throne again and beckoned her forward.

"Come here Kim," she commanded and Kim obeyed without question.

Goddess Nemesis patted her lap gesturing to Kim to climb onto her throne and sit on her lap. Kim's pulse raced with anticipation as she settled her fleshy back-side onto the cool cotton of her tunic. Kim felt the warmth of her body against her and the gentle swelling of her breasts against her own. Goddess Nemesis reached over to the platter of food Vicky was still patiently holding. Kim's chest was heaving; it felt so intimate, so wonderful to feel the soft flesh against her own. She reached out a hand and scooped up a handful of dried fruit and nuts and put them into her mouth. She fixed her inscrutable blue eyes onto Kim's; those eyes which had Kim mesmerised on their first encounter in Nemesisland and which had observed her all through her journey, sometimes cruel, sometimes mocking, sometimes affectionate.

She leaned over, the scent of her body now overwhelming the sickly smell of incense and their lips touched with a gentle kiss. Kim's heart pounded with a mixture of awe and devotion, their lips parted slightly and Goddess Nemesis flicked her tongue into Kim's mouth passing some of the sweet mixture of masticated fruit and nuts and holding their mouths together as they shared the feast. Kim was floating in heaven, locked in this embrace being fed from her goddess's own mouth like a little baby bird. She felt so warm, wanted and protected.

Then she felt it. It was the merest touch; a gentle brush of a finger against her pubic hair but it sent Kim into a swoon of erotic pleasure. Her cunt was sopping with the sensuality and intimacy of the moment, but that one touch, that one gentle touch, was nearly enough to send her over the edge. Kim said nothing but she was pleading, "touch me, please, please touch me there, please." She felt a finger run along her cunt lips soaked with the juices flowing from her and with one gentle flick, one of those long elegant fingers eased into her cunt and gently started to massage the walls of her sex. Kim pulled her lips away, swallowed the remains of food in her mouth and groaned with pleasure. Her cunt was throbbing. "Touch it, please touch it," Kim pleaded in her head. And, as if reading her mind, Goddess Nemesis, pulled her finger out of her cunt and touched Kim's clit gently, just once. It took just one touch for Kim to scream out and her whole body to pulsate with pleasure as she came. She didn't stop rubbing and Kim's body continued to writhe and shudder with sheer physical delight.

"Fuck, oh fuck. Fuck, that's so good," she gasped.

Goddess Nemesis laughed. She pulled a lock of fair hair from Kim's sweating brow and gave her a hug.

"A special treat for my special slave girl," she whispered in her ear.

Kim's head was in a whirl. All the sensations she had experienced in Nemesisland seemed to reach a climax in that one moment.

She had called her special. Nobody had done that before; all through her childhood and her disturbed adolescence, even her parents, no-one had used them expression until now, by this strange, exotic and powerful woman.

They sat for a few minutes with their arms around one another and Kim nestled into the goddess' warm embrace, tears welling up in her eyes. Finally she spoke, curiosity finally overcoming her.

"But why, please tell me, why am I so special? I still don't understand. The black cat spoke about me being chosen; he said I had been selected by you as some kind of acolyte. Is that true? How can that be? And why, why would you choose me? What could I possibly have brought to your world?"

Goddess Nemesis sighed deeply, "I think the time has come Kim for you to hear the rest of your story; the part of the tale the black cat has no knowledge of. It is time for me to restore the balance of tyche, of your fate, Kim."

"What do you mean?" Kim asked.

Goddess Nemesis let Kim get down form her lap and sit crouched at the foot of her throne expectantly before beginning her tale.

"Kim, you need to go back many centuries, perhaps to the early 16th century. You have to remember that, then, most of Eastern Europe was covered with dark and impenetrable forests. The depths of these forests were occupied by many magical spirits. You will be familiar with fairy tales from those parts of Europe, Kim, many of which have passed on in oral tradition. They often speak of the forests as being places of great mystery where spirits thrived and that was indeed true. Now, in these parts of Europe the forests were ruled over by the spirit of Samovila, a mighty Slavic goddess of the woods and a fertility goddess. She acted as a ward and protector of the forests.

"Now, it came to pass that on one day the Goddess Samovila was strolling through the forest when her leg got caught in a trap carelessly hidden in the undergrowth by a hunter. The sharp metal spikes dug into her flesh and bone causing her to pass out. Luckily, she was found by a passing woodcutter, who seeing only an injured girl who needed help, released her from the trap and carried her back to his cottage to tend to her. He put a splint on her broken bones and healing herbs on the torn flesh. The Goddess Samovila was unable to walk for some time and stayed in the woodcutter's humble dwelling until her leg gradually healed. The wood cutter was gentle and kind and they both shared a love for the forest, its trees and the creatures that dwelt in it and the Goddess Samovila warmed to him.

"Over the time that Samovila was recovering from her injuries they grew close and, being a goddess of fertility, and it not being unknown for goddesses to consort with mortals, the two fell in love and they bore one child, a daughter. They lived happily together for many years until the wood cutter died peacefully in his old age, never realising that he had shared his life with the goddess of the woods. After this, the Goddess Samovila returned to the spirit world from where she continued her guardianship of the forests but passed on to her daughter the knowledge of her true nature and also her understanding of the forest for her daughter to take up her mantle in the world of mortals.

"Now Kim, we move on a few years later, into the 1530s. You have to know that these were turbulent times. The new religion was in schism, torn apart by the teachings of the protestant faiths and, on top of that, there were those that believed the return of the new religion's messiah was imminent and who sought to build, by force if necessary, their idea of heaven on earth to receive him. All the Germanic lands were divided by conflicting faiths, war and peasant revolts. And, in amongst all this, the old superstitions remained and the new religion started to fight back to recover its control.

"This was a very dangerous time for a person such as the daughter of a forest goddess because knowledge of the woods and understanding of the herbs and plants that grew in them, even when they were used to help and heal, was considered akin to witchcraft. In these troubled times, when everybody was so fearful of the unknown and, whipped up into hysteria by the new religion's fear of heresy and revolt, women, wise and magical women, like this one, were at great risk. And so it came about that, even though living deep in the forest and trying to keep herself apart from the superstitious villagers, this woman was eventually denounced as a witch and burned at the stake. But, before that, she did have a child, another daughter, and in her the spirit of Goddess Samovila still lived on and continued to do so, being passed on generation by generation through the female line. But knowledge of this got lost in the mists of time and through the generations the connection of these women with Goddess Samovila became forgotten.

"And so we move on Kim, to the twentieth century. Here is a woman, living in the forests of Eastern Europe on the borders of what are now Hungary and the Czech Republic. She was the most fecund of women. She bore her husband nine daughters. Her husband longed for a male child, a male heir for him, but his wife only produced daughters. He could not understand it, but his wife did. Somewhere, deep in her psyche, she grasped the meaning of this. She may not have known the whole truth but she knew that nine was a mystical number and she understood that having nine daughters was meaningful and symbolic. We are now in 1944 and the family had survived most of the war as humble peasants living in the woods. But then a tragic event occurred. As the Nazis were driven back through Eastern Europe by Russian troops so they retreated through the villages and forests where this family lived needlessly ravaging and slaughtering along the way. And so it happened that they came across this particular family and, for no real reason, they were picked on and became the victims of war and were slaughtered by the German troops. Except for the youngest girl, who, still being a babe in arms, was never found by the soldiers. She survived and was brought up by another family who found her and took her in.

"Now, Kim, we roll forward another generation. The girl is now a woman; she has moved to what became Yugoslavia and, because of the spirit in her soul, is moved to live in the forests of Bosnia-Herezogovnia. And here's a curious thing Kim, unbeknownst of the life and fate of her own mother, she also has nine daughters, bearing them well into her middle age and remaining fertile as if by some curious design or fate. Her husband is uncomprehending. How is it possible for a woman to bear so many girls and no boy? But once again, the woman understands, she sees that it is fate there is something meaningful in it. And her youngest daughter is different.

She does not have the dark hair and Slavic looks of her other children; she is fair."

Goddess Nemesis stared meaningfully into Kim's eyes. Kim was transfixed. She said nothing, but her look urged Goddess Nemesis to continue the tale until its end.

"Listen carefully Kim. Would you believe how cruel fate can be? Would you believe that history could repeat itself? But this is what happened, Kim. Once again, an innocent family, trying to live the only way it knew, from the woods and forests, caught up in the ravages of war and conflict. As the Balkans were thrown into turmoil and Bosnian and Serb, Christian and Muslim fought one another in a savage civil war borne out of a poisonous mixture of nationalism and the faiths of the new religions, so this humble family got tangled in the web of war. And so it happened again, and history repeated itself. Caught in the conflict the whole family was slaughtered, except, yes Kim, except for the youngest daughter, the tiny fair haired baby girl."

"No, no. That can't be. What are you saying? You surely can't mean? That's not possible!"

Kim had been listening patiently working out where this curious tale might be going; hanging on to Goddess Nemesis's every word, trying to think through how all of this connected with her. Suddenly it hit her. The shattering conclusion of the tale struck her like a thunderbolt.

"Yes, Kim. That's exactly what I'm saying. That baby was you."

Kim was incredulous, "No, that can't be so. But, how did I end up here in England then."

"As a baby you were found in the forest and given up to an adoption agency and placed with a family in England. Did your adoptive parents never tell you anything of this?"

"No, nothing. Nothing at all. To be honest I wasn't an easy child and I was a real handful as a teenager. But no, I hadn't the faintest idea."

"But, do you not understand the significance of this Kim? The last surviving ninth daughter of a ninth daughter; the blood of a Slavic forest goddess passed on to you through the centuries. And you wonder why you would be chosen? You wonder why a pagan goddess would not want you for her own?"

"That's special, isn't it?"

"Oh Kim, you can't believe how special that makes you. The rumour had spread amongst the world of goddesses that there was a special girl, the ancestor of the forest goddess, Samovila, whose existence had been long forgotten and who had suffered much and was blissfully ignorant of who she really was. So, you were sought out and I selected you as my acolyte to be trained. But enemies of the sisterhood of goddesses heard of this tale and of the thirteen girls chosen as novices and targeted them. This was why you were taken and this takes you up to the tale you were told by the black cat; much of this had been eradicated from your memory and has been hidden from you. But now, it is time for you to know who you really are. Now it is time for your personal 'tyche', your fate, to be turned around Kim."

"Shit," said Kim, "I can't take it in. You're telling me that I'm a descendent of some 16th century pagan forest spirit?"

"Yes, that's exactly it Kim."

"The ninth daughter of a ninth daughter?"

"Yes Kim, and that's very powerful and symbolic."

"Shit, do you expect me to believe this?"

"Yes, Kim; it's all true. And you do believe it, don't you. Look deep inside yourself. Trust me; I know what you feel in your heart."

Kim felt so confused. She tried to pull up fragments from her past to make sense of it and seek any clue that might verify the astonishing revelation she had been given. But, Goddess Nemesis's instinct was right; seeking facts or evidence was pointless. In her heart she believed it. She trusted her.

"This strange path you've laid out for me; it's been to bring me to this moment hasn't it?"

"Yes Kim. Our lives are connected. I just needed to choose the right moment to bring you back and reveal it."

Goddess Nemesis got down from her throne, knelt on the floor beside Kim and took her in her arms in an embrace. She kissed her on the cheek.

"Are you alright Kim?" she asked affectionately.

"I think so. I believe what you've told me. It just feels too weird to take in."

"I'll leave you for a moment so you can have time for some solitude and quiet reflection."

She stood up and stepped bare-footed out of her special chamber. Before leaving she threw a glance back at Kim still knelt on the tiled floor. There was a tear in her eye. It was done; her purpose had been fulfilled and the balance of the fates restored. Kim had shown all the qualities she needed and expected from her and there she was, not just her slave girl, but her sister in spirit. It would be hard for Kim to take in but she had all the fortitude of the goddess spirit in her and she wasn't concerned for her. And there was the ball to look forward to; Kim would enjoy that!

Vicky led Kim out of the dungeon and into another part of Nemesisland. She was naked except for a leather metal-studded collar and lead, which Vicky was holding onto, and also leather wrist and ankle cuffs linked by chains, which were just about long enough to enable her to walk albeit with some care and effort. They passed along a dark narrow corridor through another door onto a landing. It was an area she had not seen yet; this must have been the staircase I'd been led up earlier when I was blindfolded, thought Kim. Facing her was a set of wooden shutters and Kim could see through the intricate carved gaps in the door into the room beyond. Framed in the dark mahogany she caught a glimpse of the imperious figure of Mistress Nemesis, now dressed in pure white, sat on an ornate carved wooden throne. Kim sensed immediately this was a special place, which she was privileged to look into it. She felt like she was in an Arabian palace and she was a servant granted a furtive glance into a secret place, like a harem, waiting to be called to attend an exotic and powerful sultan.

Vicky pulled the wooden shutters to one side and invited Kim to enter pulling her on by her leather lead. Her bare feet stepped onto soft fibres. Kim looked down; there was no stone floor, like other parts of Nemesisland, but a black carpet and as she cast her eyes across the floor she could see this chamber was divided into two parts separated by a low wooden partition beyond which the floor was covered in black and white tiles in a chequer board pattern. Kim smiled to herself, how apt; a chess board. How fitting that this private domain should be arraigned to represent the games the Red Queen plays with her slaves and to symbolise how they are manipulated as part of an elaborate chess game controlled by this awesome figure. And, yes, I feel like a pawn, reflected Kim. I have been led on, square by square, inexorably to this place. What purpose have I been brought here for? Have I got to end of the board and am about to be elevated to a queen in my own right to sit alongside my mistress or am I still a pawn, destined to move from square to square for ever more at the behest of the Red Queen?

Kim's initial impressions from the furtive glance through the spaces in the wooden door were confirmed. There were links set into the ceiling and floor for suspending slaves, a line of floggers on the walls and opposite the Red Queen's throne a fearsome iron bondage chair but despite these trappings of bondage and sadism this was no dark and forbidding dungeon; It was a private and personal domain. It was well lit, with light flooding through some stained glass windows and its walls were white but decorated sumptuously in black and purple wall hangings and curtains. It was full of precious objects all of which must have had great personal meaning to their owner. It was a special place exuding an atmosphere of mystery and imagination.

On the low wooden partition was an incense burner in the shape of a winged Goddess Isis figure, which sent the exotic and intoxicating scent of frankincense across the chamber. The fumes spread out from the glass bowl mounted on the burner were almost opaque in their density. By some trick of her imagination Kim could see wisps of thick air form into the shape of a hand beckoning her further into Mistress Nemesis's mystical domain.

The piercing blue eyes looked up at her. The black raven, which Kim recognised from the massage parlour an age ago, was perched on the carved scroll that formed the arm rest of the throne. Its dark eyes flicked from its mistress to Kim and back again. Kim sensed the raven knew some reckoning was about to take place and she felt it herself. She had not been brought into this special place for nothing.

"Come forward Kim and kneel before me," the voice commanded.

Kim obeyed instinctively and stepped forward off the carpet onto the cold black and white tiles and walked across to the wooden throne to take her position on her knees in front of the imposing presence she had submitted herself up to. She looked up adoringly. In her heart Kim knew this was where she wanted to be, serving her.

She sat imperiously on her throne dressed in tight tunic made of the finest white Egyptian cotton and embellished with a belt of pure gold and golden bangles around her arm. The cool white material clung to her pale skin accentuating every curve of her body and her full rounded breasts which squeezed out of the dress like two pale half-moons. The impression conveyed was both cool and detached but extremely sensuous. Kim felt her heart pounding as she tried to control the feelings of attraction, even lust, for this magnificent figure. Goddess Nemesis had a flicker of a smile on her lips, almost as if she knew what Kim was thinking. On her sleek ebony hair was perched a diadem of gold decorated with winged figures depicting Nike the goddess of victory. In her right hand she held a golden goblet decorated with beautiful engravings of deer. Behind her throne there was a mirror in which Kim could see herself and the long straight hair of her mistress reflected. To one side of the mirror was a beautiful gilded wheel, which must have once belonged to a magnificent ceremonial chariot. Kim was awe struck.

"Servant Vicky, you may bring my celebration feast in now."

She gestured for Vicky to leave them before turning her attention back to Kim.

"You see me now transformed into another guise," she pronounced, her voice clear and formal. "I appear before you as the Greek Goddess Nemesis, my name-sake, whose mantle I have assumed. You have passed through many trials in your journey through Nemesisland and now the time for revelation and judgement is nearly here. Have you heard of the Greek word 'tyche' Kim?"

Kim nodded her head. She hadn't.

"'Tyche' is the ancient concept of fate of which I am the personification. It is my place to administer fate and judgement. I am a goddess of divine indignation and retribution against evil deeds and also of undeserved good fortune. Happiness and unhappiness are measured out by me so I can restore the balance of the fates. For my male slaves I am the wielder of fairness and I bring balance by correcting them and disciplining them. For you Kim, this is more subtle; for you, I restore the balance of the fates for one who has been wronged, but to do that I must have your complete subservience. Do you understand this Kim?"

"Yes mistress." Kim was not a little bemused by this speech, "I don't know much about 'tyche' or fate but I get this; I do know that in my heart I want to serve you. I've gone through a lot and understand your power and want to submit to you more than anything else."

Kim felt that with all her heart and soul. It was hard to explain despite all the strange things that had happened to her and psychological games played on her, but she really meant it.

Goddess Nemesis nodded quietly, acknowledging Kim's expression of subservience, "that is good Kim; your declaration is sufficient for me to proceed with my purpose."

"You want to be my slave girl, my special servant."

"Yes mistress, I do."

"You want to give yourself up totally to me."

"Yes, with all my heart."

"Yes, I believe you Kim. I see you have committed yourself to me. This is a cause for celebration. Ah, look, here's Vicky with a little feast for us. Will you join me in partaking of some offerings," she said with sly smile spreading across her lips.

"Yes, of course, I'd love to," enthused Kim. She was thrilled at being invited to join Goddess Nemesis in a celebration; how nice of her to ask her to eat with her.

"Don't move Kim, you must stay kneeling at my feet Kim."

Vicky had quietly returned to the chamber carrying a silver platter arraigned with food. Kim could see a flagon of wine, grapes, nuts, a bowl of yoghurt, honey, bread; simple but tasty morsels fit for presentation to a goddess and her acolyte Kim thought. Goddess Nemesis held out her curiously engraved golden goblet and Vicky poured some wine into it. The aroma of the wine with its hint of fruitiness wafted into Kim's nose. It smelt wonderful; what I'd do for a glass of chilled wine she thought expectantly, hoping that Vicky would produce another glass so she could join in this ritual celebration.

Goddess Nemesis put the gold goblet to her lips and sipped the golden fluid. Kim looked up at her as she swallowed. Her gaze fixed meaningfully onto Kim's and she stared straight at her as if she was looking into her very soul. She put the goblet to her lips and took another mouthful. She leant forward from her wooden throne so their noses were nearly touching and their eyes gazed intently into each other. Kim felt the intensity of the moment. Then, she turned to one side and spat the fluid out of her mouth onto the tiled floor. She said nothing. She kept Kim's gaze and merely lifted a finger and pointed at it. Kim knew what she had to do.

She smiled. Why had she believed she would be offered something as simple as a glass of wine? Why had she thought that her mistress, her goddess, would make her life as her slave as easy as that? No, Kim knew what she had to do but she didn't mind; she relished in the task. She got down onto her hands and knees and put her lips to the tiled floor and slurped up a pool of the wine. It was still cool but had lost its sharp chill. It still had the fresh sharp taste of citrus but mingled with that was a hint of Goddess Nemesis's lipstick. It felt wonderful. Kim wanted to drink up every drop that had been spat onto the floor and wallow in the sensuous submissive feeling of drawing in the fluid passed through the mouth of this goddess. Yes sure, it's humiliating, thought Kim, but wickedly and gloriously so. Her tongue licked the floor avidly, greedily sucking in every drop of the precious liquid until none remained. She looked up and saw that Goddess Nemesis had been watching her, appreciating the dedication and enthusiasm with which she had carried out the task.

She took another mouthful of wine and leant forward again. This time, as Kim stared up at her, instead of turning her head to one side she raised a hand and ran her red painted fingernail along Kim's soft lips. A tingle went straight down to her cunt. God, thought Kim; that felt so sensuous. The fingernail gently parted Kim's lips in a gesture which invited Kim to open her mouth. Oh my god, is she really going to, thought Kim. Her cunt was sopping in anticipation. And sure enough, Kim was right. Goddess Nemesis leant right over her until their mouths were nearly touching and Kim could practically taste her lipstick and then she pursed her lips and let a spurt of the clear crisp white wine, swilled and warmed up in her cheeks, flood into Kim's expectant mouth. Kim nearly came on the spot. She wanted it so much, it was such a glorious and sexy act; humiliation and reward all mixed together so Kim could hardly tell where one finished and the other began. Kim rather thought it was the latter but it didn't matter to her; she just wanted to suck the fluid in and draw it down into her own body so that part of her mistress was inside her.

Goddess Nemesis turned to Vicky again, who was standing patient and erect, in more ways than one as Kim could detect a hard-on bulging through her petticoats and maid's dress. She picked up a small bunch of grapes and plucked a couple off for herself and popped them into her mouth. Kim could see some of the juice from the grapes on her lips as mistress raised a finger and softly wiped it from her lips and then held it out for Kim to suck off. Kim's heart raced. She picked up a piece of bread from the silver platter, broke it into a few pieces, offered one to her black raven and aimlessly tossed the rest onto the floor scattering them over the black and white floor tiles.

She stared back at Kim, "I hope you're enjoying your little feast Kim. You didn't think you could yet sit alongside me as an equal and share my food and drink with you, did you? You're still only permitted to eat the cast-off's from my plate. Now, crawl on all fours and eat the bread from the floor."

Kim did as she was told and crawled with difficulty, struggling with the chains between her ankle and wrist cuffs that hampered her movement. She picked it up one piece of dried bread between her teeth, chewed it and then swallowed. She crawled on all fours to pick up each of the pieces that had been scattered over the tiles before returning to her mistress and kneeling obediently before her. Goddess Nemesis had picked another bunch of grapes and had picked one off and popped it into her mouth. She took another one but this time she dropped it nonchalantly onto the floor in front of Kim. Then she gently kicked off her golden sandals and, with a bare foot, crushed the grape against a black tile. Kim stared down at the squidgy green mess. Once again, she knew what she had to do and bent down to lick the mixture of pulp and juice off the floor. It tasted sweet, all the more so for having been crushed by her mistress's bare toes.

Kim looked up expectantly again. What a wonderful feast this was turning out to be, she thought.

Vicky passed Mistress Nemesis a golden bowl with yoghurt and honey and a sliver spoon. After taking a few mouthfuls, she leant forward and tipped the bowl emptying some of its contents over her own foot. Kim knew what she had to do. She bent over her feet and started to lick them clean, eating up the cool creamy yoghurt, working her tongue into every gap between her toes until they were clean.

Mistress Nemesis lifted her feet up and Vicky poured sticky golden honey all over the soles of her feet. She stood up, as statuesque figure towering over the girl crouched at her feet.

"Follow me Kim. You must follow my tracks and lick up every morsel of honey from the floor."

She took hold of the leather lead and led Kim behind. Her ankles and wrists were still chained together but had enough slack for her to crawl on all fours behind her mistress, her goddess. It was a slow and stately procession, as after each step Kim bent down to lick up each honeyed footprint off the black and white tiles. It should have been humiliating, indeed it was, but Kim felt exhilarated by this intensely submissive and erotic task. She licked up the golden nectar left imprinted by her mistress's foot eagerly not wanting to miss any drop of the sweet sticky honey infused with aromas and warmth of the soles of mistress's feet. They walked a circle around her throne in silence, save for the sound of Kim's eager licking as she followed in the footsteps of Goddess Nemesis.

When they had completed their circuit she took up her place on her throne again and beckoned her forward.

"Come here Kim," she commanded and Kim obeyed without question.

Goddess Nemesis patted her lap gesturing to Kim to climb onto her throne and sit on her lap. Kim's pulse raced with anticipation as she settled her fleshy back-side onto the cool cotton of her tunic. Kim felt the warmth of her body against her and the gentle swelling of her breasts against her own. Goddess Nemesis reached over to the platter of food Vicky was still patiently holding. Kim's chest was heaving; it felt so intimate, so wonderful to feel the soft flesh against her own. She reached out a hand and scooped up a handful of dried fruit and nuts and put them into her mouth. She fixed her inscrutable blue eyes onto Kim's; those eyes which had Kim mesmerised on their first encounter in Nemesisland and which had observed her all through her journey, sometimes cruel, sometimes mocking, sometimes affectionate.

She leaned over, the scent of her body now overwhelming the sickly smell of incense and their lips touched with a gentle kiss. Kim's heart pounded with a mixture of awe and devotion, their lips parted slightly and Goddess Nemesis flicked her tongue into Kim's mouth passing some of the sweet mixture of masticated fruit and nuts and holding their mouths together as they shared the feast. Kim was floating in heaven, locked in this embrace being fed from her goddess's own mouth like a little baby bird. She felt so warm, wanted and protected.

Then she felt it. It was the merest touch; a gentle brush of a finger against her pubic hair but it sent Kim into a swoon of erotic pleasure. Her cunt was sopping with the sensuality and intimacy of the moment, but that one touch, that one gentle touch, was nearly enough to send her over the edge. Kim said nothing but she was pleading, "touch me, please, please touch me there, please." She felt a finger run along her cunt lips soaked with the juices flowing from her and with one gentle flick, one of those long elegant fingers eased into her cunt and gently started to massage the walls of her sex. Kim pulled her lips away, swallowed the remains of food in her mouth and groaned with pleasure. Her cunt was throbbing. "Touch it, please touch it," Kim pleaded in her head. And, as if reading her mind, Goddess Nemesis, pulled her finger out of her cunt and touched Kim's clit gently, just once. It took just one touch for Kim to scream out and her whole body to pulsate with pleasure as she came. She didn't stop rubbing and Kim's body continued to writhe and shudder with sheer physical delight.

"Fuck, oh fuck. Fuck, that's so good," she gasped.

Goddess Nemesis laughed. She pulled a lock of fair hair from Kim's sweating brow and gave her a hug.

"A special treat for my special slave girl," she whispered in her ear.

Kim's head was in a whirl. All the sensations she had experienced in Nemesisland seemed to reach a climax in that one moment.

She had called her special. Nobody had done that before; all through her childhood and her disturbed adolescence, even her parents, no-one had used them expression until now, by this strange, exotic and powerful woman.

They sat for a few minutes with their arms around one another and Kim nestled into the goddess' warm embrace, tears welling up in her eyes. Finally she spoke, curiosity finally overcoming her.

"But why, please tell me, why am I so special? I still don't understand. The black cat spoke about me being chosen; he said I had been selected by you as some kind of acolyte. Is that true? How can that be? And why, why would you choose me? What could I possibly have brought to your world?"

Goddess Nemesis sighed deeply, "I think the time has come Kim for you to hear the rest of your story; the part of the tale the black cat has no knowledge of. It is time for me to restore the balance of tyche, of your fate, Kim."

"What do you mean?" Kim asked.

Goddess Nemesis let Kim get down form her lap and sit crouched at the foot of her throne expectantly before beginning her tale.

"Kim, you need to go back many centuries, perhaps to the early 16th century. You have to remember that, then, most of Eastern Europe was covered with dark and impenetrable forests. The depths of these forests were occupied by many magical spirits. You will be familiar with fairy tales from those parts of Europe, Kim, many of which have passed on in oral tradition. They often speak of the forests as being places of great mystery where spirits thrived and that was indeed true. Now, in these parts of Europe the forests were ruled over by the spirit of Samovila a mighty

Slavic goddess of the woods and a fertility goddess. She acted as a ward and protector of the forests.

"Now, it came to pass that on one day the Goddess Samovila was strolling through the forest when her leg got caught in a trap carelessly hidden in the undergrowth by a hunter. The sharp metal spikes dug into her flesh and bone causing her to pass out. Luckily, she was found by a passing woodcutter, who seeing only an injured girl who needed help, released her from the trap and carried her back to his cottage to tend to her. He put a splint on her broken bones and healing herbs on the torn flesh. The Goddess Samovila was unable to walk for some time and stayed in the woodcutter's humble dwelling until her leg gradually healed. The wood cutter was gentle and kind and they both shared a love for the forest, its trees and the creatures that dwelt in it and the Goddess Samovila warmed to him.

"Over the time that Samovila was recovering from her injuries they grew close and, being a goddess of fertility, and it not being unknown for goddesses to consort with mortals, the two fell in love and they bore one child, a daughter. They lived happily together for many years until the wood cutter died peacefully in his old age, never realising that he had shared his life with the goddess of the woods. After this, the Goddess Samovila returned to the spirit world from where she continued her guardianship of the forests but passed on to her daughter the knowledge of her true nature and also her understanding of the forest for her daughter to take up her mantle in the world of mortals.

"Now Kim, we move on a few years later, into the 1530s. You have to know that these were turbulent times. The new religion was in schism, torn apart by the teachings of the protestant faiths and, on top of that, there were those that believed the return of the new religion's messiah was imminent and who sought to build, by force if necessary, their idea of heaven on earth to receive him. All the Germanic lands were divided by conflicting faiths, war and peasant revolts. And, in amongst all this, the old superstitions remained and the new religion started to fight back to recover its control.

"This was a very dangerous time for a person such as the daughter of a forest goddess because knowledge of the woods and understanding of the herbs and plants that grew in them, even when they were used to help and heal, was considered akin to witchcraft. In these troubled times, when everybody was so fearful of the unknown and, whipped up into hysteria by the new religion's fear of heresy and revolt, women, wise and magical women, like this one, were at great risk. And so it came about that, even though living deep in the forest and trying to keep herself apart from the superstitious villagers, this woman was eventually denounced as a witch and burned at the stake. But, before that, she did have a child, another daughter, and in her the spirit of Goddess Samovila still lived on and continued to do so, being passed on generation by generation through the female line. But knowledge of this got lost in the mists of time and through the generations the connection of these women with Goddess Samovila became forgotten.

"And so we move on Kim, to the twentieth century. Here is a woman, living in the forests of Eastern Europe on the borders of what are now Hungary and the Czech Republic. She was the most fecund of women. She bore her husband nine daughters. Her husband longed for a male child, a male heir for him, but his wife only produced daughters. He could not understand it, but his wife did. Somewhere, deep in her psyche, she grasped the meaning of this. She may not have known the whole truth but she knew that nine was a mystical number and she understood that having nine daughters was meaningful and symbolic. We are now in 1944 and the family had survived most of the war as humble peasants living in the woods. But then a tragic event occurred. As the Nazis were driven back through Eastern Europe by Russian troops so they retreated through the villages and forests where this family lived needlessly ravaging and slaughtering along the way. And so it happened that they came across this particular family and, for no real reason, they were picked on and became the victims of war and were slaughtered by the German troops. Except for the youngest girl, who, still being a babe in arms, was never found by the soldiers. She survived and was brought up by another family who found her and took her in.

"Now, Kim, we roll forward another generation. The girl is now a woman; she has moved to what became Yugoslavia and, because of the spirit in her soul, is moved to live in the forests of Bosnia-Herzegovina. And here's a curious thing Kim, unbeknownst of the life and fate of her own mother, she also has nine daughters, bearing them well into her middle age and remaining fertile as if by some curious design or fate. Her husband is uncomprehending. How is it possible for a woman to bear so many girls and no boy? But once again, the woman understands, she sees that it is fate there is something meaningful in it. And her youngest daughter is different. She does not have the dark hair and Slavic looks of her other children; she is fair."

Goddess Nemesis stared meaningfully into Kim's eyes. Kim was transfixed. She said nothing, but her look urged Goddess Nemesis to continue the tale until its end.

"Listen carefully Kim. Would you believe how cruel fate can be? Would you believe that history could repeat itself? But this is what happened, Kim. Once again, an innocent family, trying to live the only way it knew, from the woods and forests, caught up in the ravages of war and conflict. As the Balkans were thrown into turmoil and Bosnian and Serb, Christian and Muslim fought one another in a savage civil war borne out of a poisonous mixture of nationalism and the faiths of the new religions, so this humble family got tangled in the web of war. And so it happened again, and history repeated itself. Caught in the conflict the whole family was slaughtered, except, yes Kim, except for the youngest daughter, the tiny fair haired baby girl."

"No, no. That can't be. What are you saying? You surely can't mean? That's not possible!"

Kim had been listening patiently working out where this curious tale might be going; hanging on to Goddess Nemesis's every word, trying to think through how all of this connected with her. Suddenly it hit her. The shattering conclusion of the tale struck her like a thunderbolt.

"Yes, Kim. That's exactly what I'm saying. That baby was you."

Kim was incredulous, "No, that can't be so. But, how did I end up here in England then."

"As a baby you were found in the forest and given up to an adoption agency and placed with a family in England. Did your adoptive parents never tell you anything of this?"

"No, nothing. Nothing at all. To be honest I wasn't an easy child and I was a real handful as a teenager. But no, I hadn't the faintest idea."

"But, do you not understand the significance of this Kim? The last surviving ninth daughter of a ninth daughter; the blood of a Slavic forest goddess passed on to you through the centuries. And you wonder why you would be chosen? You wonder why a pagan goddess would not want you for her own?"

"That's special, isn't it?"

"Oh Kim, you can't believe how special that makes you. The rumour had spread amongst the world of goddesses that there was a special girl, the ancestor of the forest goddess, Samovila, whose existence had been long forgotten and who had suffered much and was blissfully ignorant of who she really was. So, you were sought out and I selected you as my acolyte to be trained. But enemies of the sisterhood of goddesses heard of this tale and of the thirteen girls chosen as novices and targeted them. This was why you were taken and this takes you up to the tale you were told by the black cat; much of this had been eradicated from your memory and has been hidden from you. But now, it is time for you to know who you really are. Now it is time for your personal 'tyche', your fate, to be turned around Kim."

"Shit," said Kim, "I can't take it in. You're telling me that I'm a descendent of some 16th century pagan forest spirit?"

"Yes, that's exactly it Kim."

"The ninth daughter of a ninth daughter?"

"Yes Kim, and that's very powerful and symbolic."

"Shit, do you expect me to believe this?"

"Yes, Kim; it's all true. And you do believe it, don't you. Look deep inside yourself. Trust me; I know what you feel in your heart."

Kim felt so confused. She tried to pull up fragments from her past to make sense of it and seek any clue that might verify the astonishing revelation she had been given. But, Goddess Nemesis's instinct was right; seeking facts or evidence was pointless. In her heart she believed it. She trusted her.

"This strange path you've laid out for me; it's been to bring me to this moment hasn't it?"

"Yes Kim. Our lives are connected. I just needed to choose the right moment to bring you back and reveal it."

Goddess Nemesis got down from her throne, knelt on the floor beside Kim and took her in her arms in an embrace. She kissed her on the cheek.

"Are you alright Kim?" she asked affectionately.

"I think so. I believe what you've told me. It just feels too weird to take in."

"I'll leave you for a moment so you can have time for some solitude and quiet reflection."

She stood up and stepped bare-footed out of her special chamber. Before leaving she threw a glance back at Kim still knelt on the tiled floor. There was a tear in her eye. It was done; her purpose had been fulfilled and the balance of the fates restored. Kim had shown all the qualities she needed and expected from her and there she was, not just her slave girl, but her sister in spirit. It would be hard for Kim to take in but she had all the fortitude of the goddess spirit in her and she wasn't concerned for her. And there was the ball to look forward to; Kim would enjoy that!

19: The Fetish Ball

Kim was overwhelmed with a mixture of emotions. Part of her was still confused. The bizarre nature of her story would be entirely unbelievable if she had not gone through this strange rite of passage which made her trust the Red Queen so implicitly. Exotic temples, kidnapping, strange rituals and ceremonies, Knights Templar chapels, aborted pregnancies, adventures and escapes; had all that really happened to her? And with all knowledge of it wiped from her memory? Can you imagine it, she reflected, the looks she'll get in the pub when she tells people, "Come on show me some respect here, after all you're talking to a woodland goddess you know, the ninth daughter of a ninth daughter..." No, I think I'll have trouble getting people to buy into that one.

Balanced against the maelstrom of confusion and amazement was another emotion, and that was one of a sense of belonging and it was this one that took the upper-hand. Suddenly, and perhaps for the first time in her life, she felt she had a sense of place. She had never got on with what she now realised must were her adoptive parents, never felt part of home or fitted in at school, had friends but drifted from one group to another. Finally, she took up a job that encouraged treating people in a detached way, as objects to make money out of. She was still reeling from the full significance of the revelations of Goddess Nemesis. But, there was no question that in her heart she believed them. Deep inside her the final denouement of her story had touched her profoundly. She felt something inside her, something powerful and magical. She didn't understand it fully or how she could begin to build up her new life with this knowledge about herself but she was deeply affected by the experience.

She pulled her hands up to her face and wiped away the tears that streamed down her cheeks. She couldn't explain why she was crying. She wasn't upset as such, quite the opposite; she felt elated about belonging to the world she had been brought into.

"Are you OK Kim?"

It was the Duchess's gentle voice as a kind hand reached out to touch her bare shoulder. Kim was still kneeling next to the Red Queen's throne.

"Yes, really I'm fine. A bit emotional and mixed up but no, I'm good. It's just such a lot to take in. You know, am I really that person…the descendent of a forest goddess? And what does it all mean?"

"It's all new to me too. I'm only her maid. I don't know all her plans. I knew you were something special to her. I knew she was desperate to have you enter her world and to do so of your own free will, but I had no idea why. You'll have a special place in her heart and in Nemesisland. She'll help you, I'm sure of that. And she is awesome and powerful. She communes with goddess spirits, I know she does."

Kim laughed, "Yeah, I can believe that."

"Come on Kim; let's get you ready for the ball. It's in your honour you know. It's to welcome you into her world."

"Oh yeah, I'm rather looking forward to it."

The Duchess led Kim into her mistress's changing room. There was no rush; the guests would not be arriving for a while. Goddess Nemesis had an important piece of business to attend to, though the Duchess didn't know what it was, so for the first time since her adventures in Nemesisland started Kim had some genuine time to relax and chill out and also to take stock of everything that had happened to her. She showered and had the nicest, hottest, sweetest mug of tea she had ever tasted. All her sensations were alive from the physical and mental exertions of her journey through Nemesisland.

Once again, the Red Queen's stipulations as to Kim's dress were precise and it was left to the Duchess to carry them out exactly.

"Madam wants you to go to the ball dressed as a bird of paradise," explained the Duchess.

"Oh well, that sounds interesting," said Kim.

Kim was offered a feathered mask, its brightly coloured plumage in vibrant colours of red, gold and turquoise stretched high above her head. Apart from the mask Kim was entirely naked, except for a pair of impossibly high heeled ankle boot coated with feathers matching the same shades as her headdress. Having her soft flesh so exposed and knowing that she would be in full view of all the guests should have made her feel vulnerable but strangely she did not. As soon as she had pulled the mask over her face she felt a strange sensation wash over. She felt exotically dangerous. Her alert eyes would peer through the brightly coloured layers of feather across her face watching and judging everything. The elaborate headdress towering over her made her feel tall and imposing. The naked curves of her body did not feel exposed or vulnerable but alluring and powerful like she was a magnificent totem figure to be revered and worshipped. It was as if the mask had quixotic and magical powers. Awesome, Kim thought.

Mistress Nemesis returned more imperious than ever, dressed again as the Red Queen. In addition to the red pvc dress decorated with black hearts she also wore a sweeping black pvc cloak over her shoulders and in the place of the tiara was a full golden crown perched on the top of her ebony hair. In one hand she grasped her red and black leather whip and in the other a golden sceptre. She was at her most imposing and fearsome but reserved for Kim a conspiratorial glint in her eye.

"I had an important piece of business to attend to," she said enigmatically, turning to the Duchess to add, "I trust the preparations for the ball are completed Duchess?"

"Yes, your majesty," the Duchess replied nervously, "and the guests have arrived and are waiting your entrance."

The Red Queen turned to look at Kim, "You look splendid, simply beautiful. When you are released all eyes will turn to you and you'll light up the ball with your radiant beauty and newly discovered goddess spirit I'm sure."

"Released?" queried Kim.

The Red Queen smiled, Kim had come to accept the unusual in her mistress's world.

"Oh but of course Kim," she laughed, "you have to be put in a cage and admired first before I can bring you out to play with my guests, You needn't worry Kim. I promise you it won't be an onerous ordeal. I think you'll find it quite entertaining to watch proceedings and I'll need your assistance, Kim, to dispense punishments because there will be some retribution I need to administer."

She cast a sidelong glance at the Duchess, "yes you may well look on in trepidation. But for you Kim, my newly acquired slave girl and fellow goddess spirit, the ball is what you want to make of it. You can take what entertainment and pleasure from it in any way you desire. You are, after all, the guest of honour."

Kim glowed with a sense of satisfaction and belonging at the Red Queen's words.

"Come; let us make our grand entrance."

The Red Queen threaded her arm through Kim's and they both paraded out of her dressing room. In the lobby before the Red Queen's private chamber there were two curious figures, one male and one female, both dressed in suits of the tightest and shiniest red latex. They immediately stood to attention when the Red Queen appeared. They shuffled anxiously. The tight rubber covered them completely, including their heads, with just holes for their eyes, nostrils and mouths. The rubber clung to every contour of their bodies. Kim could see the pert nipples of the girl standing proud and the voluptuous roundness of her hips and tight little buttocks stretching against the restraining rubber. The line of the man's cock and balls was clearly visible behind the latex. The girl had three black hearts and a figure three emblazoned across her chest and back whilst the male had five black hearts and the number five. Fetish playing cards smiled Kim to herself.

The Red Queen bent down and put her finger into a tiny drop of thick liquid on the tiled floor. Her eyes flashed with anger and Kim recognised the temper she had encountered herself through her journey. Her voice lashed out at her servants in a menacing tone.

"What, pray tell me, is the meaning of this?"

"Your majesty. It's red paint."

"Yes, I can see that you fool, but what is it doing on my floor."

The withering stare and malevolent tone of the Red Queen's voice elicited looks of fear and alarm from the two fetish cards.

Finally, the man stuttered nervously, "We're very sorry you majesty… but…we mistakenly ordered white roses instead of red ones and, well, we thought we could paint them red before the ball started."

"You idiots. You thought you could fool me with such an obvious deception. I saw immediately," said the Red Queen indignantly pointing a scarlet fingernail at the vase of painted roses on the sideboard as a drop of red paint dripped from a petal.

"Sorry your majesty."

"Yes, we're very sorry you majesty," echoed the man.

"Sorry is not good enough. You know this is a special occasion. What will my guests think when I have such useless slaves that they can't even order the right colour roses? You'll be punished for this."

"Off with their heads, I say," smiled Kim mischievously.

"Hmm, I don't think I need to go so far with such lowly servants. How do you think you'll ever become fully-fledged characters in Nemesisland if you can't carry out such a simple task?""

The two fetish playing cards hung their heads in shame. She took the girl's nipples between the tips of her fingers, squeezed tightly and twisted.

"Ooh, please your majesty," she squealed.

"And furthermore, you can't take your punishment."

She turned to the male figure and did the same. He squirmed uncomfortably with the sudden shot of pain in his nipples.

"The ball is about to start, so I haven't time to deal with you properly but rest assured you will get your just punishment for your incompetence."

"Yes your majesty," they said in unison.

"Right, let's carry on Duchess. I'm not going to let this little interlude spoil my pleasure. You can announce my arrival now."

The Duchess opened the shuttered doors to the Queen of Hearts' private domain where all her guests were assembled and announced, "Her Majesty, The Red Queen, mistress and ruler of Nemesisland."

Kim heard a burst of applause from inside the chamber. The Red Queen was smiling and acknowledging the approbation. Kim followed behind her.

"Today is a special day. Today is the day I welcome my special novice and acolyte back into my world. Kim is very special to me. She answers only to me in Nemesisland, and all of you will do whatever she asks of you. But for now, I'm going to put my little bird of paradise in a cage so you can all admire her."

The Red Queen gestured for Kim to climb into a large Perspex box by her side. It was hardly a cage in the conventional sense. Kim suddenly felt very exposed and on show. But all the guests applauded and looked at her admiringly as the Duchess closed the clear plastic door behind her and padlocked it.

"Let the ball begin," the Red Queen proclaimed. "The whole of Nemesisland is at your disposal for you amusement and pleasure, or pain, whichever is your particular predilection."

Kim looked out at her surroundings from behind the transparent plastic wall. The Red Queen's private domain had been decorated with wall hangings of red velvet decorated with giant black hearts. Candles in cast iron candelabra's cast an atmospheric red glow over the room. The red fetish playing cards were acting as waiters carrying trays of bright red drinks, clearly some exotic cocktail especially concocted for the occasion. Other fetish cards carried black trays with nibbles on; bright little baby tomatoes, sliced red peppers, red chilli dip, paprika dusted corn chips and slices of fiery hot raw chillies. Another set of trays had fruits on; strawberries, raspberries, cherries and pomegranates. Everything had clearly been executed to The Red Queen's exacting standards and looked perfect. Kim gazed on admiringly at how the red and black theme had been executed throughout the room.

Kim turned her attention to the guests. They clearly had permission not to dress in the red and black and for that reason they seemed to stand out all the more against the background. Kim recognized some of the characters she had already encountered in Nemesisland. The white rabbit was there; it seemed an age since her first introduction to him. Tweedledum and Tweedledee, the two curious figures who had rescued her were there; on this occasion not dressed for battle but as Kim remembered in the classic story book images as tubby little men in white breeches, winged collars, little black ties and red and white caps balanced precariously on their round heads. The walrus and the carpenter were present as well as the two slaves from the tea party. Nano, the black cat was there as well though the Red Queen had still not turned him back into a man yet.

Kim's eyes lit-up. She recognised that cock. It belonged to that sumptuous hunk of a head-boy from the headmistress's school room. He was dressed as the knave of hearts in a latex patterned jacket in yellow, blue, white and red but no trousers so his magnificent penis was left dangling for all to admire. Hmm, that's interesting, thought Kim. I'll look out for him when I get released from this cage.

There were also other guests, both male and female, who Kim didn't recognize; some dressed as characters she knew from the Alice stories and others in an assortment of multi-coloured fetish wear. For some inexplicable reason Kim's attention was drawn to a pair of tight muscular buttocks that belonged to a hooded figure. They seemed strangely familiar somehow though Kim couldn't recall from where.

Dominating proceedings was the Red Queen herself. Soon after the guests had partaken of their welcoming drink and had something to eat the Red Queen was soon orchestrating proceedings, ordering the Duchess or the black cat to put guests into various forms of bondage for her. There was one guest spread-eagled secured to links in the floor and ceiling, another hog-tied onto the floor. Other guests dispersed into the dungeon and the other rooms of Nemesisland. They helped themselves to the array of floggers, paddles and whips hanging from hooks on the wall. The party developed into a mixture of a BDSM fetish club extravaganza and orgy under the watchful eye of the smiling Red Queen.

Kim was starting to feel a bit left out when the Duchess approached the plastic cage, unlocked the padlock and released her into the throng of party guests. Kim climbed out of the cage, a little unsteady at first as she teetered on the heels of her feather covered boots and still a bit stiff from crouching in the box for a little while. She tottered towards The Red Queen who greeted her with a hug.

"Welcome, my dear. I'm glad you've joined the proceedings. All of my guests are at your disposal for whatever pleasures you wish to take for yourself or pain you desire to administer. You must have no qualms about what you do. In my eyes they all deserve to be punished, don't they Duchess!"

"Oh yes, certainly Madam," she replied warily.

"There's one more ceremony to perform," she announced.

There was a drum roll and one of the fetish playing cards, the ten of hearts, led with a snare drum around his neck followed by another fetish card, the nine of hearts, who carried a huge silver platter with a massive plum cake on it. Either side of the cake were two figures. Kim smiled; it was two of the Red Queen's slaves transformed, one into a unicorn with a long conical horn sticking out of his forehead, the other an elderly lion wearing a pair of tortoise shell glasses. The unicorn was dressed in ceremonial dress in a tunic and breeches in the bright colours of a picture card and a wide white ruff around his neck. The guests, or at least those who weren't in some form of bondage, all gathered around.

The Red Queen made a proclamation, "Today is a very special day. Today is the day I've been re-united with my own appointed slave girl and acolyte, Kim. It's a very auspicious day and I'd like you all to join with me in sharing some of my special plum and champagne cake."

The Duchess handed her a huge silver knife.

"If you would do the honours please Kim," she said gesturing to her to cut some slices.

Kim started to cut the cake but no sooner had she cut a slice as they joined themselves up again. How queer thought Kim.

"It's a Nemesisland cake," whispered the Red Queen, "you have to hand it around first and cut it afterwards."

"Oh," said Kim. "Well of course, I suppose I should have realised that."

So she did just that and took the silver platter around and the cake divided itself into pieces before her very eyes as she offered it to the guests.

"How curious," Kim commented as she took a large bite out of her own piece. She liked fruit cake.

"Is it nice?" asked the Red Queen.

"Delicious," replied Kim, "it's ever so moist and it has quite a distinctive tang to it."

"Can you guess the special ingredient?" The Red Queen smiled.

"Hmm, no, is it lemon peel?"

"...It's the champagne of course, silly."

Oh well, it tasted nice Kim thought as she took another bite.

Having finished her cake Kim was eager to join in the throng of the party. But where to start? She began by whipping the slave with his wrists secured to the ceiling and his ankles to the floor. She teased him by playing with his cock and making him hard and then hitting it with a flogger. She played with the girl who was hog-tied on the floor. She teased her by rubbing her shoulders and reaching under her to gently touch the tops of her breast squashed against the floor. She let the feathers of her headdress brush against her bare back and arse. She ran he fingers along her cunt and teased her throbbing little clit before putting her fingers up her cunt. That made her purr, thought Kim. All of this was great fun but it was also turning Kim on and she wanted to concentrate on something she could really get her teeth into. She had a thought. She'd always loved unicorns; they were magical and mystical creatures which had always appealed to her imagination. The idea of being fucked by or, better still, fucking a unicorn was quite an attractive one and the Red Queen had said she could do anything and command anyone at the party.

She strode purposefully towards the unicorn who was talking with the lion.

"Come with me. I've a use for you," Kim commanded.

He looked at Kim nervously but followed her obediently. They knew that to disobey her instructions would bring the wrath of the Red Queen down on them and they didn't want that and, besides, the tone of Kim's order was such they were never going to dispute the young mistress's order. Kim led the way to the dungeon with the unicorn following in tow.

Excellent, thought Kim, the rack was still free. Kim commanded the unicorn to remove his breeches and large unflattering white knickers underneath and ordered him onto the rack.

"You're a monster, young mistress. A fabulous monster," the unicorn cried out.

"Why yes of course I am, now shut up and do as I say."

"Yes, of course mistress," he deferred.

"Besides, it might not be all horrible for you.

Kim set to work with the ropes, pulling them through the hooks at the side of the rack and tightening them across the unicorn's body until he was secured to the rack. She leant over the unicorn's head and stroked the tuft of hair on his head and stroked his ears. She ran her hand sensuously up the twisted and gnarled horn that stuck out from his forehead.

"I've always been fascinated by unicorns," she said. "I used to dream how one would come into my bedroom at night and seduce me. And now look, what a lucky girl I am, my dream's come true, except now I've got the chance to seduce a unicorn."

As she spoke her sparkling green eyes looked out at him through the exotic feathered mask and a hand strayed down to his exposed crotch. She brushed her fingers against his erection. His cock was already taught and hard from the gentle touch of Kim's naked body against his as he was being tied onto the rack. It was also hard at the mere thought of what Kim might do to him. Kim ran her fingers up and down his shaft, occasionally digging her nails into the flesh. She didn't want to go too far in administering the pain as she wanted to make sure the unicorn retained his erection. Her cunt juices were flowing now and she wanted it inside her. She wanted to take her pleasure.

A female guest dressed as a fetish Alice in blue and white latex just had Kim had been at the fetish hatter's tea party earlier was looking on fascinated.

"Can I join in, Kim?" she asked.

"Yes, of course, the more the merrier," said Kim.

Kim went down on the unicorn. She grasped his cock in her hands and took it firmly between her lips. As she did that the Alice played with his horn running her hands up and down the ribbed ivory. Kim could see out of the corner of her eye as she was sucking cock that she was getting turned on by the act of handling the horn. Hmm, pondered Kim, perhaps that where the expression 'horny' originated from! She set to work running her lips up and down the unicorn's shaft as he groaned in ecstasy at having cock and horn played with by two dominant and sexy females.

Enough of this, thought Kim, it's time for me to take my pleasure. She climbed up onto the rack. She didn't need any further stimulation; her cunt was already wet with anticipation as it hovered tantalisingly above him.

"Yes, it's your lucky day unicorn," Kim said as she lowered herself onto him.

The unicorn gasped and Kim moaned as she drove herself down on him. She was sopping and eager and the hard cock slid straight into her, penetrating deep into her cunt. It was magical, just as she imagined fucking a unicorn ought to be.

Meanwhile the Alice at his head had her own plans. She had clearly become aroused from stroking his horn but wanted to go further. She had now mounted the rack and was wiggling her pretty little arse and pushing her fanny into the unicorn's face so she could smell the erotic scent of her sex. She pulled her latex skirt up and clambered onto the rack and to Kim and the unicorn's amazement lowered herself down onto the horn. It was too long for her to take the whole length but she used her strong thigh muscles to support herself and lower herself up and down onto the horn. What a sight they must look, laughed Kim. There was Kim dressed as a bird of paradise, her hips thrusting up and down on the hard cock, her brightly feathered headdress bobbing up and down and at the other end a fetish Alice mounting a unicorn horn.

The two women worked in unison, riding the cock and horn in tandem and running their eager cunts up and down their respective shafts. Kim loved the sensation as she lowered herself up and down the unicorn's shaft forcing it deep into her and then moving her hips sensuously in a circling motion. It was made all the more exciting for watching the fetish Alice opposite her riding the unicorn horn, her blonde hair flying around her with the exertion and her red cheeks getting more and more flushed with every motion. The two women looked across at each other and laughed.

They tried to read each other's reactions and the groans of pleasure emitted from their lips as their fucking drove them on to their climaxes. Kim was close now and she could see the other girl was too. It would be delightful, she thought, if they could time it to come together. And so they did as simultaneously they both let out a screech of pleasure and their bodies shuddered with wave after wave of orgasm. At the same time the unicorn gasped as he shot his load into Kim's cunt. Oh my word, thought Kim, suppose I get pregnant and give birth to a child that's part girl, part unicorn. How very bizarre that would be.

The two exhausted but very satisfied girls dismounted the unicorn. Kim caught a fleeting glimpse between the revellers in the dungeon of the distinctive patterned tail coat belonging to the knave of hearts; the head boy from the headmistress's study. There was a fetish playing card on her knees in front of him sucking his cock.

"Sorry Alice," announced Kim, "got to dash, just seen an old friend!"

She skipped off to renew acquaintances with the delectable Digby Everard. She wanted more of that long hard cock inside her. It appealed to Kim to seduce the jack of hearts, not that she expected to encounter too much resistance from him. But, this time Kim intended to take control. She crept up behind him and surreptitiously lifted the latex tails of his coat to reveal a nice tight back-side squirming in time to the sucking motion as the playing card girl fellated his cock. She lifted her hand up and gave a massive slap against the firm flesh. He jumped in surprise and turned his head around to see who had administered the stroke.

"I hope you haven't been stealing tarts knave," Kim sniggered, "or you'll really be in trouble with the Red Queen."

The young man laughed. He slid is cock from the paying card's mouth and with a gentle nod sent the disappointed girl packing. He turned round to face Kim, his cock stood up proud, the girl's saliva still glistening on its bulbous red tip. It looked every bit as huge and magnificent as she remembered from the school scene. He looked delicious with his tousled hair, dark brown eyes and his cocky smile.

"The girl from the headmistress's study," he exclaimed, "my you've come up in Nemesisland since I fucked you. The Red Queen's special companion and slave girl. Who'd of thought, after being such a disobedient girl?"

"You bet, and I've got a little score to settle," she replied laying another hard slap on his buttock, "I'm no naughty school girl now. Kim's the joker in the pack and I trump everyone except the Red Queen, even the knave of hearts, so you'd better do what I say."

Kim wrapped her arms around his muscular chest and pulled him tight against her breasts so she could feel the pliant latex against her body. She nuzzled the nape of his neck and planted kisses and bites as her fingers ran down his body seeking out the hard flesh of his erect cock which she could feel pressing urgently against her. They parted slightly so she could take it in her hands and run her fingernails along its throbbing shaft. It felt great to have it in her hand. She was going to have it inside her, but this time on her own terms.

Kim pushed him backwards. She had already spotted her destination as she manoeuvred him back to an arched-back chair in the corner of the dungeon. It was a bondage chair with hooks and eyelets set into its wooden arms and legs; Kim could see that but she had no intention of tying him onto it. She wanted those strong hands left free, free to massage her swollen breasts and touch her aching pussy. She pushed his chest and he slipped obediently back into the chair, anticipating where Kim wanted him to be. He'd go straight to the bottom of the class after she had finished with him, she thought.

Kim pinned him back against the chair with the palms of her hands. Their eyes met with a fusion of mutual attraction and sexual tension. Kim wanted this young man. She ran her fingers through his brown curls and then took his face in her hands and kissed him, thrusting her eager tongue into his mouth. He tasted delicious with a hint of strawberries from the trays of delicacies at the ball. They explored each other's mouths eagerly with mutual lust.

As their lips finally parted Kim lifted herself up onto the chair and held herself over the young knave's cock supporting herself by reaching out against the back of the chair. She looked down at him, strands of her wavy fair hair tumbling onto his face and into his mouth. His hands reached up to stroke her swollen breasts and a tingle of arousal went down to her cunt. But Kim was already wet, her cunt still filled with the spunk of the unicorn and sopping with lust for him.

"Fuck, I want you inside me now," she gasped.

She lowered herself onto him and he reached down to grasp his erect cock and direct it into Kim's aching, sopping hole. Kim groaned as it slid into her and she let the weight of her body drop down to impale herself on the full length of the long shaft. It filled her gloriously. Kim rode him expertly. She rocked her hips back and forth. She slid her cunt up and down his shaft and he responded with thrusts of his hips to penetrate her even deeper all whilst the young man was sucking on her nipples and using his fingers to play with her aching little bud.

She was supremely skilled at giving sexual pleasure of course but this wasn't to satisfy the needs of any paying client, this wasn't even to submit to one of Nemesisland's strange characters and bizarre human animals.

This was all for her. This was for her pleasure. This was to satisfy her needs and hers alone. She'd felt an animal attraction to this young man, gazing up at him through her legs in the headmistress's study and now she'd got what she wanted; his cock inside her, his tongue exploring her breasts and his fingers massaging her swollen clit to her inevitable orgasm.

"Hmm, having fun I see Kim." The Red Queen laughed approvingly at the sight of her young charge extracting such pleasure from the knave of hearts.

"Mmmm," moaned Kim her whole body riding on the knave of hearts cock, her tits bouncing up and down with the pumping motion and her matted hair, sweaty from the exertion, swinging.

Kim eased the pace of her fucking. The Red Queen stroked Kim's hair and planted a kiss on her flushed cheeks leaving a pursed red mark in scarlet lip-stick. Kim picked up the movement of her fucking again. This time the Red Queen's hands reached around her and took her nipples between her gloved fingers and squeezed and twisted the swollen mounds of sensitive flesh. The knave of heart's cock pressing against the walls of her cunt, his fingers rubbing her clit and now the exquisite nipple torture all conspired to catapult Kim into ecstasy. The wonderful mixture of pain and pleasure sent her squealing over the top as she finally reached a pulsating orgasm. The knave of hearts soon followed as he released himself into her with his own groans of pleasure. Kim wrapped her arms around him and pulled him tight, panting heavily with a mixture of exertion and delicious pleasure.

The Red Queen left the two young people to wallow in their enjoyment as they continued to kiss and touch each other with all the tenderness of new lovers. The head boy had met his match in Kim and yet, she reflected, it was good that she might find a companion in Nemesisland. Kim had exceeded all her expectations. She had truly entered into the spirit of Nemesisland. Kim had demonstrated all the qualities she had hoped for and all the resilience and power passed on through her distinguished lineage.

Eventually she drew their attention back to her presence.

"Well Kim, I've just been administering some punishments in my isolation room, would you like to join me?

The bird of paradise followed her mistress through into the adjoining room. It was crammed full of slaves and guests in different forms of bondage; in the iron cages, chained onto the wall, hog-tied onto the floor. The Red Queen had clearly been enjoying herself. The Duchess was there on a wooden chair her arms tied up with rope above her, her legs apart and her petticoats pushed to one side, her cock and balls exposed and two sticky pads on her balls. The Red Queen picked up the little controller and turned the knobs up high sending a tingling electric current through the Duchess's balls.

"Even the most loyal of my servants don't escape, do they Duchess?" She exclaimed. "He's being punished for playing with you behind my back Kim. Come over her, I've another miscreant here who needs punishing."

The Red Queen led Kim over to a large black wooden isolation box. There was a tiny wooden shutter door at one end which she pulled back to reveal the whiskered face and floppy ears of the white rabbit.

"I'm punishing him for being late, just as I said I would. He's been locked away for most of the ball now. I'll need him later as he's my emissary and Nemesisland's clerk of court. But, for now he has had to endure this isolation and punishment."

Kim could see he had been tied into the box with nipple clamps on. She also saw there was another little wooden door where his genitals would be and she slid that back to see a penis in a bush of fluffy white pubic hair. A wicked little thought passed through Kim's head.

The Red Queen turned the switch of the electric toy up and the Duchess in the corner groaned and twisted in pain.

"Oh do shut up Duchess. You know more than anybody else I can't have my servants interfering with my guests. You know that very well. That'll teach you for playing with Kim without my permission."

"Actually," said Kim, "I'm feeling a little bit peckish after my exertions with the unicorn and lion."

The Red Queen snapped her fingers and one of the fetish playing cards came forward and stood next to Kim holding a tray with a glass of the bright red drink and some nibbles. Kim ravenously tucked into some of the food, dipping peppers and tortilla chips into the spicy red tomato dip and washing them down with the fruity red cocktail. She picked up a long slice of the red chilli. Kim knew only to well the effect this had from when she'd once gone to the loo immediately after chopping some chillies once and inadvertently brushed her cunt with her fingers afterwards. She looked down into the open door in the isolation box and, taking the chilli tentatively between her fingers reached down to the white rabbit's cock. There was a surprised scream at the other end of the box as Kim brushed the fiery red chilli against the white rabbit's member.

The Red Queen smiled a broad grin, "That's my girl. I chose my initiate well. I don't just have a willing slave girl I have mischievous companion and a sister goddess to help out in my world."

The white rabbit was squirming uncomfortably. Tied up in the box as he was he couldn't even see the little object causing him such torment. Kim took his cock between her fingers, gently opened its end and inserted the chilli into the tip of his penis. That certainly made him jump. Kim and the Red Queen laughed together at his predicament. Kim would leave the chilli there for just a while longer. After the initial shock he would soon get used to the pain and it would serve him right for being late and for being such a blubbering idiot when Kim asked him questions to be locked away in the box with that fiery red instrument of torment in his cock. Kim slid the little door back.

The Red Queen handed Kim the electrics controller, "I'm going to leave you for a bit now Kim and see what else is happening at my ball. Are you enjoying yourself?" she asked.

"It's brilliant," exclaimed Kim, "but then what else would I expect from the Red Queen!"

"Why yes of course, thank you my dear," she said as she left the room.

Kim turned up the knobs on the control unit and the Duchess squirmed and groaned in pain.

"I'm sorry Duchess. I know you've been very kind to me but, you know, as the Red Queen says, you can't escape punishment in Nemesisland."

Kim turned the knob up a notch further.

"Ooh. Yes, I know Kim, I know."

As Kim was playing with the Duchess she glanced around and saw a black shadowy figure at the back of one of the cages. It was the black cat.

"She still hasn't turned you back again?"

"No, not yet," he replied. "Can you forgive me for my failings Kim?"

"Oh yes," said Kim. "I don't hold grudges and besides, I kind of feel now that it was all meant to work out this way."

"Yes Kim, I think you're right. After all, she is a goddess of fate as well as retribution. Are you having fun at the ball?"

"Oh yeah," said Kim, "I'm really enjoying myself!"

20: The Trial

The party was reaching a crescendo of frenzied activity. Tweedledum and Tweedledee were walking hand in hand like two little schoolboys watching proceedings excitedly when suddenly they gave a little jump in astonishment. Tweedledum looked at Tweedledee. Tweedledee looked at Tweedledum. They had simultaneously recognised the flash of the distinctive knife tattoo they had seen in the massage parlour where they had rescued Kim.

"It's him!" they exclaimed at the same time.

"We must tell mistress!" they shouted together.

They both set off in a hurry to find the Red Queen, stumbling over one another and bumping into guests in the process. They eventually found her in the dungeon busily whipping one of her guests with a riding crop. They fidgeted at her side waiting to catch her attention.

She turned to them with a look of withering disdain, "What do you fools want? Can't you see I'm busy."

"It's important."

"Yes, it's important," echoed Tweedledum.

"I've seen him."

"No-how. It was me who saw him first."

"Contrariwise, it was me who saw him first."

"Shut up you bickering clowns. Who have you seen?"

"The man who tried to attack Kim in the massage parlour!" they blurted in unison.

"Is that all?" said the Red Queen dismissively.

The mouths in their rotund faces dropped and they looked crestfallen.

"But aren't you going to do something about him?"

"Do you dare to question me?" At the merest arching of an eye brow and narrowing of the piercing eyes the pair realised their error, "You idiots. Do you think I don't know who the guests are at my own party?"

"You mean you invited him?" asked Tweedledum.

"You always knew he was here?" said Tweedledee.

"But of course you fools. I invited him specially."

The two round figures sniggered as the penny dropped.

"Then he's in trouble," said Tweedledum.

"He's in big trouble," said Tweedledee.

"Oh yes," said the Red Queen, a glint of malice in her eye, "nobody assaults my precious slave girl, my acolyte, and gets away with it. Now perhaps you fools can be of use. Gather whoever you need to help you, but I want him captured and secured in my torture chair. Do you think you can do that?"

"Oh yes mistress," they exclaimed together, excited at being of service to the Red Queen and rushing off to do her bidding.

The Red Queen turned around scouring the dungeon for Kim. She wasn't there, so she set off back to the isolation room to find her. Yes, everything was going to plan, she smiled to herself. There would soon be justice administered and retribution delivered. Kim would get her vengeance. She found Kim having just untied the Duchess from her bondage contemplating what more fun she could have with her. She sidled up to her and caught her attention.

"Beware the Jabberwocky, my girl," the Red Queen said with a gentle movement of the head and the slightest of glances across the dungeon.

"What do you mean?"

Kim was puzzled at first until she recognised the name of the dragon slain by the white knight in the Alice stories. She didn't realise the full import of the words until she followed the line of the Red Queen's gaze through the open door into the dungeon where a masked man with a blood dripped knife tattoo stood.

"Oh my god," exclaimed Kim as she saw, "that's him, the psycho from the massage parlour. Who invited him?"

"Oh, don't worry Kim, I'm sure I can find an appropriate way of dealing with him," she replied, a wickedly malevolent smile broadening across her red lips.

"I'm sure you can," laughed Kim, "I wouldn't doubt that for a second! You arranged for him to be here?"

"But of course Kim. He'll have to pay for his attempt to assault my acolyte. It's fortunate my idiotic agents got there just in the nick of time before you were defiled by him."

The two women looked on as Tweedledum and Tweedledee and a handful of guests grasped Kim's assailant. He was muscular and strong and struggled violently but they had the element of surprise and numbers and he was soon overwhelmed and dragged to the Red Queen's medieval torture chair which directly faced her throne. The heavy iron manacles were closed around his wrists and ankles and, despite his struggling and cursing, he was soon locked into the hideous piece of equipment.

"There's just one more costume change for you Kim. If you go into my changing room you'll see the Duchess has laid some appropriate attire out for you. I'm sure you'll appreciate it. I'll deal with this miscreant until you return."

Kim scuttled off, the shouted abuse of the trapped man echoing in her head. What had Mistress Nemesis got planned for him she wondered.

Whilst Kim was getting changed ready to make her re-appearance the Red Queen approached the iron chair and announced her arrival before Kim's attacker. She leant over him, a towering presence in black and red pvc.

"Who the fuck are you? Let me go," he screamed.

"I hear you've finally found your voice."

"What the fuck do you want with me, you perverted witch?"

"Oh my, now that's not very wise is it considering the predicament you're in?" she said calmly. "You are in Nemesisland now, the world of the Red Queen and the Goddess Nemesis. All do as I command in my realm."

"You're mad! What the fuck are talking about."

"Oh dear, I'm afraid I can't accept language like that. It's very rude you know, especially when you're talking to the party's host. Duchess, get my ball gag," she ordered.

The Duchess handed her a gag with a red rubber ball and leather strap. Tweedledum forced his mouth open as the Red Queen pushed the rubber ball into his gaping mouth. He had no choice but to close his mouth around it as she tightened the strap at the back of his head. Muffled noises came from behind the gag.

"Now, that's better, isn't it? I can't be disturbed by all this shouting and abuse. You see this chair," she said, leaning over him and whispering in his ear, "It's one of my very special toys. It's modelled on a real piece of medieval torture equipment you know. It's designed to keep slaves and miscreants trapped ready for their punishment. Can you imagine it? Can't you just hear the screams of agony as they are subjected to torture?"

"Nnngg," the voice behind the ball gag grunted.

"Who knows what torments men were made to suffer in devices like these? Can't you visualise the metal pincers as they closed around a man's balls and gradually crushed them or better still as they squeezed his useless and helpless cock until he screamed in pain?"

"Nnngg," his body shook violently in a futile attempt to break his restraints.

As she was speaking the Red Queen completed securing him to the chair by closing an iron band around his chest and pulling a metal bar down against his thighs and padlocking both into position.

The Red Queen continued to torment him, "And of course, there was always the red hot poker. And this neat piece of equipment offers up all sorts of possibilities, it leaves lots of sensitive parts of the body exposed," her voice rose in a menacing tone, "like your arse-hole for instance."

"Nnngg."

Finally, an iron head cage was closed around his face. The Red Queen stepped back and admired her handy work. He was shackled into the iron chair, her fearsome piece of medieval torture equipment built to her exact specification.

She continued, "But you see; I'm very fair. I wouldn't punish you without a trial. After all, that wouldn't be right, would it? I believe in dispensing justice. There'll be evidence heard and witnesses you know."

At that point the guests who had gathered around the torture chair to see what was going on turned their heads. Bless her, thought the Red Queen, Kim's timing is impeccable; it must be in her blood.

At that moment Kim entered the chamber. All heads turned and the guests gasped in approbation as Kim stood there head to toe in a white pvc skirt and basque decorated with black hearts and silver trim balanced on a pair of white stiletto heeled shoes. She had re-appeared as the White Queen. She was the mirror image of her mistress but she was pure white and blonde to her mistress's red and ebony. There was a hushed silence as Kim stepped imperiously across the floor tiles the stiletto heels clicking against the floor with each measured stride. She stood alongside the Red Queen and cast a withering look at the figure in the iron chair. He looked up and his eyes registered recognition of the girl he'd encountered in the massage parlour. She looked different now, scary and powerful. He remembered the moment well as since that day his life had followed a strange sequence of events that had led to him being knocked out by anonymous attackers, invited, quite innocently as he thought, to a fetish party, right up to his current predicament, locked into a medieval torture chair. It finally dawned on him there was a purpose to him being invited to this strange event.

"Yes, there will be a trial and then a judgement," announced the Red Queen.

"Punishment first, then the evidence," called one of the guests.

"Punishment first, then the evidence," the angry call was repeated around the room.

The Red Queen held her hand up to silence them.

"No, let it not be said that we don't do things properly in Nemesisland. White rabbit. Come forward and pronounce the charge."

The white rabbit, now released from the isolation box and in full ceremonial dressed and looking very officious, scurried forward. The Red Queen retired to her throne, summoned the Duchess to find another chair and beckoned Kim to sit at her side. The court room was soon arraigned. The accuser faced the accused and the guests formed orderly rows at either side of the chequered floor tiles to observe the proceedings. The Duchess and white rabbit acted as the court usher and clerk.

"It is alleged that the accused did try," the white rabbit coughed, embarrassed, "oh dear, oh dear, that he did try to penetrate Kim, the acolyte of Mistress Nemesis, the descendent of the woodland goddess Samovila and the White Queen up the back passage against her will."

"Do you deny this charge?" demanded the Red Queen.

"Nnnggg," he shook his head.

"Are there witnesses to this alleged foul deed?"

Tweedledum and Tweedledee leapt onto the black and white tiled floor pointing to the man locked in the iron chair.

"I saw him!" shouted Tweedledum.

"No-how, I saw him first. He forced Kim on her front and was about to take her up the arse. It was definitely him."

"Contrariwise, it was me saw him first. He was going to penetrate her up the back-side, no doubt, no how."

"And did he do this against the White Queen's will? Did he try to force himself on her?" enquired the Red Queen.

"Oh yeah, we saw it all," they replied in unison.

"Least ways, I saw it, definitely," said Tweedledee.

"No-how. And me too," echoed Tweedledum.

The Red Queen turned to Kim, "My dear, perhaps the victim could confirm the identity of the accused and recount what happened."

Kim smiled. She was enjoying this. Her newly acquired dominant streak was looking forward to the guilty verdict, which she knew was inevitable, the sentencing and then...the punishment.

"Yes, this is definitely the man who assaulted me in the massage parlour. There's no way I could forget him. I remember the smell of him and his tattoo is very distinctive. He tried to take me against my will. I pleaded with him to stop but there's no doubt he would have entered me if Tweedledum and Tweedledee hadn't come to my help."

They both looked terribly smug and pleased with themselves under their school caps.

The Red Queen rose up from her throne and in a few elegant steps glided towards the iron chair.

"So, you have heard the charge and the evidence, what is you plea?"

"Nnngg,"

"Sorry, I can't hear you. You'll have to speak more clearly than that."

The accused could only mumble his complaints into the ball gag.

"I'm sorry but this won't do. You have to enter a plea or it will constitute a contempt of court. Do I have to torture you to get a plea out of you?"

The man's eyes widened in terror; he was guilty and trapped. The malicious glint in the Red Queen's look told him she wasn't joking. Muttering rose up in the court room, "yes he ought to enter a plea, make him confess, torture him."

The Red Queen smiled, her lips broadening into a malevolent grin. Yes, this is what she really enjoyed, especially with a culprit who was guilty, who obviously deserved to be punished. And, of course, she could not take contempt of her court and failure to enter a plea or admit his guilt lightly, even if his mouth cheeks were filled with a hard rubber ball gag. She looked contemptuously down at his cock and took the hard object in her hands.

"So, your predicament excites you does it? You show so little reverence for the Red Queen's court you get aroused. That just won't do, will it? I'll have to do something about that."

She grasped the tip of his cock between two red finger nails and squeezed. The sharp edge of the hard varnished nail dug into his glans. She pressed harder until he was spluttering into the ball gag with pain. The cock had lost some it's hardness but the Red Queen wasn't finished. She took up the red and black leather flogger and held its black heart shaped tip in front of his face tormenting him with the threat of further punishment.

"You see, it just won't do. I can't put up with such defiance in my court."

The leather heart licked the waning tumescence of his cock, rolled it against its soft black leather and then pressed it against the cold iron of the chair. She was toying with him. She raised the flogger up and brushed it against his muscular arms and toned chest in a playful tease before the real pain was administered. Suddenly the flogger descended in one swift motion onto his cock pressing its softening flesh against the metal and sending a shooting pain through his throbbing member. Another four strokes followed in quick succession. It was now an object of throbbing redness as the Red Queen warmed to her task. Muffled screams were deadened by the ball gag.

"I'll make it a little easier for you. You don't have to say guilty or not guilty. I will accept a nod of the head. So, are you guilty of the offence?"

This interrogation was followed by another succession of hard strokes with the flogger. The searing pain was excruciating.

"Nnnggg."

The man's head nodded wildly up and down in acknowledgement of his guilt and to stop the cruel punishment being administered to his sore and aching cock before the red witch did any permanent damage to it.

"Excellent, now we have an admission of guilt, the court can proceed to sentencing," smiled the Red Queen.

Sentencing? If Kim's assailant believed his confession would end his ordeal he was in for a rude awakening. The Red Queen retired to her throne and turned to Kim.

"In a spirit of just retribution the court calls on the victim, the White Queen, to determine the offender's punishment."

Kim smiled. Yes, she thought, she will get her vengeance on him. It didn't take her much reflection to come up with the perfect punishment for him. From the first moment the Red Queen had pointed him out to her at the ball she knew what she'd like to do to him and her journey through Nemesisland had provided her with the desire and abilities to carry it through. She leant across and whispered in the Red Queen's ear.

The Red Queen laughed, "Excellent. The White Queen has chosen a very just and apt punishment and as the judge in my own court I will call on her to administer the sentence. Release him and take him into the dungeon."

The gag was removed, the shackles unlocked and the head cage lifted as Kim's assailant was gripped strongly by arm and leg and dragged wriggling and cursing into the dungeon. The Red and White Queens led the way in the regal fashion with a procession of Nemesisland land characters and fetish guests following the sentenced man.

The Red Queen pointed, "Face down on the whipping bench, I think."

He was forced down and hands gloved in a combination of multi-coloured latex, pvc or lace held him down as the Red Queen drew the leather straps across his body and tightened the buckles firmly so the leather dug into his muscular flesh. Bound onto the padded bench on his knees with his head resting in a wooden stock and padlocked into position there was no escape for him. Every sensitive part of his body was exposed. His arse was sticking up in the air and his cock and balls dangled vulnerably beneath him. He had ceased trying to struggle; he was so tightly bound onto the bench that resistance was futile.

He felt hands manipulating his cock. He tried to turn his head around to see what was going on or who it was that was playing with him but it was impossible. It was the Red Queen, who had a long piece of thin cord. She twisted around the base of the glans of his cock and pulled tightly. The man screamed out in shock and pain. The muscles of her wrists bulged with the strain as she drew a loop of the string around his cock and pulled again. The pain was excruciating as the string was woven in a criss-cross pattern tightly around his member each time being pulled with all her strength so he could feel the string digging into the soft flesh. There was no way he could get an erection now. When the Red Queen had manipulated the cord down to the base of his cock she grasped his balls in her hand and separated the two testicles within their sac, pulled a piece of the string across them several times pulling tightly each time making him grunt in agony. She stepped back to admire her work and observe his cock and balls wrapped in a tight web of black cord.

She turned back and resting a hand on the wooden head lock bent down to whisper in his ear.

"There, I'll not be offended by any signs of sexual arousal whilst you endure your sentence," she smiled.

"You bitch. What do you think you're doing?"

"Delivering justly deserved retribution. You are in my world and my laws prevail," she hissed quietly in his ear, "and any more language like that and I've plenty of methods to make you shut up, none of them particularly pleasant."

The man decided that silence was the best option. He knew there was nothing he could do. He could only wait in trepidation for the red witch to administer her sentence, whatever that was going to be. He heard the voice of the Red Queen behind him.

"Come forward my dear. You will stand alongside me, the White Queen to my Red Queen. I see you are ready. That object looks magnificent on you. Are you ready to deliver the punishment."

"Oh yes, I'm ready to administer the justice of the Red Queen's court," replied Kim.

He heard the click of heels against the stone floor of the dungeon. He felt the touch of stiff pvc against his side. He took in the luscious scent of her body as she drew closer. His eyes flicked to one side but all he could see at first was the white pvc of her skirt and the black hearts and then as she turned he saw the object the Red Queen had commented on. It was a huge white rubber strap on, secured onto Kim's waist with a white leather harness. The fearsome object protruded from the White Queen's crotch threatening unimaginable pain and humiliation.

"I will extract my vengeance for the humiliation and suffering you caused me."

It was Kim's voice but there was a resonance to it, something indefinably different about it compared to the young woman who this man had tried to force himself on in the massage parlour. There was a powerful aura in its tone and the expression she used that broached no resistance. She had changed. Changed beyond recognition from the person she had been. She had assumed a confidence and dominance that had not been there before. No longer could the massage parlour provide her with a satisfying occupation. No longer could she give up her body to be surrendered for the pleasure of others; others would have to bend to her will and give her pleasure.

"Let this be a lesson to you. You'll never treat women like that again. I didn't deserve what you did to me that day and you'll pay for it. You'll leave this place humiliated. And don't think there'll be an escape for you when you leave this place. She will find out. The Red Queen's spies will look out for you and they will report back to her if you stray. You've seen how cruel she can be and, believe me, this is only a taster, there's far worse that could happen to you here."

The man listened, transfixed by the powerful voice of this beautiful young goddess.

"Look at me when I'm talking to you."

His hair was grasped by her white glove and his head wrenched sharply upwards so he was forced to look at the cruel hard gaze of Kim, transformed into the fetish White Queen, a vision of gleaming white pvc with the fearsome piece of ridged and contoured rubber sticking out from her.

"I want an apology."

He drew in a deep breath, "I'm sorry."

"You'll have to demonstrate to me that you're genuinely sorry."

"Really, truly I'm sorry," he replied.

It was not a falsehood. He had capitulated. Seeing her there in all her white fetish splendour there was a change of heart in him.

"And will you take your punishment with good grace?"

"Yes."

"Good, then take my strap-on in your mouth and suck it," she commanded.

The hard object was thrust between his lips and he took it willingly into his mouth. He felt the taste of rubber on his tongue and the wide girth of the massive strap-on fill his mouth.

"Suck."

He sucked on it, tugging on the object as his lips slid up and down its length. He did it willingly, even eagerly. He did it not only because he had to but also because he desired to. He actually wanted to submit to the fair-haired girl who just hours ago he thought he could force himself on. He couldn't work out what it was, but she was different, somehow she had been transformed. She was just as beautiful as before as she stood there her hands on her hips rocking back and forth to force herself deeper into his mouth but now she had assumed this dominant and cruel streak that made you want to surrender yourself to her. He felt a sharp gagging reflex as the strap-on penetrated down to the back of his throat but then some relief as Kim pulled it back. He sucked as hard as he could bobbing his head back and forth as far as his restraints would allow him. He was now engaging enthusiastically with his task, desirous of worshipping the fair haired queen and her enormous false cock. Finally, Kim withdrew, pulling the hard object, now glistening with his saliva, from his lips.

Kim knelt down so her face was eye-level with his. Wisps of her fair hair gently touched his face. She looked stunning and smelt exotic and fragrant, every sense combining to lure him into submission to her feminine dominance.

"There's one more penance you have to pay. You know that, don't you?"

"Yes."

"I can force it on you. There's nothing you can do to stop me. But, will you receive it willingly. Do you want it inside you?"

"Yes, I do," he nodded.

Kim pulled away, the heels clicked on the stone again. She hitched up her skirt and climbed up onto the whipping bench, kneeling menacingly over the man's back-side as she adjusted her position ready to inflict her final punishment and humiliation. As she took hold of the base of the rubber strap-on to control it the White Queen reflected for a moment before penetrating him. How the tables had turned. She sensed it. Kim could see it in his eyes. She could feel the change in her and embrace how right and good this felt for her. She could sense the dominant streak coursing through her veins like a tingle that was physical and tangible. Wherever this journey had taken her and whatever this awakened awareness of who she was meant in the future she knew in her heart it was right.

She braced herself and explored the man's arse hole, rubbing the hard rubber teasingly across his back-side before finding the right spot. She pulled the flesh of his back-side to expose the orifice she was going to enter and pushed the tip of the white rubber into it. There was a little bit of resistance as the muscles momentarily tightened so she pushed again and felt the false cock go deeper. There was a gasp from the opposite end of the bench. Should she be cruel and just thrust it up his arse as hard as she could? The White Queen was feeling in a good mood and quite generous though. Perhaps, if he hadn't willingly embraced his punishment willingly she would have just pushed as hard as she could and forced herself in but now she was prepared to take her time and do it in a way that brought her some pleasure. And there was no doubt she was enjoying this. God, it felt so empowering to feel this hard appendage attached to her waist, to control it and know she could use it to extract submission from a male, a man who not so long ago thought he could force this act on to her.

OK, enough time for reflection, thought Kim, let's get down to the task. She warmed to it, pushing herself fully into him so that the massive white cock was fully inside his arse. She revelled in hearing his gasps and moans as she pushed harder with her hips. She alternated between sharp and shallow thrusts and long deep strokes. She could even feel his body responding to her thrusts and moving to accommodate the object so she could penetrate him even further. Kim leant over him, leaning the full weight of her body against his and pressing her tits, pulled up by the tight white pvc, against his back. She put his lips against his ear.

"Take it. Take the pain and humiliation from your White Queen. What do say? What do you want?"

"Yeah, please, give it to me your majesty."

"I'm going to fuck you so hard. I'm going to make you suffer. This rubber cock is going as far up inside you as I can force it."

"Yes, thank you, thank you White Queen," he gasped as Kim fucked his arse harder and harder.

It felt so good, thought Kim, to be so in control, so empowered, to know she could do what she liked. She really warmed to her task. She was young and strong and could carry on driving the strap-on into his arse as hard as she liked to her heart's content. She would give him a fucking like he'd never had before. He wouldn't forgot this day. He'd go away well and truly fucked up the arse but more than that he'd go away tamed and submissive. She'd make sure he'd never forget the White Queen as she pushed into him with hard deep strokes. She would only stop when she'd had enough after she had inflicted the pain and humiliation he deserved and she had taken the maximum amount of pleasure out of inflicting it.

Eventually she withdrew. He looked spent and exhausted with the pain and the exertion. Kim was flushed and excited with the empowering experience. She went back to the front of the whipping bench. His glazed eyes looked up at her. She said nothing but just spat in his face and watched the spittle run down his cheeks onto his lips before stepping away to join the Red Queen.

During all this time the White Queen had an audience though she was hardly aware of it as she was enjoying herself so much. They all looked on awe-struck and admiring and then broke out into a spontaneous round of applause when they realised Kim had carried out the sentence of the Red Queen's court.

"Take him," the Red Queen announced, "give him his day clothes and throw him out on the street. He has been given a just punishment. His presence will never threaten the White Queen or darken the chambers of Nemesisland again. That was an entertaining diversion. Now, my guests and Nemesisland characters you can continue the fun."

She turned to Kim smiling, "you're a willing student in the dark arts of domination White Queen."

"I've learnt from the best," laughed Kim. "It's been quite a day."

"Yes Kim, but your journey hasn't ended quite yet. There is another place you must see and somebody else who is aching to meet you. There's a very special place Kim, where no slave or character in Nemesisland is ever allowed. It's my very own place of secret resort, a mystical wood where I retire to contemplate and where I consort with other pagan goddesses. But your place in my world is special and you are permitted entry into it."

21: Epilogue

"Will she appear do you think?" asked Kim.

"Oh yes Kim, I'm in no doubt about that. As a goddess of fate I know the moment of your meeting was pre-ordained. Her life blood runs through you Kim, you must believe she would never turn down this chance to touch her sole heir with her spirit."

"I'm scared," Kim sobbed, "of all the weird and wonderful things that have happened to me in Nemesisland, this is the scariest."

Goddess Nemesis pulled Kim to her and held her in a tight hug, the warmth of her body enveloping her in the heartfelt embrace.

"Don't cry yet Kim. There will be a time for tears, but not yet. Show fortitude for just a while longer."

"This is my family isn't it, my only family?"

"Yes Kim, the Goddess Samovila is your family; you are her ancestor," she said wiping a tear from her eye, "but stop Kim, look, you're making me cry now!" she laughed through the tears.

Goddess Nemesis had led Kim into the final part of Nemesisland. They had left the confines of her dungeon domain and thrown open the doors into the open air. They had followed a curious path of hexagon shaped tiles in colours of azure blue, turquoise, yellow and white that led into a wood. Goddess Nemesis explained that this was a deeply spiritual place where she came to consort with the other goddess spirits. No mere slave or servant could progress beyond the path into the dark forbidding wood of ancient trees.

Goddess Nemesis turned to Kim, "you do understand, don't you, why this journey was necessary? Without these trials, without the opening up of your heart, without your devotion and submission to me, you would never have truly believed."

"Yeah, I get it, really I do. Hey, it's been wild," Kim laughed, "I've loved every minute of it!"

Goddess Nemesis had changed back into the purple and black pagan dress she had worn in her dungeon, but over it was a black velvet cloak and hood pulled up over her dark hair. Goddess Nemesis and Vicky had helped Kim prepare and get dressed. She was very particular about what Kim should wear and had chosen a gown of shimmering emerald silk for her and decorated her hair with a chain made of yellow primroses and insisted she walk bare-foot through the woods.

"I feel I should be wearing something darker, more sombre," said Kim.

"No Kim, that's perfect. It's the first day of spring and a night of the full moon, a very auspicious moment. It's a time of re-awakening and new beginnings. Spring green is fitting for you Kim. It's a perfect night. See how the luminous orb of the full moon illuminates our path."

They both lit candles and then the two women entered into the depths of the dark forest, Goddess Nemesis leading the way. The mystical atmosphere of the woods closed in on them as they made their way slowly through the undergrowth in the candle-lit glow. They broke through into a clearing bounded by gnarled oak trees with a broken tree trunk in its centre arraigned like an altar of natural wood. The glow of the moon shone through the canopy of trees to shed its magical glow on the scene.

"Put your candle down on the trunk Kim. Now, all we can do is wait."

She gripped Kim's hand tightly. Kim was breathing heavily. She understood the portent of this moment; she knew this was where she re-connected with her past and also with her destiny. Kim gazed into the dense forest, the tangled dark branches with their emerging buds of new growth, seeking out any hint of movement. It seemed like an age had past, though it was probably only a few minutes, Kim began to doubt whether the Slavic woodland spirit would appear before them tonight.

Then she caught a glimpse of a shadow in the midnight mist which gradually took shape and formed itself into the figure of a woman and emerged clearly into the edge of the clearing. Cloaked in dark green, she was in the autumn of her life having stalked the forests for centuries. The gazes of the two women met as the Goddess Samovila's piercing green eyes fixed on Kim appraising the young woman who stood across from her. She stepped forward into the glade and came towards them, the moonlight shining on her curly auburn hair. Kim's heart was racing. They faced one another. Kim could see clearly now the streams of tears running down the lines of goddess's care-worn visage and she felt herself welling with emotion. No words were spoken. No words were necessary. Goddess Samovila reached out a hand and gently brushed away the tears forming in Kim's eyes and took her in her arms and held her.

Samovila turned to Goddess Nemesis, "I know in my heart that it's so but, tell me, what you have told me is true then, this is my long lost ancestor, my child and heir?"

"There is no doubt sister. We both know it in our hearts but I have verified the facts. There can be no shadow of doubt my friend. This is your long lost daughter."

"Lost, but never forgotten, my spirit has always been reaching out for you and now I have found you. Come to me my dear."

And under the luminous orb of the full moon spring and autumn green met and embraced.

Also from S. Nano

You may also enjoy...

MISTRESS
OF THE
AIR

S. NANO